<u>DANCING IN GRAVEYARDS</u>

FANNIE PRICE

This is a work of fiction. All of the characters, organizations, and events portrayed in this novel are either products of the author's imagination or are used fictitiously.

ISBN-10: 1449908705
ISBN -13: 9781449908706

**Visit the author's web site at:
www.fannieprice.net**

DEDICATION

TO MY MOTHER FOR HER NEVER ENDING SUPPORT AND BELIEF IN ME NO MATTER WHAT DIRECTION MY DREAMS TAKE ME.

TO MY BEST FRIEND AND BROTHER, THANKS FOR ALWAYS BEING IN MY CORNER.

CHAPTER ONE

FOR the fourth time in ten minutes my cell phone rang as I added the final touches to my black eyeliner. It didn't take being psychic to know Finnius Macleod was on the other end this time just as he'd been the previous three times. Normally he wasn't as obsessive, but with me going to the opening of Sebastian Arroyo's play tonight, he would call me until I answered. Knowing this I decided not to answer until I was ready to walk out the door; so once again the phone stopped on the fifth, depriving the voicemail from claiming the call.

For any other man this would have been warning signs that something was slightly, if not majorly, off. But Finn's not like most guys, he's a werewolf; and werewolves tend to handle stressful situations differently than human males. If an alpha wolf, Finn, thinks his mate, me, though in werewolf cultures we weren't officially mated, is being belligerently disobedient, a stressful situation has just been created. The only thing that had him calling instead of driving to my house was being on duty as a helicopter rescue pilot for the San Francisco, Monterey Bay area.

It wasn't that I was going to a play without him; it was that I was attending a play written and directed by Sebastian. One thing I've learned; never let a vampire know what gets under you skin.

Glamorization completed, I stood in front of the antique full-length mirror to view the final product. I hadn't bought it with the bedroom set but the dark oak wood matched the rest of the furniture in my bedroom as if they'd all be purchased together. My sophisticated look of a white button-up dress blouse, and black wide-leg dress slacks, was complicated by a dash of rebellious youth in the form a strapless black satin corset worn over the shirt, and a pair of satin covered Mary Jane heels.

The top few buttons of the shirt were left undone allowing the Chakra pendant I wore on a sliver chain to direct the eye to the glimpse of cleavage the corset afforded. Straight black hair was down and kept from coming over my shoulders by the sides being pinned back with rhinestone bobby pins. My makeup, somewhere between tasteful and daring, pulled everything together. The weatherman said there would be a chill in the spring air, so I slipped my leather jacket on, grabbed my purse, both sets of keys and headed out the front door to the black Mazda RX8 parked in front of my house.

The fifth call came as I started up the car and was accompanied by a curse from my lips when I realized I'd left my Bluetooth in my everyday purse. Driving while talking on a cell phone is cumbersome enough; driving a stick shift adds another level of difficulty. I could have just ignored it, but he'd already be pissed. I didn't feel like pressing my luck.

"Slow night?" I questioned after I engaged the talk button.

"Where the hell have you been? I've been trying to reach you for the past hour."

Born and breed on the sunny beaches of Miami, Florida, Finn had no discernable accent, at least nothing I could detect with the exception of when he was truly upset. On those occasions I could almost hear a southern twang to his words. Sexy as hell but makes it hard to focus on arguing with him. Dangerous too since sometimes I piss him off just to hear that southern twang.

"Hello Finn, I'm fine, thank you for asking. Work was a bit long cataloging all the different new items that have come in for the ancient Egypt exhibit, but the reward of having everything on display will be well worth it."

"You're not nearly as funny as you think you are." Yep there was that twang to his voice.

"That's all a matter of opinion, and why are you burning up my phone line anyway? Shouldn't you be saving lives or something?"

"Is that why you didn't answer the first couple times I called?"

"Couple?" I scoffed and flicked on my turn signal as I changed lanes and negotiated my car onto the expressway.

"I wanted to check and make sure you were alright."

"In the event something happened on the way home from work?"

"Of course."

"Then why'd you wait two hours after I've been home from work to call and make sure I made it home from work?" There was a pause while he tried to come up with something. "The jig is up, Finn. We both know the only reason you called is because I'm going to Sebastian's play tonight."

There was another longer pause before he spoke. "You know he picked tonight so I wouldn't be able to go."

"Finn," I stopped myself before chuckling. "Even if Sebastian were that devious, the opening night of the play was set eight weeks ago. That's well before even you knew you'd be working."

He huffed silently on the other end.

"Besides you hate plays, only reason you'd go if you were off is to spite Sebastian."

"You say that like it's a bad thing."

I smirked, but only because I knew he couldn't see it. Although I did it more often than I care to admit, antagonizing a werewolf isn't smart. "What are you really worried about? That he has some hotel room ready to whisk me away to?"

"The thought had crossed my mind," it was my turn to sigh. "I know you insist he doesn't have feelings for you that extend beyond a deep and meaningful friendship, but I know better. I've seen the way he looks at you, Danika."

"The way he looks at me? And how exactly is it that he looks at me?"

"Like any man looks at a beautiful woman," Finn replied sharply.

The way he bit back his words, I could tell there was more he wanted to say but for reasons known only to him held back. For my part I decided against pushing him. Finn was even more stubborn than I was. Asking was pretty much pointless, if he wanted to he'd tell me, otherwise I'd never know.

"Let's say for argument sake you're right and he fancies me. What exactly has he been waiting for all these years? I mean don't you think he would have spilled the beans by now?"

"He's waiting for the right time."

That got me to laugh out loud. "Right, because in the seven years that I've known him it hasn't been the right time."

"He's the walking dead," he whispered into the receiver, "He's got all the time in the world."

"But I don't. I'm a sorcerer not a warlock; I don't know how to prolong my life any more than the next person."

"Well, maybe he's waiting for the right time to invite you onto his team."

"Sebastian isn't going to turn me."

"Know this for a fact do you?"

"I'd be willing to stake my life on it."

"I hope it never comes to that."

Another soft sigh left my lips. "Finn, stop being so dramatic. I'll concede Sebastian is devious by the sheer nature of what he is, but he's not like that with me. He doesn't have some secret sinister plot to turn me into a vampire, and you know well and good the only reason you don't like him is because he's a vampire."

"No, I don't like him because I don't trust him, and I don't trust his Murder. You don't know vampires like I do."

"And you don't know Sebastian like I do."

"So you keep telling me."

"And yet you continue not to listen."

"Maybe I'd believe it a little more if you didn't try to convince me all the time."

"Or maybe," I paused, "You know what, Finn; I've been friends with Sebastian for a long time, longer than I've known you."

"So?"

"So," I paused. "You might know vampire nature, but I know Sebastian's nature. He flirts with me to get a rise out of you, which he accomplishes… every single time. If you didn't let him he'd probably stop trying, but so long as he can continue to successfully bait you, he's never going to stop pushing your buttons."

"So you admit he's an asshole?"

"To you, yeah… but you give as good as you get so it evens itself out in the end," I made sure he could hear the smile in my voice. He growled soft and low in the back of his throat like I knew he would. "He knew I was a witch and he still trusted me enough to tell me he was a vampire, in my book that counts for something."

"I trusted you enough to tell you I was a werewolf."

"Technically you didn't tell me, you just chose not to deny it when I confronted you. And last time I checked witches can't affect werewolves like they can vampires."

Finn must have put his hand over the mouthpiece, because I heard some muffled voice in the background before his voice came back over the phone. "I've got to go; I'll call you when I get off duty."

"Fine," I replied and snapped the phone shut.

It hadn't been a question, but a statement; one he knew would piss me off. He knew if I was angry I wouldn't enjoy the play and would leave immediately after instead of staying for the wine and cheese they always served in the after party of opening night. It looked like he wasn't the only one that continued to respond to being baited.

Pulling into the parking garage for the playhouse, I pushed the button to get my ticket and continued up the circular ramp seven levels until I found a spot to slip my car into. Once parked, I turned everything off, closed my eyes and breathed. Several deep calming breaths in through the nose and out through the mouth. Try as he might I was not about to let Finn ruin my night.

There are different names for different types of witches. For example, though mainstream has labeled the male term of a witch, a warlock, it is really one that has learned the secrets of time. They're generally able to move through time; the stronger ones can move back or forward by the decade, though they often refrain to keep from creating cataclysmic paradoxes. They're also considered immortals.

It's not that they can't die. A gunshot to the head will kill them just as sure as it would anyone else, and their body still suffer the ravages of any disease, but they're so versed in the art of healing the only true way to kill them is to severe the head for the body and burn both, otherwise, it has been documented that another warlock can restore their life.

There aren't that many warlocks; they only share their secrets with their apprentices and becoming a warlock's apprentice is a herculean feat. A witch has to prove they are worthy of immortality, and worthy of immortality means different things to different warlocks. They can arrest the aging process for as long as they can find the ingredients for the potion being employed. However, they can only reverse the aging process back five years. No one outside of warlocks knows why and they damn sure aren't telling.

Wizard isn't the term for a male witch either, but for a witch apt in controlling and manipulating the natural elements. For most, younger wizards, it was the latter. They could take a light drizzle and milk a monsoon from the clouds, or pull down hurricane winds from a gentle breeze. The master wizards' control of the elements was truly scary.

They can create a storm on the sunniest days, and some can even control the very climate and temperature around them for prolonged periods of time. A good number of Native Americans are born into this form of witchcraft; it's where the rain-dancers come from. They can make just about anything grow in any terrain or condition. It's the wizards us witches go to when we need to find those rare herbs some potions demanded, always of course with a price. It's rumored in Africa there is a wizard so powerful she possesses the ability to raze the planet to the ground.

Sorcerers, meaning both male and female, are versed in mental prowess. Telekinesis, telepathy, thought transference, even mind controlling and imprinting thoughts if the witch is powerful enough. What people believe to be psychic powers is nothing more than a witch with a disposition to being a sorcerer who is unaware the ability resides in them. It's not all it's cracked up to be at times, the mind reading for example is a constant, it's not something that can be turned off, the best a sorcerer can hope for is to learn to filter it out and deaden the voices until it's like white noise in the background. It's not something that's easy to live with. A good number of schizophrenics are nothing more than sorcerers that don't realize the voices in their head are triggered by external forces. It's no wonder a good many sorcerers choose to become hermits.

No one knows why but preternatural creatures seem to be exempt, I can still read their minds, but it becomes an active concentration instead of the thoughts just flowing to me, it also makes it harder, but not impossible to control their minds and imprint thoughts.

Then there are the necromancers. Many people, even some naïve witches, believe necromancers are the harbingers of death simply because they are versed in the art of dealing with spirits, ghosts, zombies and all manner of dead things. Most can only communicate with spirits and ghosts, but there are those that have amassed enough power to control the dead.

Like Warlocks they have the ability to stave the hands of aging and their own death but the price is high.

Due to the stigma that's associated with their practice some necromancers remain silent about what they are. It's believed by some witches that vampires are the byproduct of necromantic magic worked on the dead or dying centuries ago. Vampires deny this of course.

Necromancers and sorcerers bare a distinction the other two orders don't possess; one has to be born with the ability. It's unclear why; some elders say it's because the mark of sorcery and necromancy has to be imprinted on the soul at birth.

With my mind clear and my breathing and heart rate back to normal I undid my seatbelt and stepped from my car. The garage wasn't attached to the theater, but it was only a block away.

Thirty minutes to show time and the lobby was packed when I pulled the doors open. If I looked hard enough I was sure I'd be able to spot some famous faces in the crowd. Sebastian's plays were almost legendary. I stopped at will call where Sebastian had placed a complimentary ticket for me, and produced the necessary ID to acquire it.

They were box seats, but then he always got me box seats to his plays. Sometimes he'd join me, but most of the time he was either backstage with his actors before they went on, in the booth with the stage manager, or playing nice with some pretty young woman that had no idea she was in for more than a night of hot sex.

Though I knew first hand how devastatingly charming and incredibly sexy Sebastian could be; it still amazed me, in this age of pseudo enlightenment and HIV, the number of women that were willing to sleep with a virtual stranger. As a reanimated corpse, Sebastian couldn't contract, nor could he be a carrier for anything beyond anemia. The women he slept with, however, were no more aware of his vampiric condition than they were of his clinically clean status. I've never asked how much of the sex he got was protected or not, some questions are best left unasked and unanswered.

Ordering a mojito, I made my way to my box seating, set everything down and fished through my purse until I found one of the bags of peanuts that had gravitated towards the bottom. The playhouse offered snacks in the form of caviar on water crackers, or pâté, or hummus, or other such treats that were meant to stimulate and entice the palate. I'd always found caviar to be way too salty, and even if it hadn't, it would have been impossible to over look eating raw fish eggs.

I read over the bios of the actors in the program, then the synopsis of the play itself. Sebastian Arroyo had managed to become a very famous playwright and director, an achievement that never ceased to amaze me. As a vampire I would have thought it would be his nature to shun the limelight. Eventually people are going to realize he's not aging; however, vampires don't get to be as old as Sebastian if they don't know what they're doing. He's never told me his age, and I've always thought it impolite to ask, but judging from some of the stories he's told me over the years I've estimated him to at least be a hundred and fifty though honestly I was banking much older.

I knew he's originally from Spain but re-birthed in America during a war. I knew guns had been invented, but that still left a lot of historical possibilities. America might still be a child compared to other countries but it's had more than it's share of warring.

The house lights flashed three times, a polite way of signaling all those still milling about in the halls, restrooms, and foyers they had five minutes to return to their seats before show time. Used to be the ushers wouldn't let people in after the play started. It was believed it disrupted the actors. Instead those people would be escorted to a room with a glass patrician towards the back allowing them to see the play. I guess enough people complained so the ushers now escorted latecomers to their seats. Apparently being in the right seat to watch the play was more important than potentially disrupting the actors.

With the price for theater tickets I could understand the reasoning behind it; however, with the price of theater tickets it looked like people would want to be on time.

The play was a two hour-long masterpiece divided into three acts with two intermissions. The actors took their bows to standing ovations before parting on either side to make room for the infamous Sebastian Arroyo. He took several bows, accepted the flowers given to him by the leading lady, blew several kisses, and tossed eleven of the dozen red roses to women in the audience, before taking a final bow and heading off stage.

I continued to occupy my little box as the others filed out, some going to their cars, or the taxis and limos outside, while others filtered down to the after party held in the theater. According to my watch it was already ten thirty. I figured I'd stay long enough to tell Sebastian how brilliant I thought his play was before heading home. My desire to call it a relatively early night was based solely on the knowledge I'd have to get up comparatively early in the morning for work.

When the theater was almost completely empty I finally made my way from the boxed seating towards the after party room. Located on the same level I quite possibly could have beat the crowd and been one of the first ones in, but that just would have meant a longer period of time spent avoiding pointless conversation. The room was fairly packed when I entered. Young men and women in modern tuxedos were pimping hor'dourves and champagne on silver trays.

I took a glass so my hands wouldn't be empty and continued to circle the room to avoid small talk while waiting for the cast. It wasn't that I felt out of place among the elbows being rubbing in the room; as an archeologist in the Museum of Natural History section of the California Academy of Science I had sufficient experience mingling with the influential people of San Francisco. But, it wasn't something I really enjoyed when my job dictated the need, and changing the venue hadn't enhanced my opinion.

"Quite the little gathering, isn't it?"

I was glancing out the window to the street traffic below, but shifted my attention to my right where the owner of the intruding voice stood. She was beautiful in the traditional since of the word; though her alabaster skin was made even paler by the platinum blonde tresses that curled around her face.

The blinding red lipstick would have gone better with her hair if her complexion were darker, or better with her complexion if she were a brunette. Instead it just shocked the senses and drew attention to her thin lips. It did, however, match her gown, a long red chiffon and satin number that reminded me of rose petals. The straps crossed each other in the back and front, making me realize they were the only piece of material covering her breasts while it left her stomach mostly bare. Her heels added at least three inches to her stature, but still put the top of her head, barely at my chin. I was already tall for a woman and my heels only added to my extra height.

The dress was interesting and she had enough curves to her body to show it off but again I couldn't help but think with her complexion she should have gone for another color. Her icy blue eyes bore into me when I met her gaze head on; waiting for the answer to her question as if her very life depended on it. I almost felt like I should have been replying in code with *the sick dog only yelps at the new moon*, or something equally secret agency. I decided to keep it simple.

"Yes it is, but then it is a Sebastian Arroyo play so…"

I let my words trail off with a shrug, and turned my eyes back to the room; my free arm crossed over my stomach. Despite her contrary features for some reason I still felt like the ugly little sister next to her, never mind my chocolate complexion wouldn't allow me to be confused as any of her relatives. I had to mentally remind myself to stand straight as my shoulders started rounding forward.

"You know Sebastian Arroyo?" that seemed to impress her, but I wasn't sure if that was good or bad.

"Yes, we're old acquaintances," I finally stated.

This woman was giving me the creeps and I wasn't quite sure why. Fortunately the actors and Sebastian entering gave me the diversion I needed to slip away as her attention was drawn to the opening doors. My new position put me closer to Sebastian, which played along with my plan to congratulate him and beat a path back to my car.

"Was it really that much of a bore?"

Trust Sebastian to catch me mid yawn with my hand covering my mouth.

"Some of us have to work for a living," I replied smiling once my mouth returned to its normal shape.

"Wasn't it you that said if you're doing what you love, it's not really work?"

"Don't start."

He grinned at that and opened his arms for an embrace I gladly accepted. His body was warm; I could feel the heat radiating from it through his suit. It was a trick some vampires did to make themselves appear more human, along with breathing, and blinking, and a heart beat, and remembering to fidgets slightly, and a few other things humans did without realizing they were doing them, but would miss the presence of on a conscious or more often subconscious level.

Sebastian wasn't really what would be considered the poster boy for bloodsuckers. He claimed to be from Spain, but migrated to America when with his parents when he was young. His time in the states has sense robbed him of any trace of an accent he once had. His hair was somewhere between brown and bronze, the kind of hair that probably would have been predisposed to lightening in the sun if it weren't for his severe sun allergy. His eyes were a crisp blue, and there was a dimple deep enough to be a cleft in his chin. He was a pretty boy, a little too pretty for my tastes but the women fancied him. I'd never seen him naked, but his clothes always gave the illusion of a toned body. It wouldn't have mattered; he could have been rail thin and still bench pressed a H3.

Upon my release from his hug, he traded my champagne glass for a single rose, the last of the dozen he received on the stage. I dutifully took the flower and brought it to my nose for a smell before accepting the offered arm.

"Finn couldn't make it?" he questioned looking around casually. I didn't bother answering, Sebastian knew as well as I if Finn were there he'd be Gorilla Glued to my side. "Tell me what you thought of the play."

"I loved it," I grinned, squeezing his arm. "But then you know I have a weakness for mysteries."

"Yes, that did enter my mind as I wrote the play. Not that I wrote it for you of course," he added with a grin.

"Of course not," I chuckled softly. "How presumptuous that would be on my part."

That made him smile but there was something in his eyes as he scanned the room.

It made me look around again even though I didn't have the slightest idea what I was looking for.

"Everything alright?"

"Yes, and no," he paused then looked to me with a slight frown. "Are you free tomorrow evening?"

I gave a dramatic sigh, "Sebastian you know I'm never free, though I'm sure someone with your resources will have no trouble meeting my going rate." When that only barely got a smile from him I found myself getting worried. "Alright I'll bite, what's the what?"

"It's a private matter, not something that should be discussed here."

"Okay," that wasn't good. "I get off work at five; want me to meet you somewhere?"

He shook his head. "You're home is fine, but let me ask you this… have there been any newcomers into your *community*?"

"I don't know, possibly. It's not like we really keep tabs on the who's who. The elders meet quarterly and there's the festival that happens in the fall but it's not like we keep track of the comings and goings of each other. Why?"

He was thoughtfully quiet for so long had it been anyone else I would have assumed they either didn't hear me or had fallen asleep standing up with their eyes open.

When he finally spoke he leaned into me, to the causal observer it would have looked very deceptive indeed. "Two have gone missing from the Murder; it is believed a necromancer is involved."

My head snapped back meeting his eyes. "Are you sure?"

"I'm not, but there are those among us that are already building the pyre."

"Sebastian, there hasn't been a necromancer in the area for decades, not since…" I paused censoring myself, and covering it with quiet pondering. "Not since at least the late seventies."

That brought a soft smirk to his lips. "You know as well as I just because none have claimed the title doesn't mean none are around."

I remained silent, partially because I didn't have a comeback readily on hand, and partially because I knew he was right. Witchcraft had its bases in alchemy for good reason, a great deal of what we did was potions for the body, for the mind, transmutations and the like, but there was more to being a witch than being able to cook up a love potion. With practice and the right spells from a Grimoire that each witch inherited and/or stole we could conjure things, some good, some evil, most indifferent.

I sighed softly, meeting Sebastian's eyes again for a moment. It was never a good idea to hold a vampire's gaze no matter how friendly they were; along with the sun allergy it was one of the things the books had gotten right.

"Give me as much information as you can tomorrow on the disappearance, and I'll pass it along to the elders."

"Thanks, I'd appreciate that," that slight smile ghosted his lips then retreated as his eyes scanned the room again like he was looking for something.

"Would you stop doing that? You're starting to freak me out." Again I found myself looking around as well, and again I had no idea what I should have been looking for.

"Sorry, I just..." he paused, shaking his head a bit. "We're supposed to be celebrating, why don't I introduce you to the leading man? He is quite charming and almost as handsome as me."

"Some other time, right now I have a date with a queen size sleigh bed."

"Then let me walk you to your car."

"I'm parked in the garage around the corner, I'll be fine."

"You're sure?"

"Positive," I leaned in and planted a kiss on the corner of his lips. "I'll see you tomorrow around six thirty?"

"I'll be there with bells on," he replied flashing that playboy smile that probably melted a few panties in the room.

"Good," I retorted, "I've been saying for years you should start wearing bells."

I tossed him a kiss from across the room before; I retrieved my leather and headed out.

CHAPTER TWO

VISIONS of snuggling my comforter danced through my head as I stepped from the elevator and made my way towards my car. It didn't help that I'd just purchased six hundred thread count sheets for my queen sized bed and would be test driving them for the first time when I got home.

My bedroom looked like something out of a Home and Garden magazine, the kind that shows the bed overflowing with pillows, and the comforter matching the drapes. What can I say; my bedroom really is my sanctuary.

There were considerably fewer cars on my level than there had been when I arrived, but I wasn't paying attention to my surroundings. That proved to be a mistake. Lesson one in self-defense or pretty much any style of fighting, always, always be aware of one's surroundings and those in it. I didn't notice the blonde in the red dress until I was almost standing on her head.

"Sorry," I offered, jerking to a stop just before I knocked into her.

"Danika Harlow, yes?"

I opened my mouth to ask her how she knew my name but snapped it shut just as quickly. Instead I pivoted to my left and took a few steps back, keeping the lady in red in view only to find there were two men advancing from the direction of the elevator.

Sure they could have just been heading to their car, except they'd passed all of the potential vehicles and the only one remaining was mine.

I jerked my eyes back to the woman as the silence in my head hit me full force. I hadn't noticed at the party due to the number of people present, but I should have realized no one could be that pale and still be among the living. My eyes did a quick scan of the area, but their strategy had been solidly planned. The woman stood between me and my car, while the guys blocked the stairs and elevator. I could try to blitz past them, but vampires are known for their speed. I'd have more luck trying to make it past the woman and run down the ramp to the next level.

For a moment I thought to extend my senses to try to open her mind up to me, but decided to hold off. I was tired, and if I didn't do it right, she'd know I was monkeying around in her head. Most humans can't tell; hell, neither can most lycanthropes, though they are naturally resistant. Vampires can. Possible because of the mental prowess they themselves possess.

Chances were if she knew my name she knew I was a witch, but that didn't mean she considered me a threat and I was willing to remain in the non-threatening category as long as possible. Hopefully it meant she'd be less likely to kill me.

"I'm hoping this is something that can be discussed," I stated trying to remain amicable.

"There is a proper time and place for the discussion," the blonde stated. "You will come with us."

I shifted my focus for a moment to the sound of tires on waxed pavement. The two goons split like the red seas making room for a sleek black Lincoln Town Car limo that cruised to a stop between them. The blonde gestured with her hand towards the car; my cue to head in that direction.

"And if I decline?"

Those thin lips of hers, if possible became even thinner as she pressed them together. "It is not a request, Miss Harlow." Again she gestured to the limo, impatiently this time.

She was ready; the goons were ready; everyone was ready for me to make my move. Chances were they wanted me alive, which meant they had questions and believed I had the answers. If they wanted me dead they would have killed me already.

A couple of witty remarks about not getting into cars with strangers flirted with the tip of my tongue, but this wasn't the time for pithy comebacks. I focused on a picture of Sebastian at the party, imagining him moving around the room. It worked better with my eyes closed but I wasn't about to open myself up to a blind attack.

Soundless my lips moved around the words and mentally pushed the urgent message to the only person close enough to help.

"Parking garage! Level seven! Vampires! Help!"

"Grab her!"

The acoustics of the garage sent the blonde's voice bouncing off the walls. I reached out with my mind, throwing a kinetic blow that caught the blonde in her hip, and another to knock back the two goons that began moving forward on her command. My first couple of steps were lurching. The alcohol combined with already being tired caused more of an energy drain from those three uses of power than I expected. One of the main reasons why it's always a good idea for a witch, especially a sorcerer, to get as much rest as possible.

I heard the tires of the limo squeal but didn't bother to look back. It would only slow me down and I was pretty sure they weren't about to run me over with the car. Vaulting the guard railing to the next level, I chanced a glance over my shoulder to see the blur of movement from one of the male vampires. I barely twisted my body out of the way as he launched himself at me and caught nothing but air. My victory was short lived as the other vampire made his play.

If it was just one, I might have been able to hold him prone while I made my escape, instead I used his movement against him, shoving him into the pathway of the goon that regained his footing and sending them both to the ground. I didn't bother to hang around for the aftermath. Unfortunately the diversion was enough for the blonde to catch up with to me.

She held her arm out and let my momentum do the rest; a perfect clothesline that would have made any ECW wrestler proud. My legs went out from under me so fast I didn't have time to try to catch my fall even though it felt like I was moving in slow motion. I felt myself go airborne, my weight carrying me to the ground; then I felt nothing at all.

* * * * *

I'm not sure what woke me up; maybe it was the voices that spoke around me in heated, urgent tones. I should have been able to understand them, the words sounded English, but it was distorted as if they were talking through water. I continued to lie where I was struggling through the mental haze of my last memory; it took a while before the parking garage came back to me. The blonde, the goons, the limo; as each bit filtered back my heart rate increased until my own blood roared in my ears.

"Silence," a female voice hissed.

I tried to move but someone was holding my shoulders down. It occurred to me I might want to open my eyes, but that inner voice in the back of my head warned me that might be a bad idea.

"Relax, Dani," the words would have been ignored if they hadn't been spoken by Sebastian's familiar voice. "Can you open your eyes?"

"Not sure that's a good idea right now," I whispered simply because I was sure if I spoke too loudly my head would explode.

"She will answer for her crimes," that same heated female voice from before hissed.

I smirked. I couldn't help it. I was pissed and in pain and the only way to lash back right now was verbally. Like I said, there's a time and place for wit. "What, my contribution to the Vampire League didn't come through on time?"

I felt the air rush around me followed by a hard smack and a hiss that came from the other side of the room.

"You said you brought her here to question, not to attack. I suggest you remember you place."

"I suggest you remember yours as well, Sebastian." Another voice, this time male entered the picture. "Your word is the only reason she is not dead yet."

Now seemed like a good time to open my eyes. I cracked first one, then the other, but the lights wherever I was weren't bright enough to bother my eyes. I was in a room, an expensively decorated one from what I could see. There was thick carpet the color of blood on the floor, the kind that begged to be treaded on in bare feet.

The walls were a nice crème hued contrast lit by floor lamps strategically placed to provide optimal lighting to accompany the chandelier, but still managed to leave some of the room in shadowy darkness. I focused on the crystals, trying to count them but stopping when I reached fifty. I was lying on some sort of chaise lounge; extremely comfortable but it left me feeling all shades of vulnerable.

Encouraged by the success of my eyes, I decided to push the limits and sit up. It was a bad idea, even with the inching slow movement and the aid of Sebastian. It felt like my head was on tectonic plates; each movement issuing a quake that sent them scraping against each other.

Sebastian must have expected it, because he pulled me forward, holding my hair back as I wretched into a trashcan he provided. My stomach didn't have any contents to empty but that didn't stop it from heaving until it was good and ready to stop. Taking a seat next to me, Sebastian waited until I was finished before offering me a glass of cool water. A sip was all I needed to swish the liquid in my mouth and spit it into the trashcan.

"Are we quite ready?" the woman hissed. "We've wasted enough time tonight."

"If you were in such a hurry, Brenda, perhaps you should have taken more care in the manner in which you obtained her," Sebastian replied calmly.

He moved the trashcan to kneel in front of me again, a handkerchief in his hand pressing against my lips. I knew he was trying to comfort me, but the last thing I wanted to do was appear weak in the face of enemies, even if that's exactly what I was. I leaned back, away from him; grateful the chaise had a back I could rest against. Slowly I turned my eyes to my would-be captors.

Brenda, it turned out, was the name of the woman in red. Glaring at me, arms folded over her chest from across the room she looked, if possible, even paler than she had earlier. She must have used a lot of her reserved blood to bring me down and that thought alone brought joy to my heart. The other male vampire that spoke stood just over Sebastian's shoulder and glared at me as if he'd be just as happy, if not happier, to see me dead. He wasn't ugly, at least not entirely, but he definitely would never be called handsome. He looked to have been in his mid thirties when he was turned, but his features still appeared too big for his face. His mouth just a hair too wide, his eyes stopped just short of bulging from their sockets and his nose seemed to spread a bit too far and come out too long. Staring at him I decided maybe ugly really was the best word to describe him.

There were at least a half a dozen other vampires in the room that I could see; the two goons from the garage, who turned out to be twins upon closer examination, a man and woman that sat on the bed intertwined in each others arms, which wouldn't have creeped me out if they hadn't been staring so intently at me. A girl that couldn't have been older than sixteen and young man that was so damned skinny if he turned sideway he'd disappear. I had no idea if there were more behind me or not, but at this point it didn't matter. The eight in front would have stopped me before I could do anything anyway. Besides, my head was sliding apart too much to work any magic.

"You won't be able to cast," the ugly vampire informed. He could have easily been reading my mind, but chances were he just took an educated guess. "The copper bindings on your wrists and neck negate your abilities."

I lifted both wrists to eye level and found there was indeed copper bands around them about an inch wide and half a centimeter thick. They looked like nothing more than two matching bracelets with some sort of ancient hieroglyphics etched into the metal, but they were anything but harmless. I could feel the magic in them humming against my skin where they touched. Turning my wrists over and examining them completely, there didn't appear to be a clasp on them; though I noticed on both, a sun hieroglyph indented deeper than the others. Raising my fingers to my neck I felt the same type of collar there as well.

"What the hell have you done?" I demanded in a low voice.

"A necessary step to keep our Murder safe from you, witch," he spat the word at me as if it were a substitute for something else that rhymed.

"Dani, please," Sebastian stated to return my focus to him. "The jewelry—"

"—Shackles," I corrected.

"…Only temporarily counteract your magic. Once they are removed your abilities will return."

"You knew about this?" I didn't bother to hide the accusatory tone of my voice.

"No," the only thing that prevented me from holding his gaze was my own fear of becoming entrapped in it. Without my magic I was even more susceptible. "When I left for the theater this evening it was with the understanding I would be allowed to speak with you first," he paused and glanced at the others, "Tomorrow."

"That was before Alexander was discovered to be missing," Brenda hissed.

"I don't know anything about that," I stated.

"Lies," came a unified voice from the two vampires on the bed.

The ugly vampire growled and moved forward, only Sebastian standing kept him from reaching me. I didn't bother moving, my legs were already letting me know they wouldn't co-sign vertical movement. Besides, there was nowhere for me to go.

"Get a hold of yourself, Peter."

Peter snarled at him, and then wrenched his arms free of Sebastian's grip. "Your word carries weight but even your pleas will not stay the hand of judgment."

"There will be no judgment without proof," Sebastian stated.

"Exactly what is it I'm being judged on?"

"Alexander!" Brenda yelled.

Despite my best efforts I visibly winced at the effect her shrill voice had on my pounding head.

"Where is he? What have you done with him and the others?"

"One more time for those who English is obviously not a first language; I don't know anything about Alexander or the others."

"Lies," the choir on the bed chanted softly again.

At the sound of their voices pain, like a thousand needles erupted at the sight of the shackles on my wrists and throat. I was able to catch the scream before it ripped from my throat, raising my wrists again, only this time blood trickle in thin lines down my arms; could feel it going to same down my neck.

"What the hell is this?" I let me gaze drift to Sebastian.

He raised his right arm encasing it with the fingers of his left hand where the shackles on my wrist sat. "Living metal," he answered softly. "They have bewitched it to seek the truth."

"To punish those who lie," Peter amended. "With each lie you tell the teeth will lance deeper into your flesh," he moved closer, his body sinking to the floor as his too wide mouth split into a grin. "Tell the truth, and I promise to kill you quickly. Continue your lies, and your death will be slow, painful, and by your own lips."

My eyes narrowed, but the effect was lost since I refused to meet his eyes directly. It was a word game; the truth could be interpreted as a lie if the wrong words were spoken. I'd just have to make sure I chose the right words. The good news was the new lancing pain in my neck and wrist was lifting the fog in my head.

"Okay," I took a deep breath and let my head lean back on the lounge. "This has to do with what you were telling me about at the theater, right?" my eyes opened to linger on Sebastian.

"Yes," he answered with a nod.

"We ask the questions here, not you!" Peter shouted.

"Then ask one I can answer, because beyond the teaser trailer Sebastian gave me tonight I don't know anything of what's you're talking about."

I would have said the room collectively held its breath and waited for the device to impale itself further into my skin, except not a one of them, even Sebastian who practiced so hard to appear human, seemed to be breathing. When nothing happened, Peter's mood seemed to darken.

"Of course she can lie, a question was not put forth," Brenda pointed out.

"Then ask the questions so we can be done with this," came from Sebastian. I could tell from the tone in his voice he was about as fed up with this as I was.

"Did you take part in the disappearance of Alexander?"

I jumped. Not because the devices tightened, but because the voice didn't come from anyone in the room. At least no one I could see. Nor did the voice come from any one direction but surrounded me. The vampires in the room reacted as well; Sebastian, Peter, Brenda, and the pair on the bed bowed their heads. The other vampires in the room actually seemed to shrink back and attempt to disappear into the shadows, as if they didn't want whoever was speaking to even notice them.

"Answer please," came the urging of the voice.

"No, I didn't."

"Did you take part in the disappearance of Stanley?"

"No," I replied again.

"Did you take part in the disappearance of Matilda?"

"I don't even know who these people are."

"Dani, please," Sebastian's voice was soft and rushed and held a note of urgency. "Answer his question."

"No, I didn't."

"Know you of any witches that practice the art of necromancy?"

"None that are alive," my reply was softer than the others, and I could feel my body tensing up for further mutilation. I'd answered his question truthfully, but there was a gray area to my words the device might read as a lie.

"Your words," the voice began with a moment of hesitation, "Ring true. Remove the restriction."

"But my lord," Peter began. He didn't turn in any direction so I assumed he was no more aware of where the owner of the voice was than me. "I must protest; she has already proved herself a threat to us. She used her powers against Brenda and the twins."

The voice chuckled, "Because she would not allow herself to be taken like a lamb to the slaughter?"

"But my lord…"

"Remove the restraints," he repeated in a curt tone. Whoever this guy was, he wasn't in the business of repeating himself. "Brenda, leave the room. Your control is unstable and I do not wish the scent of *Senorita* Harlow's blood to send you into fury. Take the twins with you."

Her lips peeled back from her teeth to reveal razor sharp white pointed fangs where her eyeteeth used to be. I wondered if her teeth were like that before or after the statement about my blood. I hadn't noticed before, but then I hadn't been paying attention to her either.

Peter produced something from his pocket and moved forward, but Sebastian stepped in his path again. Without a fuss Peter relinquished the object. It looked like a charm of some kind on a key chain, but when Sebastian fitted it into the compressed etching of the sun there was a releasing click. A counter clockwise twist pulled a barely audible hiss form my lips as the blades drew out of my skin, leaving rivets of blood and ten symmetrical incisions in my wrist. With nothing else to hold onto the claws retreated to lie against the flat of the bracelet. He removed first one then the other before finally removing the one from around my neck.

I must have been expecting it, or else I was just too tired to react to the vampire materializing behind Sebastian. He was as handsome as Peter way homely; from the lines in his face he must have been turned at an older age, but if anything it just made him look that much more distinguished. In his right hand he held three strips of clothe offering them to Sebastian. Judging from the frayed ends I was guessing they'd been ripped from something. Vampires don't often need first aid.

"My apologies, *Senorita* Harlow," his voice was the same, even though he was standing in the room it still seemed to come from everywhere. "We are not used to dealing with wounds in the same manner as humans. I'm afraid this is the best we have to offer."

"If you're not used to dealing with them, maybe you shouldn't inflict them," I returned, only to receive a warning from Sebastian in the form of a slight shake of his head. My friend took the strips one at a time securing them around my wrists and neck.

"Danika, allow me to introduce you to the leader of our Murder, Juan Ortiz."

"I wish I could say it was a pleasure, but all things considered…" I held up my covered but still bleeding wrists.

He bowed his head a bit. "Perhaps under different circumstances I could have made it much more pleasurable for you."

I kept my eyes averted from his; I didn't like the way my body was already responding to his presence and his voice, I didn't really need visual contact to seal the deal.

"I've answered your questions," I began with all the respect I could muster. "I'm tired, my neck hurts, my wrists hurt, my head is conducting its own Sheila E. drum solo, and right now I'd really just like to go home."

"Of course," he inclined his head in my direction. "But if I may make a request, *Senorita*?"

I really wanted to tell him to go to hell and that I'd had about all the requests I was going to take from him and his ilk for the night, but something in Sebastian's eyes told me smarting off to this guy would be about as sensible as running down a narrow street in front of a fleet of pissed off bulls.

"Yes?"

"Meet with Sebastian and myself tomorrow. If you do not feel comfortable meeting here you may pick the place, so long as it will afford us privacy to speak freely on delicate matters."

Again I managed to stave off my smart-assed reply for a general nod of compliance.

"Gracias *Senorita*," he nodded then bowed deep at the waist.

All it took was shifting my attention to Sebastian, when I returned it to the spot Juan stood he was gone. No puff of smoke, no spark of any kind, not even a sound. It was like he'd never been standing there at all.

Sebastian picked up an oak box at his feet; I manage to see the shackles inside before he closed the lid and handed the box to Peter who all but snatched it from his fingers.

"By the very definition of what she is, she should not be allowed to leave these walls," Peter spat; his words almost caused the air around him to crackle with energy.

"You wish this to be the cause of a war with every witch on the west coast?" Sebastian asked.

"They're killing us already, if you weren't so blind you'd see that."

"That," Sebastian began in that veiled warning voice again. "Is an assumption that has yet to be proven."

Peter hissed, like a cat, opening his mouth to show elongated fangs. Oddly enough it was when Sebastian returned his hiss that I found myself getting creeped out.

It was a cross between a mountain lion and a rattlesnake. It was also a sound I hoped not to hear from him again in the near or distant future.

"Can you stand?" Sebastian asked his attention back on me, his face a perfect mask once again.

"I need to get my car."

"Your car is here, I'll drive you to the nearest hospital. I believe you suffered a mild concussion at Brenda's hands."

"And how do you plan to explain this?" I asked holding up my wrists. "Take me home, I have herbs that will help."

"Alright," he conceded holding his hands out to help me to my feet. "Home it is."

CHAPTER THREE

SEBASTIAN must have arrived before Brenda and her thugs hauled me into the back of the limo and followed with my car, because it didn't appear to have been broken into... that and he had the key that was in my purse. He also had the good graces to remain silent as he drove; only giving me the occasion corner of his eye glance when we pulled to a light.

The streets were clear, but it still took a good thirty minutes to make it from the fancy mansion on the outskirts of San Francisco to my urban dwelling. The two times I tried to nod off to sleep Sebastian gently shook me awake again. I managed to catch myself before cursing him out. The digital clock on the dash displayed 2:43. The relief I felt at it not being as late as I originally thought was short lived by the sight of Finn's Challenger. I didn't see him inside his car, but the lights in my living room were on and I knew I'd turned them off before I left.

"You might want to leave," I muttered while still in the safety of my car.

Sebastian chuckled. "You think I'm afraid of the big bad wolf?"

Always one to repeatedly test fate, Sebastian handed me my keys and opened the door stepping into the crisp night air. I followed suit, swaying a bit as my head adjusted to the change in altitude.

I took a few steps but had to stop again and steady myself on the car's hood. My equilibrium was already dodgy and my street being on the upward slant of a hill didn't help matters. Sebastian had the good graces to wait until I made it to his side of the car before he hefted my arm around his shoulders and helped me. He was counting so softly I almost missed it.

"Five…four…three…two…"

He finished to the tune of my front door flung open and Finn's body filling the doorway, haloed by the hall light. Anger rolled from him in near suffocating waves even though I was still outdoors. He was off the porch and standing in from of me in movements too fast to visually track, fingers pulling at the makeshift bandage around my neck. If it was anything like my wrists, blood leaked through staining the fabric and outlining where the cuts were.

"What the hell happened?" he reached a hand out shoving Sebastian's shoulder. "Are you responsible for this you undead son-of-a-bitch?"

"When *exactly* was the last time I hurt Danika?"

"You think this is funny?" he snapped at Sebastian before turning his anger to me. "How the hell did this happen?"

I remained purposefully silent for several seconds as my eyes shifted from him, to the sky and finally to look up and down the street. "How about we continue this inside where the neighbors can't hear?"

Instead of answering, Finn stepped to the side and gestured for us to lead the way, however, Sebastian didn't move, at least he didn't move forward. His face turned to the sky as he closed his eyes and breathed deeply.

"Unfortunately I can't stay," he began with a regrettable tone. "Dawn's approaches and I have to speak with Juan before he beds for the day."

Finn gave a very nasty sounding grunt, accompanied by an eye roll. He bodily checked Sebastian out of the way as he took my arm from around the vampire's neck and settled it around his completing the Dani transfer. If I weren't sure I'd fall flat on my face without the help I would have opposed.

"I believe she's got a concussion," Sebastian informed casually. "Though she refuses to go to the hospital."

"Hospitals ask questions," I sang softly.

"The device to detect untruths has been removed," Sebastian countered.

Sebastian placed a kiss on my cheek as the werewolf gave a soft warning growl.

"Call me after sundown this evening and let me know where you wish to meet."

I blinked and he was gone, just as Juan had done earlier. I'd witness Sebastian perform that disappearing act before, but that didn't make it any less creepy. That wasn't my normal reaction, but then on a normal night I wasn't kidnapped by pissed off vampires.

I have to give Finn props, he managed not to say a word or utter a question until after he closed and locked the door.

He helped me to the kitchen and parked me on one of the benches in my breakfast nook. Dropping to the balls of his feet he undid the bandages and began inspecting the wounds.

"I suppose you've got something to put on these?"

I smirked and managed to remember in time not to nod. "Yeah, but I'll need some gauze. Upstairs bathroom, under the sink."

Rising to his full height, Finn left the kitchen, taking the back stairs to the second floor. Meanwhile I regained my footing and slowly made my way to where my pots and pan hung on wall hooks and removed a small cooking pot. Filling it midway with water, I set it on the stove, and then stepped into the pantry, which I'd converted to a green house/herbal garden. I knew the recipe for healing wounds by heart, not because my life was so dangerous, before tonight I'd never been kidnapped or personally met another vampire than Sebastian. Nope, I was just that accident-prone.

I had just finished sprinkling the herbs I collected into the water and adjusting the fire when Finn returned.

"What are you doing up?" he barked. Not waiting for an answer he took me by the shoulders pushing me back to the bench he deposited me onto earlier. "Is there anything else you need to add to this?"

"Nope."

"Anything you need to say?"

I glared at him. "Yeah, abracadabra, presto-chango."

"Cute."

I gave one of those smart-ass smiles. "Just stir it with a wooden spoon and when it starts to steam add the gauze you'll use to cover these," I held my wrists up in case he wasn't sure what the gauze would be going on.

"What are you doing here?"

"I called you -like I said I would- when I got home from my shift. You never answered."

I sat patiently waiting; sure there was more to his story that was coming. Two minutes later I realized that was all there was.

"That's it? I didn't answer my phone so you decided to what get the drop on me? Does that even sound like the actions of a sane, rational person to you? You do realize being a werewolf doesn't mean you get to abandon all semblance of good judgment, right?"

"I called at eleven, and again at twelve, and again at one before I came over to find you front door partially open. By the scent, I'm guessing vampires since I know you'd never leave with your front door unlocked, less on sitting open. Nothing was broken, and it doesn't look like anything was taken," he added quickly. "I was worried about you," his voice softened as he added the gauze to the water and turned the fire off. "That's what happens when you care about someone and they aren't where they say they'll be at a given moment in time."

I gave a soft sigh before finally relenting and relaying everything that happened after leaving the theater, though my memory of the parking garage was sketchy at best. It was like watching a movie that was missing some of the reels. You know something important happened on the missing reels but damn if you know what it is. While I talked, Finn covered my wrists and neck with the gauze saturated in the herbal remedy, and covered those with thicker bandages. He then checked for the severity of my possible concussion, which included a bright penlight shone into my eyes, probing fingers, and a balance test I failed.

"I can't believe these words are coming out of my mouth, but I agree with Sebastian, I think you should let me take you to the hospital. You've got a mild concussion at best, at worse there could be something else scrambled in there," his fingers lightly touched my temple.

"I'll be fine, I just need to sleep."

"I know," he dropped his voice to a soft whisper, the hands that skillfully tended to my injuries cupping my jaw. "But you really shouldn't. Not with a concussion."

"I can't go to the hospital right now. They'll keep me twenty-four hours at least, and I've got a meeting tomorrow night... this evening... you know what I mean."

He sat back on his heels and passed a hand over his face. "You don't owe them anything."

"I never said I did."

"Then why are you helping them?" he snapped. "Because of Sebastian?"

A battle of wills quietly began as we locked gazes. Finn rose slowly giving himself a height advantage over me. He knew I would look away first, hell I knew it too.

It was just a matter of how long I would make him wait. There were two dominant parties in the kitchen but there was only one Alpha werewolf.

"You really don't want to challenge me in your current condition, Dani," he warned softly when the minutes began to tick by and my gaze didn't waiver.

When I finally did look away I made sure not to lower my eyes in submission, but focus them past his shoulder. He'd won and proved to be more dominant, without me declaring to be submissive. Technically he hadn't won, I withdrew, but a submission by withdraw was still a submission.

"You still haven't answered my question."

"Because it might be a necromancer, Finnius. Do you realize the impact that could have upon safety of the witch community?"

"You don't know that it is. You don't know what it could be. There are a lot of creatures out there between heaven and hell that could take out a vampire besides necromancers."

"I agree, however, the only way to find out is to meet with them and see what evidence they have."

"Fine, what if it turns out not to be a necromancer, will you promise me you won't go after it?"

I didn't bother answering right away; Finn would know if I lied to him. There was nothing stronger than werewolf's senses. They were able to scent the change in pheromones and hear the increased heart rate that accompanied a lie, especially in those they were familiar with. I didn't want to lie to him, but I didn't want to piss him off anymore than I already had. Finn cut me slack because I wasn't a werewolf, and he cut me even more because of the feelings he had for me, but he could still be pushed too far.

"I don't know Finn."

His cerulean blue eyes closed in a blink and reopened to the translucent almost glowing green of his wolf. His nostrils flared as paced the length of my kitchen. I called his name once, but he didn't stop pacing. When I called it again and those wolf eyes focused on me, I wished I'd left him be. He stalked forward, slow enough for me to run; slow enough for him to regain control of his wolf... neither happened. The rim of those burning green irises had trimmed themselves in black. He and his wolf were battling and the wolf was winning.

He stopped his advance, as he reached the island in my kitchen and pivoted his body; palms pressed flat against the countertop.

"If it's not a witch dropping vampires this quickly, it might be in our best interest to find out what is. Who's to say it views vampires as its only enemy."

I watched him finally regain composure. The sound of bones cracking filled the kitchen as he closed his eyes and rotated his neck from the left to the right.

"You're right," his voice was once again soft and in control. The blue eyes that met mine as he spoke were pure Finn. "But I don't like you working that close to anything that's hurt you once."

"Well, they surprised me. I wasn't paying attention; I wasn't ready. Next time I will be."

"How long has it been since you woke up?"

"I guess a couple hours."

He gave a slight nod to that answer. "Why don't you let me take you upstairs so you can get some rest?"

"I thought I wasn't supposed to go to sleep."

"Technically you're not, but I'll let you sleep if you'll let me wake you every hour without curse me out or try to take my head off."

I smirked, but when I realized I was too tired to even think up a decent comeback I just nodded and pushed myself to my feet. I waved him away when he moved close to take my arm around his shoulders again. It wasn't that I didn't want him to help; I just wanted to see if I could make it alone. The pounding in my head had lessened considerably, and the dizziness was just about gone completely.

Finn helped me out of my shoes, corset, and pants leaving me clad only in my underwear and the white dress shirt before literally tucking me into bed. He lay down behind me. The blankets may have separated our bodies, but it didn't keep him from nuzzling his face against the bandages around my neck. Catching a nose full of the herbs he gave a disgruntle snort before readjusting his nose into my hair. I just smiled and snuggled closer to him enjoying the warmth his body, and the security his scent brought.

* * * * *

Finn tried everything short of threatening bodily harm to get me to stay home from work. We compromised on me arriving three hours late, and him stopping by with lunch. I didn't really need him to bring me lunch, our cafeteria was surprising good, but he would have come to check up on me anyway, besides any excuse was a good excuse to see Finn.

Lunch consisted of baked chicken and potato salad, both made by Finn who, I had learned in our first month of courtship, was an exceptionally good cook. I'd forgotten I hadn't eaten since early yesterday evening, but at the smell of the food my stomach felt the need to remind me loudly. Werewolves were voracious eaters on a regular day, so by the time we were finish so was the chicken and all but a half serving of the potato salad.

Sitting out on the quad of the museum we watched each other in silence for a while. Finn usually kept his hair in a neat close cut, but for some reason had dodged his barber the past two months. Blonde hair that normally held the illusion of being straight had been allowed to grow long enough to begin to how its true curly nature. The sun managed to leak through some of the leafy coverage in the tree we rested near and fell upon the short curly locks transforming them to the color of melted gold on fire.

"How are your wrists and neck doing?" he finally asked breaking the silence first.

"Itching, but that's a good sign."

He nodded then fell silent again as he stretched out on his side, leaning on his elbow with his head resting in the palm of his right hand. The bandages around my wrist were safely hidden under the sleeves of my shirt, but the one against my neck stood out like a beacon. If it had been winter or a mild spring, I could have at least hid it under a turtleneck, but the weather was closer to summertime. Most people actually didn't ask, I suppose it was considered rude. The few that did I just told them it was a rash brought on by allergies. If they didn't buy it, they didn't question it any further.

I knew if I lay down there was a good chance I would drift off to sleep. I was still tired from the previous night, and this night was promising to be fairly trying itself. The near constant throbbing in my head seemed to ease at it rested against the cool grass, and my eyes hurt less protected behind closed lids.

"You're staring at me," I stated; eyes still safely sealed behind my lids.

"I can't help it, you're beautiful."

I gave a weary smile as I felt one of his fingers trace a path from my forehead, over the bridge of my nose to the tip, across the center of my lips and down to my chin.

"I don't feel very beautiful right now," I confessed opening my eyes.

He had moved, his body now laying very close to mine in the grass though he was still propped up on his elbow as he stared down at me.

"No one feels beautiful with a concussion," he grinned. "I guess that means you'll just have to trust my opinion then won't you?"

I wasn't surprised when he leaned down and dusted his lips against mine. I wasn't a fan of public displays of affection, but no one else was present on the green where we lunched, and my concern didn't extend to anyone passing by the upper windows that looked over the campus. Besides, I wasn't ashamed to admit, when Finn kissed me, the world ceased to exist beyond his lips.

His weight shifted as he deepened the kiss. Knowing my potential reaction he restrained his hands from wandering over my body and instead moved the fingers that had been toying with my nose and lips to glide into my hair. Finn was nothing if not an excellent kisser, but the moment the tips of his fingers came in contact with the rather large lump on the back of my head I yelped in protest.

"Ah, baby, I'm so sorry. Are you okay?"

"Yeah," I raised my hand to the bump carefully letting my fingers explore the edges, and it still brought a hiss to my lips. "It's just a little sensitive right now."

I waited for him to lay down pillowing his head on his hands, before I curled on my side resting my head on my arms watching him this time. Staring at Finn up close it always hit me how devastatingly handsome he really was. It was a realization usually accompanied with me wondering what the hell someone as gorgeous as him was doing with me. He could have easily been a high fashion model as opposed to a rescue helicopter pilot, though saving people fit his personality far better than posing for a camera in Calvin Klein tighty-whities.

Being supermodel hot, however, didn't always work in the favor of being an Alpha werewolf. Finn did what he could at times to try and take away from his physical beauty and make himself look more rugged; the two day old growth he sometimes left on his face, keeping his hair trimmed, and the stern expression he kept over his features when we were in public or around his pack. Finn could look down right menacing when he needed to, and when he stood at attention with that towering height, forget about it.

"I've been thinking about what you said this morning," he began, "You're right about the vampire problem potentially being a problem for the rest of us," he turned his head so our eyes met. "You're still meeting with them tonight?"

I nodded. "Sebastian will be there and a guy named, Juan who I think is like the head vampire of San Francisco's Murder. At least that's the impression I got last night."

"He's not like the head vampire, he is the head vampire," Finn confirmed, angling his head so he was once again staring up into the trees.

"You've met him?"

"No, but he's the head of San Francisco's Murder; I'm the alpha of San Francisco's wolf pack. I know who he is, just as he knows who I am."

"Do you trust him?" He glanced at me and gave a smirk to which I rolled my eyes. "You know what I mean, Finn."

"Yes, I know what you mean, as far as trusting him goes… I trust him to act in a manner he sees best for his people."

"Care to be just a little more vague on your answer?"

He chuckled softly. "Let's say he happened upon you being held up by a gunman that was obviously going to kill you and his actions could either save your life, or condemn it. He would save it, but only if it was to his benefit or he thought he could get something out of it. He wouldn't do it out of the goodness of his heart, or because it was the right thing. The thing with vampires is you never know what is to their benefits and what isn't. Have you decided where you're going to meet with them?

I nodded. "Here. I don't want him at my home and I figure this will give us some privacy and still be on fairly neutral ground."

"I could have Luke stand with you. I'd come myself but more than likely he'd interpret that as a challenge, and I don't think we want a power struggle just yet."

Luke Harris was Finn's best friend and his Beta; second in command of the pack. We got on great so long as dominance never came up. Finn's declaration of me as his mate was a two edged sword; on one side it meant anyone that messed with me would have to deal with Finn's wrath, on the other it also gave me next in line control over the pack under Finn. Female werewolves hold the rank of their mates, as Finn's mate –even though I hadn't officially claimed the status- I had dominance over the other females in the pack. In Finn's absence, that dominance moved over the men as well.

It would have been a bitter pill for the men to swallow by itself; the fact that I wasn't even a werewolf caused it to get lodged in some of their throats. Finn's declaration was meant to protect me, but it really just secured my spot in the line of fire.

"I don't know; it might be best if he doesn't know the werewolves know anything about this yet."

"Good point, still, I'd feel better if you weren't alone on this."

"I know you don't trust Sebastian, but I do."

"I know you do, Dani. As much as it pains me to say this, I believe under normal circumstance he'd keep you safe from harm, if for no other reason then the threat of what I'd do to him if he didn't. However, these are not normal circumstances. Juan is the equivalent of an Alpha in the vampire world, and no matter how much you mean to Sebastian or his ultimate agenda, if Juan orders him to kill you… he has to obey. I don't think even Sebastian is strong enough to go against Juan."

I sighed, closed my eyes, and rolled onto my back. Things really did have a way of turning complicated quickly. I decided to let the remark go about me being a part of Sebastian's ultimate plan, because part of what he said made sense. Sebastian was old, and he was strong, but the power that washed over me from Juan last night was stronger than anything I've ever felt. If he said to kill me, or tried himself, would Sebastian really be powerless to stop him? It was a question I didn't want answered, and a test I didn't want our friendship to endure.

"What about one of your elders?"

I scoffed at that shaking my head slightly. "You're kidding right? They'll not so politely remind me that the only troubles they concern themselves with are witch troubles, and until this is proven to truly be a witch problem they'll not concern themselves with it."

The elders were nothing if not predictable, and in this instance, their line of thinking was parallel to the thinking of vampires. If it didn't affect them it wasn't their problem, and wouldn't become their problem until it affected them. If it turns out to be a necromancer they'll step in guns blazing if only to keep the tenuous peace between witches and vampires. If it turned out to be anything else the chances of them helping were hinged on the benefits they received. So I was waiting until I had a better understanding of what we were up against before asking for their help.

I closed my eyes and sighed softly. Sitting up, I began gathering the leftover foil and used plates and utensil, shoving them into the plastic bag they came from.

"Danika?" Finn sat up as well, watching me. "What is it?"

"Nothing, I just thought of who I could ask."

"Who?"

I hesitated because I knew what his reaction would be. "Kailani."

"Kailani," he repeated letting the name roll of his tongue several times. I could tell the way his eyes grew larger he finally realized exactly whom I meant. "The only Kailani I know of is a sea dragon."

"That's the only one I know of too."

CHAPTER FOUR

IT took twenty minutes to calm Finn down enough so I could explain my rationale of involved Kailani. He still didn't agree, but since he wasn't able to offer an alternate plan that wouldn't involve a power struggle or all out massacre, he finally relented.

After Finn was on his disgruntle way I placed a call to Kailani to make sure she was around. During the winter she tends to migrate back to her homeland of Hawaii, not that I could blame her. If given the choice between spending winter in San Francisco and winter in Hawaii I'd definitely take the latter. When she did stay in San Francisco she dwelled along the Warf.

The sun hadn't quite gone down by the time I got off of work so I left a message with Sebastian telling him to meet me at the employee entrance in the back of the museum after seven. I wasn't sure how long it would take to convince Kailani to come along, or if she would. I wanted to have time to come up with a back up plan just in case.

Pulling up in front of her condo, I climbed out of my car and walked to the front door, pushing the button next to the name Kailani. She didn't have a last name, at least not one I or apparently anyone else knew. Though I suppose when you're a sea dragon all you really need is one name.

Chances of Kailani helping were pretty high. She owed me a favor; technically she owed me three, though I would never mention the debt to her. As her culture dictated it was her job to remember or risk bringing dishonor to her family. If that weren't enough the intrigue alone would be adequate to rouse her curiosity to accompany me. Out of all the dragons, sea dragons had the most insatiable curiosity. The promise of meeting the head vampire of San Francisco would probably be enough of a lure itself, but the promise of an intrigue would only sweeten the deal.

Buzzed through the outer door, I took the stairs to the third floor where the sea dragon resided. She'd already opened the door to her unit allowing me to walk on in.

"I'll be right with you, Danika," she called out from somewhere towards the back of the condo.

The sea dragon definitely knew how to live in style, I'd give her that. Her condo was located directly across from Fisherman Warf. The smell of fish would have been too much for me, but I suppose for a creature of the sea it's perfect. The building was nothing to look at from the outside, but inside she had only top of the line furniture, appliances and electronics. Did I mention sea dragons could assume human form?

Legend has it, as legend has everything at some point; that hundreds of years ago a sea dragon and a sorcerer went into battle allying together against a spectacular foe. Depending on the version the foe ranges from another dragon to an army of demons. At any rate the sea dragon could only accompany the sorcerer when the battle was in the water. Seeing victory easily obtained the foe -dragon, demon, or other- took the battle to the land.

Knowing she would never survive fighting alone, the sorcerer cast a spell over the sea dragon allowing him to take human form, and thusly they won the battle.

After the battle, as a token of appreciation for their help, sorcerer taught the sea dragon the ritual to perform to allow him to come ashore whenever the mood struck, though they would forever have to wear the symbol of their true vessel. Should they be in human form and the symbol lost, they would lose the power to return to the sea.

As gratitude for freeing him from the confines of the sea, the sea dragon granted the sorcerer the mental prowess our sect is known for. In exchange, the

I don't know how true the legend is, I suspect it has roots in fact though it might have been embellished over the generations. I do know I've never seen Kailani without this excruciatingly long seashell necklace.

I had just walked over to peer through the telescope set up on her patio when Kailani came bouncing out of the back covered only in a tube top that really was more like a strapless bikini top, and an asymmetrical whimsical skirt that could have doubled for a barely opaque sarong. Outwardly she had the appearance of a Hawaiian female in her early twenties. Truthfully, Kailani had pasted twenty back in the fourteen hundreds. Dragons live an incredibly long time, some even believe them to be immortal.

The front of her black hair was done in intricate tiny braids the led into more intricate tiny braids, some accompanied by delicate small violet flowers others not. The rest of the long black tresses hung straight and full almost to her waist. Kailani had the stunning beauty that could have been on the cover of magazines, walking down a runway, or launching ships to war. On the couple occasions we were actually in public together, men literally fell over themselves staring at her. I was counting on her beauty captivating Juan tonight.

"It's been too long," she purred after embracing me in a hug tight enough to crack my back. "Come, sit. I must admit our conversation on the telephone earlier left me near bursting with curiosity."

Led to her couch, I took a seat next to her, waiting for her to get comfortable before speaking. "Unfortunately I don't know much more beyond what I've already told you."

The bright grin never left her face. "*The* master vampire will be there tonight? You are certain of this?"

I nodded. "According to our brief conversation last night, he will give me as much information as they have, which the more I think about it the more I doubt will help. I get the feeling this Juan is pretty old, and if he doesn't know what's taking his vampires, the chances of me knowing are slim to none."

"You have not heard of Juan Ortiz?"

I don't know why, maybe it was the way she said it or the look in her face but her statement made me feel as if I had just kicked a puppy, laughed, and walked away. Still, I couldn't help what I didn't know.

"The only Juan Ortiz I've ever heard of is a Spanish conquistador that went searching for the lost members of the Narváez Expedition."

She grinned brightly at that. "You *have* heard of him then. Good, I feared perhaps you were not as knowledgeable as I'd come to expect."

"Hold up, you're telling me the Juan Ortiz I learned about in my early American history class at Berkley is the same man that's calling himself the master of San Francisco's Murder of Vampires?"

"Yes, you thought perhaps there was another Juan Ortiz?"

"I… it's just…" I paused, pulling up the date I remembered him dying and calculating the math in my head. "That would make him four hundred and eighty-eight years old."

"Yes, magnificent isn't it?"

Magnificent was definitely one way of looking at it, not exactly the way I saw it but definitely one way of viewing it. The amount of power and energy rolling from Juan last night made more sense though. I didn't image one got to be almost half a millennium old and not be powerful. It also made me think meeting him anywhere was a bad idea.

Everything was suddenly in a new perspective, and I couldn't help but wonder; why did a five hundred year old vampire need my help?

"It's... definitely something," I concluded.

"And you have told him of me, and he wishes to meet me, yes?" she added just as enthusiastically as before.

"Not exactly, he doesn't actually know about you."

Confusion caused her brow to crease in a frown. "Then why does he wish to meet me?"

"He doesn't know you're coming. He knows I'm bringing someone, but not who the someone is."

"Your Finn, he does not wish to accompany you to meet Senor Ortiz?" her head tilted to the side as if she were still having a hard time grasping the situation. I guess I should have expected it; sea dragons didn't rationalize things the same as people.

"He wanted to come, but bringing the Alpha werewolf of San Francisco could potentially be like throwing a lit match on an open powder keg."

She nodded finally understanding. "Ah yes, they can be such silly creatures. I wonder if they realized the power they could share jointly if they only worked together," she sat quietly for a moment pondering that. "No, it would be too strong I think; perhaps it is best it remains unrealized and untapped."

"Right," I nodded pretending to follow when I didn't. "The thing is, he doesn't think it's a good idea I walk into this meeting alone, and the more I learn about Juan, the more I'm agree."

Her entire body jerked upright as she beamed. "You wish me to be your muscle?"

I probably wouldn't have suppressed the amused smile on my lips even if I could have. "Something like that."

"I'm not very intimidating in this form, but perhaps my presence will encourage him to behave like the gentleman I have heard him to be."

"As long as I don't end up dead or worse that works for me."

She clapped her hands. "I will come; an exchange for the many times you have aided me."

"Thank you, Kailani."

"We meet tonight, yes?"

I nodded and looked to my watch. "Yeah, in about oh… two hours."

"Excellent!" she jumped into a standing position from the couch. "We have time to eat. There is a sushi bar that has been established around the corner while I was away. I'd very much like to try it tonight before our meeting."

* * * * *

If I had expected Kailani to change into something more conservative for the meeting I would have been disappointed. Fortunately I knew the sea dragon well enough to know the strapless, lightweight, cotton sundress was about as conservative as she got.

The material was fine enough to catch and fly in even the gentlest breezes, while the color along with the strappy sandals on her feet matched the flowers in her hair.

I was grateful I had a big lunch, because sushi definitely wasn't my thing. I ate a bowl of rice and a few noodles, but mostly just made polite conversation and listened to Kailani's stories about her recent travel to Hawaii. We were about forty-five minutes early arriving at the museum for the meeting, with Kailani still providing detailed description of her exploits, and me wishing I new a spell off hand that would temporarily rob me of my hearing. It was a good reminder of why I didn't hang out with Kailani on a regular basis. By the time Sebastian and Juan arrived I was just about ready to throw myself onto the mercy of their fangs.

Don't get me wrong, I liked Kailani, and I sure as hell respected her. She was over a millennium old and I was willing to bet that was based on neither luck nor chance. But sometimes her energy was more than I could bare, especially working on truncated sleep and a slightly aching head.

The vampires pulled up with Sebastian behind the wheel of his dark maroon BMW M5, and Juan riding shotgun. Both men disembarked the car as if the movement had been rehearsed; doors opening and closing at the same time, both walking around the car to the front then continuing forward towards me and Kailani.

Sebastian was dressed much as he usually did when not attending opening night to his plays, a pair of dark blue jeans, a dress shirt with the first few buttons left undone, a pair of black loafers, and a leather jacket to stave off the cool night breeze that wouldn't have affected him anyway. Still as he's told me several times, appearance is everything. Juan was much more conservative wearing a tan three piece suit, white shirt san the tie, and camel colored loafers.

Looking at him again, I assessed his look was more distinguished than actually being attractive, though he was definitely easy on the eyes. He was shorter than men I was generally attracted to, a fact that was magnified as he stood next to Sebastian who topped out around six-two or so, Juan was doing good if he reached five-eight. His nose was a bit long for his face, his lips far too thin, and his eyes too small and shifty, yet there was no mistaking the magnetism about him. I wondered if it was because he was almost half a millennium old, or if it was something he possessed while he had a pulse.

Forcing myself to look away, I instead fixed my gaze on the safer target of Sebastian. Sometimes I was attracted to this vampire, but we were really too good at being friends for me to attempt to muck it up with complications a relationship would bring. Not to mention the little factor of being in a relationship with Finn. Not to mention the little factor of vampires not really being relationship prone. Monogamy wasn't really in a vampire's vocabulary, and honestly who could blame them.

Eternity is a long time to be with the same person, no matter how deep and endless the love.

Sebastian once told me in one of our many heart to heart conversations that vampires love humans for what they represent, mortality. They love in humans all the things they no longer possess themselves. The only problem with that is humans die. Rather the vampire loses the human to a mortal death or turns them, they ultimately end up losing the very thing they fell in love with. Rather sad.

I remember being depressed several nights after that conversation. Immortality is one of those ideas that are great on paper; not so great in practice.

Meeting Sebastian's gaze, I watched a slow smile creep across his lips as his left eyebrow shot up. Try as I might, I couldn't keep the blush from shooting up from my neck to the rest of my face and burning the tips of my ears. Smug bastard knew exactly what I was thinking.

"*Senorita* Harlow, thank you for agreeing to meet with us."

Juan held his hand out to me, which I inspected for several moments before accepting it. I went in for a handshake but he changed his hold bringing the back of my hand to his lips for a kiss. I could feel his eyes on me but refused to meet his gaze.

"And your friend?" he released my hand and turned to Kailani. "I trust discretion was used in your selection?"

"Kailani, this is Senor Juan Ortiz, head of San Francisco's Murder. Senor Ortiz, Kailani is…" I glanced at the sea dragon, hesitated, and mentally booted my behind for not having asked Kailani earlier her position on Juan knowing what she was. "Very wise and experienced in many oddities of the world."

"It is acceptable for him to know, Dani," she began as Juan took her hand and kissed it much the same manner he'd done mine. She met his gaze before giving a bow and lowering her head. "I am one of the few remaining sea dragons of the west."

"Truly?" his eyes looked over Kailani again as if the rarest gem had been revealed to him. He released her hand so he could walk around her, taking every inch of her in as he gazed in wonder. "I have heard many times of the legend of sea dragons but never in all my years have my eyes laid upon one until now."

He looked at me and for the moment I found myself caught in his gaze. I could feel my knees weaken. I looked away quickly, taking a sudden interest in the sidewalk.

"I must say *Senorita* Harlow I am truly impressed. For you to have such a creature as your acquaintance, less on willing to accompany you is remarkable indeed. I am beginning to understand Sebastian's fascination with you."

"Only the tip of the iceberg I assure you," I could hear the amusement in his voice. I didn't have to look at Sebastian to know he was enjoying the hell out of this.

"So, um, why don't we take this inside?" I posed it as a question out of sheer courtesy; after all it wasn't like we were about to discuss the absence of vampires and possible necromancers in the parking lot of the museum; even if it was after hours.

Using my keys, I unlocked the employee entrance and lead the way down the hall and down the stairs to the broom closet that was currently doubling as my office. I didn't like having Juan at my back but it wasn't like he knew which way to go.

After I took the chair behind my desk there were only two other chairs to be had on the other side. Juan stood behind one, his hand placed on the back as if holding it for Kailani as she took a seat. He claimed the last, putting him closest to the door with Sebastian standing behind his left shoulder.

I told myself there was no cause for me to be concerned over him being in the way of me and the only exit to my office. And currently he seemed to be more interested in Kailani than either the original reason for his visit or me.

"It is not often one meets a creature with your distinction and grace," Juan began, crossing one leg over the other and shifting in his seat so he faced Kailani more. "If I may be so bold as to ask your true age?"

Kailani gave a rather coy smile as she tilted her head and lowered her eyes to the side. She could unintentionally flirt better than most people who put whole-hearted effort into the act.

"Senor Ortiz do you really think it polite to ask a lady her true age?"

He chuckled and took her hand between both of his again for a light kiss. "Of course not, but you can't blame a man for trying."

"Let us just say," she began covering his hands with her free one, "That I had already hit my stride when you were but a babe dreaming of adventures as you slept in your basinet. Still it is an honor to meet one as accomplished as you."

"You pay me a great service with your compliments, *Senorita*," he bowed his head. "You are too kind."

I glanced to Sebastian in time to catch the faint smile flirting with his lips and his quick wink in my direction. I also couldn't help but realize how tired I was starting to feel or how my wrists where those damn shackle things tore the flesh was starting to hurt like hell.

After clearing my throat I spoke. "Mind if we cut to the chase? I was up rather late last night."

Juan's eyes flashed in my direction and he gently inclined his head. "Of course, *Senorita* Harlow, my apologies."

He settled back into his chair, his hands folded delicately over his knees, fingers clasped together. It was eerie to watch him; he didn't move, he didn't blink; there was no steady rise and fall of his chest, no slight flutter of movement that is innate in all mortal creatures. Maybe he felt comfortable enough not to pretend because everyone in the room knew what he was. Maybe he just didn't care to play human as Sebastian did.

"First, allow me to apologize again for last night, and for Brenda's behavior," he began. I know he was looking at me, but I was looking at a point just beyond his shoulder. I'd almost perfected the art of meeting a vampire's gaze without meeting their eyes. I also noticed like Sebastian there was very little trace of an accent, save when he said words with R's in them or those belonging to his native tongue. "Alexander is her brother by rebirth; she's taking his disappearance rather hard. That in no way excuses her actions, but gives you insight to the reasoning behind them."

I nodded. It didn't make me like her anymore but at least I could understand why she was a bitch. I was an only child, but I had a few friends as close as sisters to me, and I could imagine how I'd feel if one of them disappeared.

"What about Peter?"

"Peter I'm afraid has no justification," Juan stated and unless I missed my guess there was a disapproving tone in his voice.

"Peter's always been a loose canon," Sebastian stated.

"He does have his redeemable qualities," Juan stated, though I got the feeling it was more for Sebastian's benefit than mine.

"Which are far to fleeting and don't outweigh the bad."

"*No ventile nuestro lavadero sucio delante de extranjeros, Sebastian*," Juan stated softly. Sebastian smiled but fell silent with an inclination of his head. I made a mental note to brush up on my Spanish.

"Last night you mentioned two other names in addition to Alexander, a Matilda and Stanley?"

"*Sí*, you have a good memory."

"Served me well in college," I leaned back in my chair, "Why don't you start from the top and tell me everything you know."

"Unfortunately that is precious little," he stated. "Matilda was the first to go missing over two months ago. About six weeks after that Stanley disappeared, and most recently Alexander."

"How much time lapsed between Alexander and Stanley?"

"Close to three weeks."

"Any idea where they were when the nabbing happened?" I fished through the top drawers on my desk before coming back with a notepad and pen jotting a few notes down along the paper.

"Matilda and Stanley we are not sure, however, we know Alexander was taken from his sanctuary."

Nodding I added those notes to the list. "How do you know that?"

"Because he shares it with his sister. Brenda has stated when she bedded down at dawn, Alexander was in his room, when she awoke he was gone."

I looked up at that, forgetting whom I was talking to for a moment and meeting his eyes. "Whoever took him came into a sanctuary occupied by two vampires?"

He nodded, "It would appear so."

"Maybe he left and was taken then."

"Vampires are creatures of habit, Dani," Sebastian cut in, "Alexander and Brenda have hunted together every evening since they were re-birthed over seventy years ago. It is very remote he would suddenly decide to leave his sister behind."

"Alright, fine, how does your suspicion of necromancers play into his disappearance?"

"There was a residue left behind at Brenda and Alexander's sanctuary... a magical feel in the air."

"There are many creatures capable of wielding the type of magic strong enough to incapacitate a vampire," Kailani stated.

"Very true, but I have smelled this residue before," Sebastian stated.

"Care to elaborate?" I pushed, shifting my eyes to Sebastian.

The vampire paused, his eyes falling to the back of Juan's head. It wasn't until the head of the Murder gave a slight nod that my friend continued.

"The scent of a witch is very distinctive," he began softly. "When I was younger I had a run in with a death de—" he paused, his eyes flicking to mine as he caught himself before completing the derogatory statement, "—A necromancer. For those with the nose to catch it, the smell of jasmine and decay is very distinctive indeed. It is a smell that permeates Brenda and Alexander's sanctuary."

I pressed my lips together, letting what they said sink in as the room fell into silence for a few minutes. The air in my office was charged, but it was hard to tell if it was from me, Kailani, the vampires, or a combination of the four of us. More than likely it was the really just Juan by himself.

"Alright, for argument's sake lets say that it was a necromancer, have you or anyone in your Murder pissed any off lately?"

"No," Juan answered quickly.

"Then why would one take the risk of going into the sanctuary of two vampires? Doesn't make sense."

"I assure you, *Senorita* Harlow if I knew the reasoning behind the deaths or kidnappings I would more than likely have the culprit behind it by now."

"And you've not received any contact, demands, nothing from whoever is taking your vampires?"

"No, there has been no communication from the person or persons responsible."

"You said that Alexander and his sister are both over seventy years old?" Kailani stated looking to Sebastian with her large brown eyes. I watched, as the other vampire almost seemed to melt under her gaze, smiling softly and nodding his head. I'd have to remember to tease him about that later.

"It would take an experienced necromancer to engage a vampire of that age. Especially one that may risk running into two adolescent vampires."

I nodded to that. "Good point," I nodded and jotted down a few other notes.

"How old were the other two?"

"Matilda was nearly a century and a half; Stanley was barely two decades into the new life."

"Has anyone been to their sanctuaries?"

"Of course, *Senorita*," Juan nodded.

"And no scent of jasmine and decay there?"

"None that was detected, though Matilda's absence was not noticed for almost a week. Since Alexander has gone missing I have had my vampires check in nightly with Sebastian or Peter, and they in turn check in with me."

"Who are the oldest among you?"

I could feel his eyes on me, but didn't dare meet them. "How is that relevant?"

"I'm not sure yet, I'm trying to establish a pattern. Maybe it has something to do with age, especially if Matilda was one of the older vampires."

"There are those older than Matilda in the Murder, *Senorita* Harlow. Much older, myself included."

I knew a hint to back down when I heard it, but I couldn't help but wondered if I told him I knew who he was and exactly how old he was would it loosen his tongue at all.

"Okay, did the other two live alone?"

"*Sí.*"

"Was it common knowledge that Alexander lived with his sister?"

"Among the Murder, *sí.*"

I drummed my fingers on my desk, my eyes casting from Juan's general direction to Sebastian. "Why me?"

"I beg your pardon?"

"Why are you coming to me for help? I'm sure Sebastian's told you I'm a sorcerer."

He chuckled, letting his elbows rest on the arm of the chair while his fingertips barely touched against each other. "There are multiple reasons behind my heeding Sebastian's advice and employing your services to track down this rogue necromancer, not the least of which is the implication something like this could have on the witch community. I would hate to think of what could happen if word got out that a necromancer had been unleashed upon us without provocation. The last time that happened in the late 1600s it had dire effects on your community, *sí?*"

I pressed my lips together, my posture suddenly becoming very straight, my eyes almost meeting his but staring at his ear instead.

"Are you threatening me?"

"On the contrary," he stated in that suave voice, "I am giving you and yours a chance to clear your names before I am forced to take this matter to the Council of Councils."

Momma always said if you give a person enough time they eventually show their true colors. For all his refined manners he really was just a conquistador at heart. For a moment I'd forgotten that.

"I'll want to take a look inside all the missing vampires' sanctuaries."

Juan gave a quick nod of his head. "That can be arranged."

"Great, now if you'd be so kind, please get the hell out of my office."

He gave a smug smile as he stood. With his hands placed squarely on my desk he leaned forward causing me to either hold my ground or lean back in my chair. I chose the latter. I hadn't wanted to be close to him before, and I damn sure didn't want to now.

"Anger suits you, *Senorita*," I tried to ignore the way his words echoed against my ears; the way it felt like his voice was physically sliding down and caressing my body. "It brings out the fire in your eyes."

I remained silent, partially because I couldn't think of something snappy, to hurl at him, but mostly because trading insults with a five hundred year old vampire just didn't seem like a good idea, especially not one that had just indirectly issued a threat of that caliber. If the Council of Councils was brought into this a lot of people would get dead very quickly regardless of innocence or guilt.

Standing straight, he smoothed his suit jacket out as he turned to face Sebastian.

"*Hijo*, if you would assist *Senorita* Harlow in anything she needs."

Sebastian gave a slight nod of his head accompanied by a bow, as Juan shifted his attention to Kailani.

"*Senorita* Kailani, may I be so bold as to request the pleasure of your company this evening?"

I watched as he bowed deeply at the waist extending his hand to Kailani and maintaining the position until she slipped her hand into his. I think I should get points for not hurling on the spot.

CHAPTER FIVE

SEBASTIAN agreed to let me know when I'd be able to tour the sanctuaries of the vampires, before he left to play chauffeur for Juan and Kailani. I didn't bother asking Kailani if she would be alright in Juan's company. The chances of a vampire, even one of his age, besting a millennium old dragon were so low they weren't worth calculating.

I just nodded and remained in my office until they left trusting them to find their own way out. I was pissed at Juan for his blatant threat and arrogance, but I was more pissed off at myself for reacting as I did. What was I, a schoolgirl, sneaking a peak of Henry Miller's _Sexus_?

Placing a call to Finn as I headed out I got his voicemail, and left a message letting him know where he'd be able to find me when he was off duty; a little place called _No.9_.

From the outside _No.9_ looked like any other dive bar in a semi-questionable neighborhood. On the inside glamour magic and a good paint job created one of the hottest and extremely posh nightclub in San Francisco. It was also owned and operated by my best friend Nancy Keller, who like me was a witch, but subscribed to the Warlock lineage. By Warlock standards she wasn't at all old. Though she was only a year or so away from her bicentennial birthday, she didn't look a day over twenty-five.

Nancy's complexion was darker than mine, the color of a Special Dark Hershey's bar with skin that was just as smooth. She had high cheekbones, full lips and a mouth full of perfect white teeth. I'd once heard a guy say her laughter was like the music from a lute, not that he'd probably ever heard a lute before, though oddly enough he was right.

Her thin locks were usually tied back together, or held back by some artificial means but on occasions she let them fall loose and free around her face. She'd been a model when she was my true age; the money had paid for the club.

Sometimes I'd enter the club to find her working behind the bar serving up drinks to satisfy her enjoyment of socializing with the patrons. Other times she'd be in her special booth towards the back of the club, enjoying a drink or two, sometimes alone, sometimes not, sometimes doing bookkeeping, though how she concentrated with the pulse pounding sounds vibrating around her was beyond me. It's amazing what a person can get used to, another pearl of wisdom from my mother.

At the door I slipped the bouncer a ten as he pulled aside the velvet rope. Despite the neighborhood being somewhat on the seedy side Friday and Saturday nights were always crowded inside and outside *No.9*, and this Friday night was no exception. Good tipping and being friends with the owner helped to keep me from ever having to wait among the masses. It was the doorman just inside that told me where to find Nancy, her usual booth at the back.

The good thing about *No.9* was there wasn't really a dress code, or moreover the code was dress to impress. My khaki business slacks and matching heels didn't have me standing out too much. By undoing the top three buttons on my shirt it almost looked like the outfit was planned and not a left over from the workday.

I was hoping to find Nancy alone, I wanted to discuss the events of the evening without having to ask her to send her date away or speaking in code, hell I wasn't even sure I'd be able to relay what I'd learn into any sort of code she'd be able to understand. Fortunately upon my arrival to the back booth she had her bookkeeping ledgers spread over the table and glasses perched on the tip of her nose, despite her vision being twenty/twenty.

She looked up as I approached; the smile that began spreading her lips quickly halting and retreating in the opposite direction. When I was close enough she grabbed me by the arm and yanked me down next to her.

"Oh my god what happened to you?"

Without waiting or asking for consent she tilted my head and pulled the bandage around my neck down just enough to reveal the wound underneath. Anyone else I would have protested, hell anyone else I would have flat out stopped, but Nancy was the one that gave me the recipe I used last night.

"I was abducted by vampires last night," I informed frankly.

She blinked looking at me as if I'd just told her I was abducted by aliens. "You were what? Why?"

"Some vampires have gone missing, three to be exact in the past couple of months. They think a necromancer might be involved, so they decided to ask... rather forcefully... if I knew anything about it."

That was another good thing about the club. The back of the booths were high enough to give the illusion of being in a private room and the music loud enough where a private conversation would easily remain private, even out in the open as we were.

"Are you okay? I mean I know that's a stupid question, obviously you're not but..."

I held a hand up staving off further inquires to my current state of being. "I'm fine mostly, a little banged up but..." I was able to keep my fingers from reaching for the lump on the back of my head.

"I thought you were cool with vampires."

"I'm cool with Sebastian. Until last night he was the only vampire I knew."

"So why grab you? He knows you're a sorcerer, not a necromancer."

"It wasn't Sebastian's idea," I stated. "He wanted to talk to me, not accost me…anyway; the bottom line is I need your help."

"I got your back girl, you know this," she finally smiled and gave me a quick wink. "But if necromancers are involved shouldn't you be telling this to the Elders?"

"If they're involved yes, but right now all we have is the testimony of a vampire based on smell not actually proof."

"Ah," she gave a nod to that.

"Right, so what I need is something solid to go to the Elders with. Oh and did I mention when I met with the head vampire in charge tonight he hinted if something doesn't happen fast enough he might be 'forced' to go to the Council of Councils?"

"Let's worry about one thing at a time," she gave another nod, but frowned slightly as she tapped in quick successions a perfectly French Manicured finger against the table. "How *do* you plan on proceeding? There haven't been any necromancers in the area since before I moved here in the late eighties."

"They know for sure one of the vampires was taken from his home, I figured I'd start there and see if anything was left behind."

"Like a card with his name and address on it?"

I made a face, reaching for her drink, but ended up setting it down before I took a sip. In addition to lunch, Finn had dropped off some pain medication. It wasn't as strong as Vicodin, but something told me mixing it with alcohol was still a no-no.

"I don't know what might be left if anything is left at all, but I figured two eyes were better than one."

She took her glass back and drained the contents. "You know I enjoy a good Nancy Drewing, just let me know when and were and I'll show up with my Sherlock Holmes bag and a magnifying glass."

"Tomorrow night probably, if I don't get some sleep soon I'm going to fall over."

"If it's any consolation you don't look like death on a stick."

I cracked a smile. "Thank I think, though that leaves a lot of ground left uncovered."

"Incidentally, how does Finnius feel about your new found partnership with the undead of San Francisco?"

I rolled my eyes leaning back against the booth. "He loves it like jock itch, but what can he do?"

"You think it's a necromancer?"

I gave a shrug without really thinking about the question or the answer. I didn't want to think about the implications and was willing to deny it as long as humanly possible.

"I think there are too many things under God's creation and the Devil's to narrow it down to one without any real proof. Sebastian said he based his beliefs on the scent of jasmine and decay."

"It is a scent associated with death, and necromancers are associated with death."

"This I know, but it still doesn't provide it was necromancers. Zombies, some pixies and faeries, gargoyles, trolls... especially trolls, all of these are also associated with death. Hell who's to say it's not a troll; they like the counterpart of vampires."

"Because trolls and subtle are never used in the same sentence," she paused and gave a smirk, "Come to think of it trolls and higher intelligence don't belong in the same sentence either. On the off chance he lucked upon the sanctuary of a vampire there would be evidence of the fight all over the place."

"Good point, still..."

"I know, I know, I'm just saying once you've removed the impossible, whatever remains, no matter how improbable must be the truth."

"Thank you Dr. Watson."

"I'm Holmes, remember? You're Watson."

"You realize Watson was the brains of the operation, right?"

"Spoken like a true sidekick."

We grinned at each other before lapsing into a comfortable silence that stretched the seconds into minutes. I was the one that broke it first.

"I'm going to take off," I stated leaning in close to be heard again.

She gave a sly smile to that, "Finnius waiting for you at home?"

"No," I denied quickly. "It just so happens he's at work, I'm going home because I'm exhausted."

"Right," she nodded, but she was still smiling that devilish smile. "How is Finn these days? Has he asked you to marry him yet?"

"Bite your tongue."

"Oh what, like you wouldn't say yes if he got down on one knee, looked at you with those amazingly hypnotic eyes of his and asked for your hand."

"Finn and I haven't talked about marriage."

"You guys have been dating for a year and a half; you mean to tell me in eighteen months it's never come up?"

"No, not really," I could tell by the way she was looking at me she wasn't buying it. "Alright fine, there were a couple of times we discussed the topic of marriage but it wasn't really in a '*we* would get married' sort of thing, it was just a general discussion."

"Right," she continued to eye me.

"What?"

"You realize I don't believe you."

"There's nothing wrong with our relationship as it is right now. We see each other when we want and when we start to get on the others nerves we each have our own homes to go to for solace. Besides, Finn has enough on his plate being one of the youngest Alphas to ever hold a pack in a city this big. Add marriage to that and the poor man just might snap."

"Sure," she nodded, the smile that crept across her lips still pulling the corners as she regarded me with interest.

I made a face. "I'm going home."

"So you've said."

"I am," I repeated scooting to the edge of the booth. "You'll miss me when I'm gone."

Nancy winked before lifting her hand to wave at me as I departed. The temperature outside had dropped enough to have me fastening the buttons I'd undone to blend into the atmosphere of the club. I sent a text message to Finn letting him know I was leaving the club in favor of my bed. Normally I didn't text him my every move but I knew he would be worried about me until this necromancer business was settled.

I told myself I was cutting him a break, that I hadn't texted him where I'd be in hopes he'd come over after his shift ended.

Truthfully I wasn't sure what my answer would be if Finn asked me to marry him. A large part of me wanted to say yes. For all our issues and problems I did love him, but I had a hard time believing love would see us through every problem. A few people in his pack already had a problem with him dating a non-werewolf and weren't shy about expressing their dislike of me.

Those that did tolerate his mate claim over me, might not be so understanding if we were to get married. I failed to relay all the details to Nancy, but Finn's claim of me being his mate so far was verbal only. There was a ceremony that needed to be performed before I could truly be his rightful mate, and it wasn't something to be entered lightly. Two lawyers and a signed piece of paper was all it took to end holy matrimony. 'Til death' was a very literal meaning for mated werewolves. When werewolves mated it wasn't a contract that bound them together but a union of their spirits. There was also the chance that it might not even work with humans.

Unlike last night I realized something was off as I pulled my car into the driveway in front of my garage. As soon as I opened the door the feel of magic having been cast prickled over my skin and caused the hairs on the back of my neck to rise. I muttered a quick incantation of protection, if the witch was still around he would know I'd just cast but safety took precedence over surprise.

Pulling the messenger bag I used for work from the back seat I rifled through it until I found the small canister of pepper spray. The first thing I noticed was the front door sitting open; it wasn't swinging back on its hinges but it was definitely ajar.

Standing at the bottom of my steps I closed my eyes for a moment and extended my senses inside the house until I touched another mind. I debated calling the cops for about five seconds before deciding against it. It's generally not a good idea to involve civilians in preternatural problems; things have a way of getting complicated and unexplainable.

This would be the point where, if I were watching a horror movie, I'd tell the actress not to enter the house. This being my house made things a bit different. I wasn't scared that someone was inside, I was pissed. Whoever it was, knew that I was outside, I could feel them moving from the attic clearing the second landing, and that's when implication of where they had been propelled me forward.

I had assumed last night's break in had been the vampires looking for me since nothing had been taken, but forgot to confirm it with Juan. But what if nothing had been taken because they hadn't the time to search the house thoroughly? For all I know Finn coming over could have interrupted the plundering. There was only one thing in my attic worth taking... the Grimoire my mother left me.

Bolting up my front steps I shoved the front door open and continued full speed to the second floor. I reached out again with my mind grasping a mental hold of the witch bolting down the hall towards the backstairs leading to my kitchen, but the hold slipped and when I reached out again it was like trying to walk through a door that was closed.

There weren't that many creatures that could effectively close off their minds from a mental attack. One would have been another sorcerer, but I would have been able to detect that. The other was a vampire.

We squared off at opposite ends of the second floor hall from each other. The only light in the house was the foyer lamp on downstairs, which put us both in the dark, but I was at a greater disadvantage. From the streetlights filtering in from the window I could make out his general shape; male, and that he was crouching low with his hands extended in a primal battle mode.

He, on the other hand, I was sure could see me just fine. Not only was there the light from the foyer filtering up to halo my outline, but vampires had night vision to rival any feline. That left one question though. Where was the magic coming from?

"Who are you?" I demanded taking a step towards him. His reply was to bare his fangs and hiss. I decided to try for question number two, though I didn't have any higher hopes at getting an answer. "What are you doing in my house?"

He rushed forward then; a surge of air and blur of movement. I had time to plant my feet before I felt his hands gripping my shirt pushing me to the ground. I used the momentum, controlling the fall into a tuck roll that flipped us over and had me pinning him to the floor. My jujitsu training was being put the practical testing these past two nights.

He literally threw me off of him before I even had a chance to settle my position into any sustainable joint lock, but a quick telekinetic blow forced him backwards. He teetered on the top step for a moment; I sent another powerful hit to his midsection sending him backward down the stairs.

It only took me a couple of seconds to secure my footing but the foyer was empty upon my arrival. The front door stood open from when I had burst in but that didn't mean that he had left through it. I shifted my body, pressing my back against the wall as my eyes searched the dark. When they came up empty I extended my mind, and a hand wrapped around my throat hoisting me into the air.

I couldn't scream, it wouldn't have done any good anyway and it also required air, something that was effectively being blocked as he tightened his grip. Thin lips pulled back to bare fangs in a feral hiss. The vampire extended his arm straight up with me dangling at the end like a fish on a line.

Staring down at him, I was able to get a bird's eye view. Baby fine, red hair hung straight to his shoulders in such a mass quantity that it actually had the appearance of being thick, his features were Nordic; high cheekbones, stout nose, square chin, wide full mouth surrounded by a flaming red Van Dyke, and piercing blue eyes. Likewise his body had the wide girth and muscles of a Viking. I might have thought he was handsome had he not been choking the life out of me.

I stopped struggling and focused all my energy against his chest, but it was like pushing a car uphill. He slammed me back against the wall for my efforts. The back of my head cracked against the drywall and sent a borage of dancing lights through my eyes.

"Where… is… it?"

I watched his mouth form around the words but they didn't seem to come from him, and I felt a swell of magic spill from his body that shouldn't have been there.

Vampires are reanimated but they aren't magical.

"Where… is… it?" he repeated.

I gasped, as if trying to talk. It was enough for him to loosen his grip, and that was enough for me to summon every ounce of strength in my body and transfer it into a telekinetic blow that lifted him from his feet and sent him flying backwards into the opposite wall. We both dropped to the floor me gasping for air and trying to back peddle into the living room for distance, him picking himself out of the debris of drywall and splintered wood.

He was pissed, blue eyes glowed like flames at me as he climbed to his feet, but he was also injured. There was a nasty gaping wound on his shoulder where a piece of wood was protruding though flesh and muscle. His nails extend into claws; his head jerking quickly to right… and then he was gone. In his wake the sound of wood splintering and glass shattering as he literally ran through the back door.

CHAPTER SIX

ONE of the advantages of living in a relatively safe neighborhood; the neighbors tend to call the police when they hear a disturbance or see something unusual. Conversely one of the disadvantages of living in a relatively safe neighborhood; the neighbors tend to call the police when they hear a disturbance or see something unusual.

About thirty seconds after I picked myself up off the floor I could hear the sirens in the distance, though in actuality it took longer than that as I almost hit the floor a moment after standing. It was either the lack of oxygen, the blow to the head, or a combination of both that had me light-headed and dizzy again.

Despite my assurance that I was all right, the medics insisted that a trip to the hospital was required. The huge knot on the back of my head and the double vision went a long way to convince them, and the nose bleed only added to their claim. After the police took my statement and my next door neighbor's husband assured me he'd put plastic up at my back door I was loaded into the back of the ambulance and carted off to San Francisco General Hospital.

A CT scan was my first stop, followed quickly by a MRI once the doctor learned the blow to the head tonight was the second in as many nights. I heard the phrase Second Impact Syndrome tossed around as the doctor spoke with the nurse, who immediately took several samples of my blood to have tests run on them. The only positive was I was allowed to keep my clothing on instead of having to trade them for one of those breezy hospital gowns.

Reclining on the bed with an arm flung up to shield my eyes from the near painful glare of the florescent lighting when Finn burst into the room. I can't say I was surprised.

San Francisco General Hospital was the only hospital in the area with a helipad. It's where he and the crew hung out when they weren't out on a call, and according to the clock on the wall his shift ended five minutes ago. More than likely someone had bumped into him on his way to the locker room and informed him I was there since he was still in his flight gear.

I can count on one hand the number of times I'd seen Finn in his flight uniform. It was rare enough for me to forget from one time to the next how good he looked in his blue jumpsuit. Sometime between leaving me after lunch and going on call he'd gotten his hair cut. Those adorable curls clipped away giving his hair the illusion of being straight as it was brushed down flat against his scalp.

Finn knew I loved when his hair was long enough so I could play with the curls, but it seemed the need to look the part of a badass alpha trumped my love of playing with his hair, at least for the moment.

"What happened? Are you all right? Why didn't you tell me you were here?" the questions tumbled from his lips faster than I could keep up with them.

"Finn, please slow down," I soothed grabbing hold of his arm and giving a tug so he sat facing me on the bed. "I took a blow to the head... again. I think I'm all right but they haven't told me anything yet. I didn't tell you I was here because I've been ferried from one test room to another. And besides, you were on duty."

"You think that matters?" he chastised.

"And you would have done what? Stand around like a worried boyfriend in the waiting room while they ran the tests?"

He frowned, but he didn't argue. Score one for Danika. Grasping my chin, he angled my face upwards and tried to take his revenge in the form of a bright penlight in my eyes, I managed to turn away before the assault.

"How long have your eyes been sensitive to bright lights?" he asked staring at me with concern.

"Since birth."

"Danika," he sighed my name looking at me with a very serious expression.

"Finn," I know the smile was only irritating him more but I couldn't stop it from spreading my lips. "No one likes a bright pen light in their eyes."

"This isn't a joke," he snapped softly. "It hasn't even been twenty-four hours since you got the first concussion and you suffered another blow to your head. People have died from that."

"Alright, fine, I get it, it's serious. What exactly do you want me to do? It's not like I go around bashing my own head against walls and grounds you know."

"So who did it this time?"

"A vampire," I replied and waited for the eruption of Mount Finnius.

Rage flashed over his face, turning his tan complexion a bright red but his verbal tirade was put on hold as the doctor entered. Finn stood and retreated to the other side of the room, staring out the window. He didn't want the doctor to see him, and frankly neither did I. I didn't want to have to convince him my boyfriend didn't cause the concussion. Even though it was the truth I didn't think he'd believe me. Explaining why his eyes resembled two glowing orbs would have been a might difficult too.

"We got the results back, you do have a fairly severe concussion, but then you were aware of that, correct?" he looked at me, his eyes occasionally glancing in Finn's direction, watching his back.

"Yeah, Finn," I gestured to the back at the window, "Tried to get me to come to the hospital last night."

"You should have, a concussion is a very serious thing; the dizziness, the nauseous the sensitivity to bright lights are all signs your body gives letting you know something's wrong."

"Give it to me straight, doc," I requested with a poker face. "How long do I have to live?"

"Damnit Danika!" Finn barked, turning to glare at me. "People have died from concussions." At least he'd managed to regain composure enough so his eyes were once again pure blue.

"And you said yourself last night that it wasn't too bad."

"That was before you took another blow to the head."

"Are you familiar with something called Second Impact Syndrome, Miss Harlow, or SIS?" the doctor interrupted.

"About as familiar as I am with any other medical term, though I've heard it tossed around several times tonight."

For the next twenty minutes or so the doctor lectured me, with the occasional butt-in from Finn, on the dangers of head injuries, as if I were a Martian transplant that didn't realize the severity of them. I'm not sure if they relented because they felt they'd finally driven the point home, or if it was because they realized I'd stopped paying attention five minutes into the conversation. I was released into Finn's custody, and yes those were the doctor's exact words. I'm fairly certain if Finn hadn't been connected to the medical profession I would have been held over night for observations, even if that meant putting me in restraints.

"You're coming home with me," he snapped, once we'd pulled out of the parking lot.

"Which would explain why you're driving."

"Damnit Danika is everything a joke to you?"

"No, but I am starting to wonder if there's a quota you have to reach for saying Damnit Danika tonight."

He remained silent after that for the duration of the ride to his home, which considering his house was outside city limits was a fairly long duration. When we left the hospital the anger emitting from him was thick enough to choke a horse; it had largely dissipated by the time he pulled into his circular driveway. When he cut the car off but continues to sit behind the wheel I didn't rush to open the door either.

"I love you."

Had he whispered the words any softer I wouldn't have heard them, and even still in the silence of the car they sounded like a shout. Despite the duration of time we'd been together, neither Finn nor I were the type to daily profess our feelings.

"So much so that sometimes there's an actual physical aching I feel when we're apart, or when I haven't seen you in a few days. It's why I get so crazy sometimes," I felt his eyes on me before his finger touched my cheek and turned me into his gaze. "Even though we haven't formally been joined sometimes I feel like I'm already mated to you…in more than just words. The thought of losing you—"

"—You're not going to lose me—"

"—Is more than I can bear."

I held his gaze for as long as I could before that blue-eyed gaze grew too intense for me and I had to drop it or risk being burned from the inside out.

"What do you want me to say, Finn? I don't know how to respond to that. I can't promise you nothing will happen to me, no one can make that promise."

"I know," he spoken softly and pulled his key from the ignition. "I didn't say it to get you to promise me anything, Dani. I just thought it was something you should know."

Even as I watched Finn climb out of his Challenger I continued to sit in the passenger seat for a few moments. I should have said something, the man just poured his heart out to me, and I just sat there like a lump of coal. I should have said something, anything, but I couldn't think of a single thing that wouldn't sound like it came straight off of a Hallmark greeting card. By the time I'd made up my mind to bite the bullet and tell him how I felt he was already unlocking the front door.

Finn lived in a fairly huge house considering he was a bachelor. Actually it might have been a mansion, I'm not sure where the cross over was, or how many rooms it took to convert a home into mansion status. I did know there were four and a half bathrooms and six bedrooms inside, in addition to the standard living room, dining room, kitchen, study and a few other rooms with interchangeable names.

Finn owned his own condo in the heart of the city, but the only time I'd been there was during the beginning of our courtship; I'm pretty sure he's currently renting it out to someone. The pack house was just one of the perks of being an alpha. It changed hands with the change of the title, which wasn't that often. Finn had received it from the previous alpha, and when he either stepped down or was forced down it would pass to the next. It had been in the Alcatraz Pack -yeah named after the island- since they moved to the area in 1947.

Most of the wolves of Alcatraz had their own apartments, houses, or condos, but occasionally some would stay in the house with Finn. Anywhere from the newer wolves that were still learning control, or still trying to get their feet under them, the occasional teen that had a tiff with their parents and needed a safe place to stay while all parties cooled down, to an injured wolf that couldn't be alone.

It was the sight of where their pack meetings were held or where they could come to change into wolf form unseen and run free… or at least to the line of the property. The house was pretty secluded in one of those neighborhoods where the nearest neighbor's property was next to yours but the house could have been a city block away. The trees he kept full and thick by his fence helped to shield his grounds from prying eyes.

"Finn," I called jogging to catch up with him as he walked through the doorway. "Finn I'm—"

My apology froze on my tongue as I entered the house to see a girl clothed only in a pair of cotton micro shorts with the waistband rolled down, a halter top and a mega-watt smile bouncing down the stairs. She looked Asian, Japanese by my guess, approximately in her late teens or early twenties. She had the small, lithe body of a gymnast, her dark hair pulled back into a ponytail that bounced as she moved.

The silence in my head told me she was a wolf, but her face didn't look familiar. I might not have known all the names of the people in Finn's pack but I knew the faces.

"I was beginning to worry something happened to you," she stated without the slightest trace of an accent. She bounced to a halt directly in front of Finn; head tilted back, hands placed on her ass so she could easily push what little chest she had in his face. "I thought I was going to have to send out a search party.

I'm not sure if it was her completely ignoring me standing there, or if it was her attempt to scold him that was pissing me off more, and sent my arms crossing over my chest.

"An emergency came up," Finn answered softly.

"Oh, well in that case I suppose you're forgiven," she continued to grin up at him, slightly twisting her body from one side to the other. "You hungry? I could fix you something to eat."

"No, but I want you to meet someone," he reached for me with his right hand, lacing his fingers through my left. The gesture made the tramp's eyes narrow, which brought a smirk to my lips. "Simone this is my mate, Danika Harlow. Dani, this is Simone Matsamora, she's the newest member of the Alcatraz pack."

Neither of us pretended to be hospitable or attempted to shake the other's hand. She stared at me and I met her eyes unflinching. Her weight shifted legs as she crossed her arms over her chest and I lowered my hands to rest on my hips.

"Simone, Dani is my *mate*; you will extend to her the courtesy that title demands."

It was a gentle warning, but a warning all the same. Had Finn not said anything the two of us might have been standing there all night having a good old-fashion stare down. Simone showed no interest in conceding dominance to me, and I wasn't about to concede it to her. Finn's declaration made me her dominant; to look away first would have caused all kinds of problems.

She didn't so much lower her gaze as she just looked off, a trick I'd used on Finn too many times to count, but despite the defiance of her face her shoulders rounded forward a bit; a posture of submission. With wolves every gesture meant something, werewolves were no different.

"Simone's new to the area," Finn explained. Finally remembering the door was still standing wide open, he moved to close and lock it before letting his gaze drift over the house. I'd seen him do this before; it was the werewolf equivalent of making sure no one was inside that should have been outside. "She's staying here until gets settled."

Which meant until she was ready to move. Finn would never tell a member of his pack they had to leave unless the circumstances were extreme.

"Actually," she continued with her eyes for Finn only, "I was thinking about college. I'm only two semesters away from my bachelor's. What do you think?"

Finn closed his eyes, nostrils flaring with a deep intake of breath. His fingers tightened around my hand before he brought it to his lips for a soft kiss. "I think I'm going to grab a shower."

"Want some company?" Simone slipped quickly back into some smitten schoolgirl roll, posing the query with a quick bat of her eyes and a toothy grin.

"You little…"

Finn moved quicker than I could, turning his body so he stood between Simone and me, denying my hand the taste of her cheek. I found myself wrapped in his arms, his diversion to keep me from wringing Simone's neck.

"Next time," he warned her, "I'll let her hand fly."

His grip loosened until he was just holding my hand again, a hand he used to pull me upstairs with him rather I wanted to go or not. It was probably for the best. The doctor warned a side effect of the concussion was irritability. With the mood I was in, if he left me alone with Simone I couldn't guarantee her safety.

"You didn't tell me you had a house guest," I stated once we were behind the closed door of his bedroom.

"She's only been here a week."

"And that's supposed to makes it better or worse?"

"Do you really want to fight about this right now?" his question was asked as he rummaged through one of his drawers and pulled out a pair of boxers and a white t-shirt.

I didn't answer; I just glared at him, snatched the clothing from his hands and went into the adjoining bathroom, slamming the door behind me.

As much as I loathe admitting it, I knew Finn was right. I didn't want to have a screaming match about him not mentioning Simone being there while she was within earshot of us. I also knew it wouldn't have stuck in my craw as much if Simone's name was Simon, or if she wasn't advertising her desire bed Finn.

I pulled extra towels from the linen closet to the left before stripping down, and turning the jets on. I loved the shower in his master bathroom; it was along the lines of those found at ritzy spas that had multiple jets from various directions. There was a dial on the wall to control the stream of water ranging from the pulsating jets meant to simulate a shiatsu style massage, all the way to a steady contemporary spray. It was near impossible not to relax once inside his shower.

Hands touched my back; a bar of soap against Finn's palm trapped next to my skin. I hadn't heard him open the bathroom or shower door, he was just instantly behind me. His scent filled the air, mixing with the steam.

This was how Finn and I communicated best, through body language and unspoken words. Neither of us were verbal wizards, I know I wasn't. I always felt speaking my heart and feelings left me open for some sort of attack; been like that since I was a kid. I'm sure a psychologist would equate it to not being hugged enough as a child or my dad dying when I was young or my mom not saying 'I love you' enough. I like to think it's because I was a believer that actions spoke louder than words. Anyone can say I love you; all it takes is forming the proper sound and stringing continents together with vowels. Saying it and showing it were two different things.

I rounded my shoulders; letting my head hang forward as his hand moved across my back downward in circular patterns. His hands stroked my body with the soap; moving from between my shoulder blades slowly working down my spine to the small of my back, my buttocks, my hips. I was gradually being undone by the tenderness of his washing.

He wrapped his right arms around my shoulders, pulling my body back against him. The tip of his nose traced the edge of my ear before being followed by the gentle brush of his mouth. His lips moved softly against my ear, murmuring foreign words in a guttural language I couldn't understand. I'd heard him speak the language before, usually to his wolves, though the frequency of him speaking it during sex was increasing, as was the gentle whispers he laid against my ears when I drifted to sleep nestled in the protective cocoon of his arms.

The pitch of his voice implied he'd asked a question as he continued to speak softly into my ear while his left hand lathered the front of me. He moved the soap across my shoulders, washing my breasts, around them, under them, slowly working the lather over my stomach and belly. Kneeling behind me he carefully washed my backside, moving the soap between my legs, over my thighs and down my calves.

I waited until he was standing again before turning to face him. My finger pressed against his lips as soon as he parted them to speak. I used my loofa and the shower gel I kept at his house. Tomorrow he'd smell like citrus fruit, but I didn't think he'd mind, it was partially my scent after all.

Times like these I loved when he looked at me; the tenderness, the love, and compassion held in those blue depths were almost overwhelming. I switched our positions, pushing him into the center of the multiply sprays to soak his body before beginning to wash him down. His eyes closed, but only for a moment. Water clung to those dark thick lashes, clumping them together. I started with his right arm, running the loofa over the forearms, elbow, bicep, tricep, shoulder and underneath, repeating the process on the other arm.

I stared into his eyes as I washed his chest, moving the sponge over his torso and downwards to his flat toned abdomen, before I slipped behind him to cover his broad shoulders and back. I knelt behind him; pressing my cheek against the small of his back and listening to the soft sigh escape his body. He was trembling slightly; that one gesture excited me almost as much as his gentle washing.

I washed his buttocks, the inside and outside of his thighs, and his calves before coming back up having saved the best bits for last. He knew it was coming as he placed his hands against the wall to steady himself. I moved the loofa delicately over the twin sacks and up to the soft hair against his pubic bone before stroking the increasing length of him to the sound of a deep bass-filled groan.

"If you tease me," he breathed out, his voice deep and husky, "I can't promise I'll be gentle."

"Did I ask you to be gentle?" I listened to his soft panting as I gave a couple more strokes before releasing him.

"You have a concussion baby, the last thing you need is me banging your skull against the headboard."

He pulled away as soon as I released him, preventing me from any further torment or torturr. My eyes focused on a scar on his right hip. It started at his pelvic bone and ran upwards across his stomach towards his navel, and stood out a bit paler than the rest of his flesh. He touched his finger under my chin; just light enough to get my eyes to focus up on his.

Finn knelt down in front of me. His eyes moved over me, followed by fingers that traced down my shoulders to my arms, before his lips tasted what his eyes and fingers had already touched. Arms that he wrapped around his neck before guiding his hands down to my waist, round the small of my back, and over my buttocks before coming to rest on the back of my thighs. I was the one that touched our lips together, or would have, had I not pulled away just before his mouth claimed mine. I felt his lips curl into a smile, his fingers tightening on the back of my thighs in protest.

Finn stood slowly, hoisting me into the air, using nothing but his thighs to raise us. As he rose he pulled me close to him, the hands on my thighs guiding my legs around his waist. I gripped the back of his neck with one hand, skimming the other between our bodies to wrap my fingers around the meat of him.

The first squeeze had him sucking his breath in through his teeth. The second had him grunting, pressing his nose against my throat and pushing against my hand. The third almost caused his legs to buckle; the pressing of his nose became gentle nipping from his teeth.

Part of me wanted to continue, to press my luck and see how far I could take him before he went over the edge, but teasing him had gotten the better of me as well. I knew we weren't going to make it to the bed; only thing left to do was to make sure he understood as well. I unhooked my ankles from his back and shifted my position, angling my hips downwards, just enough to rub my lips against the sensitive tip of him.

"Dani... please..."

His body went completely ridge and still, as time seemed to freeze for that span before I found myself propelled backwards. His right hand abandoned my thigh and cupped the back of my head, absorbing the blow as he crushed me between his body and the shower tiles, sheathing with one thrust into my body. It was my turn to gasp, the intrusion sudden and complete. I tightened my legs around his hips again; heels pressing against the small of his back while my fingers clung to his neck and threaded into his hair. He moved slowly, pushing up with his knees, rolling with his hips, rubbing so perfectly against me, my body shook with each slow rhythmic thrust.

I pushed at his chin until the lips that were buried against my throat were vulnerable. His eyes focused on me for a moment; the desire showing inside pulling another moaning quiver from my lips and body. I gasped, my body jerking as another skillful thrust stroked and ignited a burning need deep inside.

"That's it baby," he whispered softly, "Open up for me."

My tongue licking against his lips brought a feral growl from his throat, his hips shoving harder against me. I tried to kiss him, but each retreat rubbed against my sensitive bud bringing a gasp from my lips, and each returning thrust hit a different sensor coaxing waves of pleasure.

My voice battled over the pelting shower around us, my head throwing back into his palm as his lips once again attacked the expose flesh of my neck. Finn was everywhere, surrounding me, inside me, I clung to him, trying as much as possible to move with him, my hips catching his rhythm only for a skillful nibble to knock me out of tune again. His growls were lost against my throat as he buried his teeth into my shoulders biting down; pulling, nipping, licking.

He could feel it building inside me, the pressure of my muscles squeezing him tighter. It only egged him on to go faster, my shoulders slapping the tiles with the force of his thrusts. It hurt, but the pain wasn't enough to tell him to stop, wasn't enough to distract me from the tightening in my womb, or the burst of pleasure that pulsed outward.

Finn road the orgasm out and pushed through it. He forced past the muscles that tried to cling to him and hold him in place, causing a series of smaller quakes on the heels of the first.

His own release took him by surprise. He tightened his arms around me, around my bottom where one hand continued to support my weight, the hand on my head pulling my face against his throat. He shouted my name, his legs finally gave out and we both sank to the floor of the shower.

The hand on my bottom moving to splay, fingers wide against my back. I could feel his pulse still hammering under my lips, his body twitching inside mine as I placed a tender kiss there.

"Don't," he whispered, his hands moving to hold my hips still when I attempted to shift on top of him. "Please don't move. Not unless you're trying to screw me to death."

I grinned at that, sitting up enough to kiss the tip of his nose while combing my fingers through his hair. "Are you saying you have objections to death by shagging?"

"With you? Never."

I watched him watching me, or he watched me watching him, either way I felt myself falling into his eyes. I couldn't stop touching him, his hair, his face, his shoulders. Like I needed the contact to remind me we belonged to each other and even that wasn't quite enough.

"You know I love you, right?" I whispered softly.

"You definitely just cleared any doubts I had."

"Finn I'm being serious." The words followed by a pinch to his shoulder.

"You drive me crazy enough to murder you sometimes with that macho, borderline misogynistic attitude, but despite all of that, I do love you."

He chuckled, his fingers moving from my hips to comb down my back, "Am I really that big of a boar?"

"You can be pretty tough to take sometimes," I teased. "But I know I'm not a walk in the park either."

"I love every bit of you," he answered quickly. "Your flaws, your virtues… there is nothing about you I would change."

"Not even me not being a werewolf?"

He sighed softly, his right hand lifting to push my damp hair behind my shoulder.

"I can guide you through the change, Dani. It doesn't have to be overly traumatic."

"Will you be the one to maul me too?" I countered our gazes still locked. "What about when I can't do magic anymore? Will you comfort me through that as well?"

"You don't know for sure that you'd lose that ability."

"When was the last time you heard of a witch-wolf?"

When he didn't answer I stood, pushing the shower door open and wrapping one of his fluffy robes around my body before I continued to his bedroom. With the return of reality every ache in my body seemed magnified, along with a couple of new ones against my back and shoulder.

I heard the absence of water and a few moments later he stood in the doorway, a pair of pajama pants riding low on his waist, arms folded over his chest as he watched me turning the covers down and crawling into bed still wearing in his bathrobe.

"You don't know what will happen after the change," he stated softly.

"And you don't know for sure that I will change. How many times have you told me if you're not born with the werewolf DNA you have to undergo a near death attack to get the genes into your system?"

"I wouldn't hurt you," he snapped, almost immediately looking away as the absurdity of his statement hit his ears. "You know what I mean."

"Finn I know you wouldn't set out to kill me, but the thing about near death attacks is you can't control them. And it's not just about me potentially dying. What if you don't do enough damage to infect me and I live? What if you do enough damage, I live but I still don't contract the strand of DNA?"

"I just want…" he paused pulling his eyes from mine again. A sigh left his lips as he pushed his hands through his hair.

"I'm really tired, Finn. Let's just go to sleep, okay?"

Nodding, he moved to the light switch on the wall while I climbed into the center of the bed, tossing the robe to the floor after I was nestled under the covers. With the room in darkness I listened to his feet on the carpet, felt the depression of the mattress as he climbed in next to me. He pulled me close until my head was pillowed on his chest, while his fingers rubbed my back and combed through my hair. I fell asleep smelling the scent of my body wash on his skin and listening to the slow rhythmic beating of his heart.

CHAPTER SEVEN

THE following morning I woke in the bed alone and lying on my stomach. The clock on Finn's night table read three fifteen, but I had already guessed it was late in the afternoon. Finn's bedroom balcony and window had a western exposure and the room was brightly lit from the sun. I was betting that was what had woken me.

The mouth-stretching yawn I gave was followed by a slow stretch of my body, and finally me burying my face in the pillow next to my head. Finn's scent mixed with my bath gel filled my nose and brought a smile to my lips. A smile that slowly faded when I remembered the conversation we went to bed on.

I hated arguing about my status, or lack there of in his werewolf community. It was the only part of our relationship I didn't feel rock solid about. Finn took three things in life ultra serious: his job, our relationship, and his pack. His pack life and job life coexisted harmoniously as did his relationship and his job. If anything it made him that much more attractive; I was a sucker for a man in uniform. His pack and I though caused major friction. It was an external element that could potentially split us apart.

Finn was probably at work. Tonight would be his last three to eleven shift. He'd have tomorrow off, and then return to his normal seven to three time slot. I wanted to talk to him about it, but it would probably end up waiting until tomorrow since I had no idea how long it would take to tour the three sanctuaries of the missing vampires.

Rolling out of bed I made my way into his bathroom and examined the damage in the mirror. There were new bruises forming against my shoulder blades that looked much worse than the felt, along with bruising around an imprint of his teeth. It was one of the prices to be paid with having sex on hard surfaces with a werewolf. Werewolves are extremely hearty creatures and heal typical injuries like love bruises almost instantly.

Most sex between werewolves is rough sex. Finn practically handles me with kid gloves when we make love, but there were still occurrences of injury. I refrained from letting him see them when I could; his apologies were usually followed with him mentally tearing himself apart. I remember asking him once if sex was enjoyable for him since he had to restrain himself so much with me, his reply: being with me was worth any sacrifice… not exactly the answer a girl wants to hear.

I climbed into the shower again and turned the setting to gentle rain; smiling softly as I looked to the tiles he had me hemmed up against last night. It's a good thing he protected my head or I might have suffered from Third Impact Syndrome. Several months ago Finn had cleaned out a couple drawers for me, where I kept several pairs of panties, socks, bras, and various articles of outer clothing. There was also a pair of gym shoes and sandals in his closet.

I pulled on a pair of jean shorts, but despite having my own shirts slipped on one of his Colorado State t-shirts. It smelled like him, and I needed to have that reassurance, especially knowing when I left the room I'd have to deal with Simone. I towel dried my hair as best I could and packed last night clothing in the over night bag that traveled between our homes. The last thing I did before leaving the room was to call a cab.

For about twenty minutes I thought I had gotten off lucky enough to make it out without a Simone run in. The cab company's estimated time of arrive was only ten more minutes away, and although the Jane Fonda workout video playing down the hall alerted me to Simone being in the house, I thought she was avoiding me. I was wrong.

I heard her coming down the hallway poorly singing Beyoncé's *Crazy in Love*. I didn't think it was just a coincidence she was singing that particular song.

"Oh," she gave an overly exaggerated sigh when she stopped in the living room and saw me sitting on the couch. "You're still here? I thought you would have gone home by now."

"Funny, I was thinking the same thing about you," I replied not bothering to look from the magazine I was leafy through to her.

"This *is* my home, in case you missed that last night."

I would wait outside. It was obvious the only reason she'd come out was to pick a fight and I didn't feel up to a verbal sparing match with a teenager, or someone barely out of them.

"You're just holding him back," she called following me from the living room to the foyer.

"Excuse me?" I stopped in my tracks and turned to face her.

"You heard what I said."

"Yeah but I think maybe I shouldn't have."

"I've heard about you," her eyes moved down sizing me up. "Big bad witch, right? Well Finn doesn't need a witch; he needs a werewolf that's going to understand what he's going through. He needs a mate that's going to be able to keep the pack in line when he's not around, not one that needs him to protect them from the pack."

"Let me guess, you're that person, right?"

"I fill the bill better than you," she snorted back crossing her arms over her chest. "Face it, you're weak and—"

Her head snapped to the side, words cut off by the taste of blood in her mouth left by my fist. I turned completely into the punch putting as much power behind it as possible.

The shocked look on her face was well worth the effort and the bruise that would be on my knuckles later.

Simone stared at me stunned and caught completely off guard, though the eyes staring into mine weren't brown but the amber hue of a wolf. She snarled and I got a glimpse of elongated eyeteeth, but when she tried to rush forward she was, once again, surprised. I reached out with my mind; an invisible hand wrapped around her throat and held her in place. Her hands flailed, reaching up to claw at something that wasn't there.

I squeezed; she coughed and gagged, gasping for air as she stared wide-eyed at me. I watched the wolf in her bleed away, replaced by a terrified young woman.

"You feel that?" I asked squeezing harder. She nodded. Outside the cab driver blew his horn. "You remember this the next time you want to challenge me. Do you understand?" Again she nodded, mouth open as she choked down small breaths of air.

Taking no chances I didn't just release her, but flung her down the hallway. By the time she got up I was already getting into the cab.

* * * * *

When I got home I called a repairman to come replace the entire door. The way the vampire broke through it last night there was no way I could have gotten away with only replacing the glass panel. The wall under my stairs was a different story. I wasn't sure how I was going to patch that up, but since it wasn't like someone could come in my house through the hole it could wait until this necromancer/missing vampire thing was put to bed.

I couldn't do anything until after sundown, so I spent my time doing mundane tasks around the house. Every time I thought of the surprised look on Simone's face, a smile touched my lips. I wasn't sure if she would tell Finn what happened, but it wasn't like she would get any sympathy from him. He had warned her last night. She'd definitely think twice before mouthing off to me in the future.

Sebastian showed up thirty minutes after sundown dressed in jeans, steel-toed boots, and a hoodie. Not very vampire chic at all. He knocked on my door to the tune of *Shave and a Haircut,* and was already walking back to the car by the time I opened it.

"What if I was going to invite you in for a quick bite to eat?" I asked getting in on the passenger side door he held open for me.

He didn't answer, at least not with words. Climbing behind the wheel it was my turn to be surprised as I found myself in the passenger seat one moment, and pulled across his body with my neck exposed the next. I didn't even feel him take the seatbelt off, he moved that fast.

"Didn't your mother ever tell you it's not nice to tempt a hungry vampire?" he queried.

He'd balled my hair into his fist, exposing the pulse in my throat. As he spoke his lips brushed the skin covering the beating artery, causing a shiver to run the length of my spine.

"My bad," I tried to keep my voice as neutral sounding as possible. "Didn't realize you hadn't gotten your grub on yet."

About three tense seconds passed where I was beginning to wonder if Sebastian really was going to bite me before he quickly hauled me back into my seat.

"You know," I began refastening my belt, "For a moment there I thought you were going to bite me."

He smirked as he started his car and pulled onto the streets. "For a moment there, so did I."

I glanced at him, but it was impossible to tell from the smirk if he was deadly serious or pulling my leg again.

"I'd like to start with Alexander's lair," I began deciding the best route was to pretend what happened five seconds ago never happened. "We also need to swing by *No.9* and pick up a friend of mine."

"Your warlock friend?"

"Yeah, you remember Nancy, right? I'm sure she remembers you. She's been around longer so I'm hoping she's more experienced. You should know a vampire was waiting for me when I got home last night."

"What? Why didn't you call?"

"Someone called the police and there was this big circus afterwards, but it also occurred to me that he might have been sent by Juan."

"Why would Juan send a vampire to your house?"

"I don't know… maybe he was sent to leave a message, though I think he was sent to retrieve something."

"Retrieve what?"

"I don't know. He didn't tell me what he was looking for, damn rude of him wasn't it." Sebastian frowned at that. I shrugged. "Only thing he did say was *where was it.*"

"Where was what?"

"Did you miss the part where I mentioned he didn't say what he was looking for?"

That earned me a look of reprimand that was mostly wasted, before he returned his attention to the streets. He maneuvered expertly through the traffic of the streets, gliding his German car from one lane to the other as if he were on the streets by himself.

Watching Sebastian drive never ceased to amuse me, it was the vehicular version of a gazelle gliding through the Savannah. He pulled up in front of the club and I sent a text to Nancy's phone letting her know we were outside.

"Did he hurt you?" Sebastian asked turning to observe me, though inspecting me was more of what he did.

"No, not really, beyond violating my home, choking me, and slamming my head against the wall." I think it was the last two lines that made him frown. "I'm fine, but you know there was something weird."

"Other than a vampire breaking into your home?"

"Yeah," I nodded. "When he talked, his lips moved, and it seemed to be his voice, but it didn't seem like it was him."

"I'm not sure I follow you."

"I'm not sure I follow me either. I felt the pull of magic too coming from him, but I thought vampires couldn't work magic. I mean I know you guys have some abilities with mind reading and stuff, but this wasn't mind reading magic. It was something else."

"Have you felt it before?"

I shook my head.

"Very curious indeed," he glanced at me, and then gestured out the passenger window with his chin. "Here comes your friend."

Nancy was definitely dressed better than Sebastian and I put together in a pair of red leather pants, yellow halter-top and red strappy heels that showed her pedicure matched her manicure. Sebastian slipped out from behind the wheel and walked around the front of the car, opening the back door behind me for Nancy.

Kisses on the cheek were exchanged before she climbed into the back of the car and he reclaimed his position behind the wheel before pulling back into traffic as smooth as glass on a beach.

"Thought you were going to start swinging by the club, Mr. Arroyo," Nancy spoke softly. I recognized her flirtatious voice when I heard it and looked away to keep the smile spreading across my lips from being visible to all.

"Apologies," he replied, "My schedule has been rather strained as of late."

"You keep avoiding me and I might think you don't care anymore."

"I promise you that is not the case, my dear."

I couldn't take it anymore as the laughter bubbled from my lips.

"So," she began leaning forward as much as the seatbelt would allow. "Is the plan still just doing a supernatural CSI to the crime scene or...?"

"CSI," I nodded. "Hopefully we'll find something useful, though with Stanley and Matilda it's less likely since they've been missing the longest and we don't know for sure were they were taken."

"CSI?" Sebastian questioned glancing in the rearview mirror. I noticed he was heading south, the opposite direction from the mansion I was taken to two nights ago.

Not that it really mattered. Vampires, like werewolves weren't required to live with or near the Master of the Murder.

"You don't watch TV?" Nancy purred to Sebastian.

He chuckled softly. "My nights are usually spent out for the evening."

"You're not missing anything," I informed. "If it's not a variation on the CSI formula it's a lawyer show, police show, or doctor show."

"You forgot reality shows," Nancy chimed in.

Sebastian pulled the car up to a rather small but tidy looking house. The front yard was well maintained with weed free green grass, edged sides and surrounded by a white picket fence. There were flowers lining the walkway from the curb to the stairs that led to the porch, and bushes planted neat and evenly spaced in front of the house.

The porch lights on either side of the door were on as if company was expected, but the rest of the house was dark.

"Whose house is this?" I questioned climbing out of the car to take an uninterrupted inspection.

"Alexander and Brenda's," he replied. He and Nancy followed suit climbing out of the car so we could assemble on the sidewalk.

"This is where Alexander and Brenda live?"

"You sound surprised?"

"I am."

He chuckled, leading the way up the front walk to the door. "You were expecting what, a gray-stoned mansion with a tower in the back?"

I narrowed my eyes a bit climbing onto the porch and peaking into the windows. "I wasn't expecting *Pleasantville.*"

Bending down he retrieved a key from underneath a brown rubber mat with the word 'WELCOME' etched in black, and fitted it into the lock. Sebastian led the way inside the house, bathing the foyer in a soft yellow light and motioning us to enter.

"I'm beginning to see why it was so easy for whoever broke in to break in."

"I asked Brenda to leave the key," Sebastian stated letting his gaze move over the home. "Given your past I thought it would be best if she wasn't around while you and Nancy went over the home."

I couldn't argue with that logic. I wasn't sure Brenda believed in my lack of involvement, or if she even cared and just figured I was guilty by virtue of being a witch.

"Any idea what we're looking for?" Sebastian queried.

I shook my head. "I guess anything that looks like it might not belong."

The inside of the house looked vastly different than the picture that had been painted outside. If the outside looked like *Pleasantville*, the inside was a smaller scale of *People Under the Stairs*. Behind the curtains covering the windows were some sort of steel covering that was nearly invisible when viewed from the outside, at least I hadn't been able to see them through the window when I looked.

The walls were a dark cherry wood that made the house look smaller inside than it really was. There were stairs directly in front of the door leading to the second level, a hall that stretched out to the right of the stairs and rooms to the right and left of the foyer.

The furniture was antique possibly from the Renaissance area or maybe even beyond that, but it appeared to be in good condition. Likewise the hardwood floors in the living room and dining room were covered with area rugs that were clean but worn, and a worn runner stretched from the doorway to the stairs were it split, covering the center portion of the stairs and down the hallway to the back. There was a musty smell, as if the place was usually kept locked up, but there was another scent as well, like burnt charcoal.

"Where's Alexander's bedroom?"

Sebastian motioned us to follow him down the hall. It was obvious the trail would have ended in the kitchen, but it was a doorway under the stairs that was our destination. There was a keypad to the right of the doorway where Sebastian pushed a series of numbers to the tune of a phone dialing. When the last number was pushed there was a beep and a click sound as the door was released and opened a crack inwards towards the stairs.

"Brenda sleeps upstairs in a similar chamber," Sebastian explained as I examined the keypad.

"How many people generally have this code?"

"Before tonight, to my knowledge it was only Alexander and his sister."

I examined the door next, running my hand against the section that fit into the frame before rapping my knuckles lightly against the middle.

"Titanium?"

Sebastian pressed his hand against the door. "Perhaps."

Nancy looked at me then the door. "So we've got an intruder that not only managed to break into the house, but also made it past this door, obviously without damaging it, and without the access code?"

"It would appear so," Sebastian nodded. "Would they know a spell to manage this feat?"

"No. There's no magic potion or spell that could actually pick a lock. For something like this," Nancy gestured to the keypad. "There's a pretty universal spell that could show the natural oil residue from fingers left on the correct buttons—"

"—But since vampires don't have that residue…" Sebastian broke in.

"Let's take a look at his lair," I suggested feeling against the wall for a light switch and flipping it up when my fingers touched it.

The stairs led down to a room that definitely looked more like a bedroom than a remodeled basement. Thick light blue carpet greeted the feet upon stepping from the last stair. The way it gave under my weight I had to assume there were at least two layers of padding underneath to take away the shock of walking on concrete covered floors.

Likewise, even the walls seemed to have some sort of light blue cashmere covering, it almost felt like touching velvet as I ran my hands over the material.

It looked like the French Renaissance exploded inside the room. Actually it looked like someone took the bedroom of King Louie, and transplanted it into Alexander's. There was a huge four poster bed in the middle of the room that looked too large to be just a king size mattress. Against the walls were an armoire, chest, dresser, vanity table, and a few other bedroom accessories I'd never seen, all done in this shiny oak that looked like it had to weigh a metric tone each.

There was a sitting section done in the basement as well, complete with area rug, a couch, two high back chairs all surrounding a table. The couch and chairs of course matched with a sort of baroque appliqué. The television looked boldly out of place, the only modern appliance other than the lamps inside the sanctum.

There were a few paintings hanging on the wall of various outdoor sceneries. I noticed all but one, a cemetery scene, were daytime paintings, and all included the sun hanging brilliantly in the sky. However, it was the painting behind the television, the portrait that had me walking over to inspect it closer. The portrait was of a woman and man done in either the late 1600s or done to replica that time period.

The woman was obviously Brenda, just as blonde and pale in the painting as she had been standing next to me a couple nights ago. Thin lines representing her lips were painted a blinding red, that contrasted her pale skin and hair and only helped to make her look, even more, like the walking dead. The man, however, as I stared at his face I was staring at the face of my attacker. His hair was longer and done in such a perfect wavy texture that might have been a wig, but not far from it, but the rest of his face was the same.

"Sebastian," I called softly. He was still standing by the stairs while I wondered around looking the place over, and Nancy searched for any hard evidence. "Who's the guy?"

"That is Alexander."

"I've seen him before."

"Really? When?"

"Last night. In my house."

"What?" came from Nancy.

"Beg pardon?" came from Sebastian.

"This is the vampire that was in my home last night."

"You're certain?"

I nodded. "Yeah, I got a good look at him while he was choking me and slamming my head through the wall."

"Why was he in your house last night?" Nancy asked halting her search and moving to join us.

"He was looking for something. At first I thought he was trying to steal my Grimoire, but that wasn't it. Whatever it was he didn't find it."

"But you're certain this was your intruder last night?" Sebastian questioned again.

I met his eyes biting back the less than pleasant reply on the tip of my tongue. "His face was a foot from mine, Sebastian. I'm positive it was him."

"Yes, but you also said you felt magic coming from him as well."

"You felt magic coming from a vampire?" Nancy piped up frowning at that. I nodded my answer. "Are you sure it was a vampire?"

"He had fangs like a vampire," I stated thinking back. "And when I tried to read him mind there was a black box around. I know that doesn't mean he was a vampire but I've never known a witch to sprout fangs. Not to mention he had the strength to go along with the rest of the package."

"Neither have I," Nancy's agreed.

I looked to the painting again, my head canting to the side a bit. "What if this isn't a witch we're looking for at all." I began folding my arms over my chest. "What if it's really just another vampire?"

Sebastian scoffed at that. "Why would a vampire kidnap other vampires?"

"Why would a necromancer?"

"Off the top of my head, to use them in crimes. Vampires leave little to no trace in their wake."

I rolled my eyes at that, walking away to look at the items on top of the vanity.

"Matlilda was kidnapped over two months ago and there've been no rash of inexplicable crimes. Not to mention why kidnap the other two if they've already got Matilda. Holding control over one vampire is already difficult, but three? Two of which are adolescents?"

Nancy nodded. "That is true. Your average necromancer wouldn't have the strength to control more than one vampire at a time, and the older they are the harder it is to maintain that control over them."

"And," I continued. "So far we've yet to find any trace of anything magical being in here, which is directly in line with your observation about vampires leaving little to no trace behind. Not to mention there's still remains the mystery of how anything got in here without the code."

"A sorcerer could have plucked it from his head at anytime."

"So now there's a sorcerer *and* a necromancer working together?" He remained silent for a while, turning a bit to regard Nancy and me. "Not to mention he probably would have known if a sorcerer was rummaging around in his head. If he and his sister are as close as you say, don't you think that's something he would have mentioned to her, which in turn she would have mentioned to Juan?"

"Vampire blood is highly coveted by necromancers," he stated simply, switching to another argument since the first one wasn't serving him well.

"That still doesn't explain what Alexander was doing in my house last night. Or what he was looking for."

"And the magical charge coming from him? Do witches not possess the ability to take on the appearances of others for a short time?"

"The appearance yes," Nancy stated. "A Necromancer feasibly could have gotten his or her hands on a spell to temporarily take the identity of another, right down to the fangs, but they couldn't have duplicated the strength. Doppelganger spells work on outward appearance only. Most of them can't even match up voices."

"It still doesn't change that the most likely suspect at abducting three vampires successfully is a necromancer."

I scrubbed my hands down my face, sighing softly. I really hadn't expected anything other than this from him. The vampires had already decided what was responsible, and changing a vampire's mind or opinion without anything to back it up was a monumental act.

CHAPTER EIGHT

WE searched the rest of the house to the exclusion of Brenda's bedroom but came up with as much as we found down in Alexander's room; nothing. The whole thing actually turned out to be a big bust, raising more questions and answering none, save to identify my houseguest from last night.

Sebastian dropped Nancy back off in front of *No.9* after leaving Alexander and Brenda's place. He stood outside the car flirting with her for several minutes before they went their separate ways; Nancy into her club, Sebastian into his car. He remained quiet for quite some time, just sitting there, staring out into the street. I decided whatever he was thinking it was best if I not interrupt.

"Juan will want to speak with you on your findings," he stated softly.

"You mean what we didn't find."

"That too," I felt him glancing at me from the side of his eyes but didn't bother meeting it. "He'll also want to know about Alexander being in your home last night. You still think vampires are ultimately behind this?"

"I don't know, Sebastian. That's part of the problem; at this point it really could be anything including a vampire and necromancer working together."

"You think that's possible?"

"I don't know what to think. I'm an archeologist, Jim, not a detective."

"But isn't part of what you do also determining what happened in the past? What an object was last used for, when and why?"

"That's different."

"Perhaps," he stated, starting the car and pulling back out into traffic. "But perhaps not quite as different as you believe it to be."

I didn't say anything, just sat there staring out the window. I remained quiet the entire car ride back to my place, except we didn't go to my place. Instead Sebastian drove his car into the heart of Nob Hill, pulling to the curb in front of the Ritz Carlton.

I glanced at Sebastian as he undid his belt. "Let me guess, we're here because you're hoping by taking me to the Ritz Carlton and not some sleazy cheap hotel I'll have sex with you?" of course joking… mostly.

"Are you saying my dastardly plan is flawed?"

"Actually it's perfect except for the sex part," the valet opened the door and actually held out his hand for me, though I ignored it and climbed out myself before following Sebastian inside the over priced hotel. "So… when you said Juan would want to speak with me about what we found you meant…"

"Tonight," he concluded.

We bypassed the front desk and headed straight for the elevator, which let me know the vampires had already planned this out before hand. I guess it was written on my face; he decided to fess up once we were on the privacy of the elevator.

"Juan thought this would be an acceptable alternative to the mansion."

"Smart man, but you could have told me."

The elevator slid to a silent stop and we disembarked heading for the presidential suite, to which Sebastian produced a keycard from his breast pocket.

The suite was as huge as I expected it to be complete with an area to hold board meetings in a separate room, a living room, small kitchenette, and a couple bedrooms.

The carpet was a rose hue, thick without being overly so, while the walls were the standard eggshell white that seemed to be taking the place of plain white hotel rooms across the country. There were also the same scenery pictures on the wall of fuzzy flowers or a horse pulled wagon.

Juan sat at the head seat of the table, wearing a suit that was similar to the one he had on a few nights ago save this one was navy with gray pinstripes. He stood when I entered, the weight of his age settling against me like the tide, and with it that stirring I was becoming familiar with in his presence. Despite my best effort to the contrary my heart sped up.

Brenda stood with her back to the window; arms folded glaring at me with all her might. I thought different colors might help with her look, but the pale blue satin shirt, and darker blue pencil skirt didn't help her look less like the queen of the damned. All it did was bring out the brilliant color of her eyes more.

"*Senorita* Harlow, thank you for coming tonight."

"If I knew I would be speaking with you tonight, I might have dressed up for it."

He smiled and gestured to the chair closest to his left side. As with the night in my office, he waited until I was seated before he reclaimed his chair, with Sebastian on his right. Brenda remained standing and glaring; she'd be lost without her glare. Both Juan and I remained silent as Sebastian shared the events of the evening, along with my surprise visitor the night before.

"You saw my brother?" she finally spoke taking a half a step forward, only to have Juan halt her movement with an upraised hand.

"Yeah," I answered. "Did you miss the part where he broke into my house?"

"But you have no idea what he might have been looking for," Juan stated, tenting his fingers.

"He kind of failed to mention that."

Juan gave me a look that was probably meant as a warning. I almost forgot and met his eyes. I wanted him to see I wasn't afraid of him, but it's hard to show defiance when you can't meet someone's eyes.

"Dani," Sebastian concluded, "Is under the impression there could be a vampire behind the disappearances in addition to, or instead of a witch."

"Really?" Juan stated with no small amount of amusement. "That is an interesting theory but what proof do you have, Senorita?"

"The same proof you have that it's a necromancer," I replied. "Oh and there's also Alexander who happens to be a vampire, breaking into my home."

"You said yourself you felt magic originating from his being," Brenda stated. "And what proof do you have that it was really him?"

"I have a big hole in a wall in my foyer if you wanna check it out."

"You could have done that yourself," she accused.

It was one of those statements that brought silence to the room. It was also a statement that had Juan shaking his head.

"Alexander was the smart one, right?"

Her eyes narrowed and her lips drew back over her teeth but she didn't charge me, she didn't even budge from her spot.

"You have a knack for upsetting, Brenda, Senorita. It is a dangerous skill to possess," Juan stated.

"Brenda gave me a concussion and her brother tried to multiply it, I could give a shit about upsetting her."

"So you believe that because Alexander broke into your house that vampires are responsible for the disappearance of our own, sí?"

"Yeah that and the fact that his bedroom was virtually impregnable by anyone that didn't have the code. There were no signs of forced entry either to the house in general or his bedroom specifically. A bedroom that showed absolutely no sign of a struggle."

"All of what you have said is true," Juan stated, "However that does not negate the fact that I detected the lingering presence of a necromancer inside of the home, and that you yourself said you felt a swell of magic emit from Alexander. Vampires, as you are more than well aware, are impotent to magic."

I lowered my gaze before looking to Sebastian. I didn't have an argument for that, he was right. There was no logical way Alexander could have produced the magical charge I felt coming from him last night, not if that was really Alexander. On the other side, there was no way a witch could have imitated the superhuman strength coming from him either, or mask from me their general presence at point blank range.

"It would seem that we are at a crossroads, my dear *Senorita*," Juan stated pushing back from his chair to stand.

He didn't walk far, simply moved from his seat at the head of the table to sit on it beside me. He rotated my chair so I was facing him, meant to connect our gaze had I looked him in the eye, which I didn't. Instead I focused on the tip of his right ear.

"A witch is behind the disappearance, of this I am sure. Rather it is a necromancer, or warlock or another faction matters not."

I opened my mouth to object but found one of his slender aristocratic fingers pressed to my lips. It was enough to make me jerk back with a frown, but not to promote eye contact.

"What matters is your kind has violated the agreement set forth by the Council of Councils. That I do not believe this violation was sanctioned by your elders is the only reason I have not taken this matter to the CoC."

"So take your beef to the elders, this is not my problem."

"I am making it your problem," he countered.

I heard the warning in his voice, and the buds of anger but I was at that dangerous point where I was beyond caring.

"Get yourself another witch; I'm not your lackey."

I tried to stand but his hand shot out wrapping clawed fingers around my throat. I was hauled from my chair only to be slammed onto the boardroom table. I was barely able to get my arms up before he straddled my waist.

One hand went to the fingers around my throat; the other went for his throat only to be pinned to the table by his free hand. From the corner of my eye I saw Brenda charging forward, but Sebastian was on his feet hemming her back up against the wall.

"*Padre, no por favor!*" Sebastian's voice rang out, though he made no attempt to move towards Juan.

Juan squeezed, not enough to choke me, only to get my attention as if having him straddling my waist on a boardroom table hadn't accomplished that.

"Let there be no mistake, the only reason I suffer you to live is because Sebastian pleaded for your wicked life. Had he not begged to give you a chance, I would have already turned this over to the Council of Councils requesting the witches of San Francisco be terminated from existence. I understand the obsession he has with you," he continued, still holding me prone. "You are very intelligent, charming when you wish, and fairly attractive in your own way, but your garish attitude is trying my patience."

He gave a final squeeze for emphasis, cutting off my air supply for a second before letting me go completely. He crawled from over me like a cougar toying with its pray.

My hand went to my throat; only believing it was intact after feeling it in place. Slowly I climbed off the table, ignoring the hand he offered for my assistance. If I had a stake I'd been hard pressed not to shove it into his chest. I moved away from him, my steps putting an unobstructed path from where I stood to the door. Sebastian no longer held onto Brenda but remained standing in front of her.

"You have ten days, *Senorita*," Juan began, smoothing out the sleeves and front of his suit carefully before his fingers plucked at lent I'm sure was not really there. "Prove that witches are not behind this, or to bring the one that is to justice."

"And if I can't or don't?"

A smile touched his lips, which was more evil than amused. "Then I will follow through with my petition to the Council of Councils and the matter and fate of yourself and all the witches of the area will be out of your hands."

"You realize when I speak to the elders of this; they will have reason of their own to go to the Council."

That amused him enough to laugh. "*Senorita*, I have faith in the wisdom of your elders, to discern the difference between a shrewd decision and an utterly foolish one."

I could feel his eyes on me, but didn't dare meet them. I didn't even study his ear, just kept my gaze focused on the distorted reflection of his in the glossy finish of the table.

"Shall we say your ten days begins tomorrow at sundown?"

I didn't give him an answer, but then he wasn't waiting for my agreement. I left the suite. I tried to slam the door but the spring-loaded hinges prevented that satisfying clap of door meeting frame. The elevator door slid open as soon as my finger hit the down button. Sebastian was quick, but not quick enough to make it to the doors before they closed. My insistently pressing the button to close the door as soon as I was inside might have helped him miss the cart. I watched the numbers decrease on the digital read out above the buttons, as my anger threatened to increase.

I was furious at Juan for his words, his attitude, and generally being the manipulative bastard he was. I was furious at Sebastian for even getting me involved in this mess in the beginning, good intended motives be damned. I was furious at myself for not being smart enough to clear myself from the mess. One thing was for sure; first thing in the morning I'd be going to the elders.   If I was going to be stressed for the next ten days I wasn't going to be the only one.

The elevator dinged its arrival to the ground floor, and I was moving to the main entrance as soon as the doors opened enough for me to walk out. My anger must have showed on my face because the few people loitering in the lobby made sure to stay out of my way. The sound of Sebastian calling my name didn't quicken my gait, but it didn't make me pause or slow it in the least.

Despite it being almost midnight or possibly because it was Saturday night there were cabs waiting outside the hotel. As soon as I pushed outside the revolving doors the doorman signaled the first in line to pull forward and moved to the back door.

"Danika, would you just wait a minute?"

Sebastian attempted to seize my arm but I jerked away the moment I felt his fingers make contact. It served its purpose; however, it got me to stop and whirl around to face him. His hands were up in the international sign of peace but I still felt it necessary to issue the warning through partially clenched teeth.

"Touch me again and I swear I'll kill you."

"I'm not here to hurt you," he stated as simply as possible.

"No, you'll just let Juan do it for you."

"That's not fair."

"And what he's demanding of me is? And now I find out I have you to thank for that?"

"You think I would have volunteered you for this if I knew it would end up this way?"

"Ten minutes ago I would have said no. Of course ten minutes ago I would have thought you would have tried to do something."

"What would you have had me do?"

Neither of us paid much attention to the doorman still waiting by the cab, but neither of us dismissed him to the point of speaking too openly about it.

"I couldn't have stopped him."

"Because you've tried it before, right?"

"You don't understand," he paused for so long if I hadn't been staring at him I might have thought he left. "I *can't* stop, Juan."

"Why? If he's that much stronger than you why the hell did you get me involved with him in the first place?"

"It's not because he's stronger," he said in a hushed voice.

"Then what?"

He gave a bit of a frustrated sigh before looking over my shoulder. "Dani, please. Just let the valet get the car and I'll explain as much as I can on the way to your house."

"I got a better idea. Stay. The hell. Away. From me," I turned away from him and climbed into the back of the cab. I didn't bother to look back as he pulled from the curb.

True enough it wasn't Sebastian I was really angry at, but since I couldn't yell at Juan like that he had became the whipping boy. Not to mention I still wasn't ready to let him off the hook completely.

The cabbie wasn't one of the talkative ones, which was perfect because I wasn't in a social mood. I gave him the crossroads of my house, getting out at the corner and walking the half block to my front door. It was closed and locked; always a good sign especially since lately it seemed to have turned into a playpen for the undead.

Locking the door behind me, I headed into the kitchen and put on the teakettle. I fired off a text to Finn telling him I was fine and going to bed, then left a voice message for the sorcerer elder before turning my phone off for the night. On the cab ride home I'd decided to spend the night at Finn's place, and just as quickly changed my mind once I was inside my house. I didn't feel like explaining the evening to him, nor did I feel like rehashing the conversation between us from last night.

Most of all I didn't feel like dealing with Simone. I wasn't in a very forgiving state of mind, which meant if she said the wrong thing -which for her would be anything- I couldn't be held responsible for my actions. I was in the mood to hit something and she'd make a perfect target.

I grabbed a teabag from one of the boxes on the shelf that had a bear napping in a chair. Relaxation was definitely on the menu tonight. In another saucepan I poured the left over concoction from the other night before adding gauze to cook with it. At two days old, the wounds were nearly healed. By tomorrow morning if I were lucky there wouldn't even be any scarring.

I turned the pots down low so they would do little more than simmer, before I headed upstairs, stripping from my clothing along the way to the bathroom. What can I say; one of the joys of living alone is walking around the house completely naked whenever. I pinned my hair up before turning on the shower and stepping under the jet stream. It was a long cry from Finn's spa jet-stream shower.

I turned the hot water up as high as I could stand it without scalding myself. It would dry my skin, but any damage done would be corrected by a good application of Shea butter. I tried to shut my mind down as much as possible and just concentrate on the feel of the water and the scent of the shower gel, but of course my mind was determined not to let go.

Sebastian didn't deserve my anger, or the dig I tossed in about Finn being right. He had stopped Brenda from charging forward and assisting Juan or getting her own licks in while I was unable to fight her off. He had asked Juan to stop. I knew enough Spanish to understand what *Padre, no por favor* meant, but why To my recollection Juan Ortiz hadn't been a priest before death, and he damn sure didn't seem like one now. Maybe it was some title of respect.

Clean and less achy than before I hopped into the shower, I pulled the towel from the nearby rack and dried myself off before slipping into the bathrobe and fuzzy slippers I kept in the bathroom. With the door closed the bathroom retained the heat and steam from the shower turning it into a mini sauna. I grabbed the Shea butter from under the cabinet applying a generous coating to my body. It was when I finally stood to exam my neck in the mirror that I noticed it.

The glass was completely covered in steam; well, all of it was covered save the word 'FIREPLACE' neatly lettered across the center of the mirror. The chant for a shield flew from my lips without even thinking, the area around me giving that crackling buzz only another witch would be able to feel.

It was tragic how quickly my instincts were adapting to me being in dangerous situations. I extend my senses into my house, the effect originating in the room and pushing outwards until the whole of the house was encompassed. Nothing answered back. No crackle of magic, no feeling of another presence until I reached the neighbors on either side.

The word on the mirror was already fading as the heat in the bathroom dissipated.

Despite the check of intrusion coming back all clear I padded quickly across the hall to my bedroom and slipped into a pair of sweats. My magic was pretty reliable, but then I'd never had to test it to this degree before, and there was the possibility that someone with stronger magic was concealing himself or herself. Maybe that had been what happened the other night. Maybe it wasn't that the magic came from Alexander, but someone hiding in the shadows near him.

As soon as the notion entered my head I dismissed it. The surge of energy hadn't come from around him, it had come from him; rolling like waves of water onto the beach, not like rain falling from the sky or being blown sideways by the wind. I checked the attic first; making sure my Grimoire was safely hidden, something I'd done since the second break in. The next stop was the front door, followed by the back door, along with all the windows on the first floor, all of which were locked.

"Great," I muttered turning both eyes off on the stove. "On top of everything else, I have an American haunting happening in my bathroom."

There were, in fact, two fully functional fireplaces in the house. The first was of course the main one located in the living room on the first floor. I backtracked into the living room, turning the overhead light on before crossing to stand in front of the fireplace. I stood there like an idiot, staring at it, not really sure what to expect, but halfway expecting to look down in the few ashes that remained to see some word scrawled there. The ashes were annoyingly silent.

Flicking on the lamp I moved the clear gate in front of the opening before getting on my hands and knees and peering into the pan were the logs rested then up into the open flue.

Nothing was there, no ghost hanging in the chimney ready to pounce or slime me with ectoplasm. I held my hand into the open, fingers splayed wide, but no answering breeze came back.

Upstairs was my next stop. Despite having inherited the house after my mother's death a couple years back, I still slept in my old bedroom while the master bedroom was used as a guest room. At least it would have been used as a guest room if I actually had any guests. The second fireplace was located across from the bed. I was a bit more cavalier in my inspection of the second fireplace, turning the light on and moving the glass shield in front of it without the pause.

Everything was identical to the fireplace below. Since I didn't use the room there was virtually no ash build up, save for some residual soot left behind as the smoke made its way up the chimney. No words were marked out through the soot, no ghost lingering as a partial apparition, not even so much as a cold spot greeted me.

"Hello?" I called out feeling completely silly speaking to nothing. "I'm at the fireplace. I don't see anything." I waited, my eyes moving around the room looking for the anything that could potentially be a sign and frustratingly finding none.

"I have no idea what you're trying to tell me," I called out again.

I turned off the light in my mother's old room and closed the door moving back down the hallway. I stepped into the bathroom but the mist over the mirror was gone along with the word. It would have been convenient and easy to just say I imaged it, but you have to be pretty damn gullible to successfully lie to yourself. I stared at myself in the mirror for quite sometime, again waiting to see something, anything that never happened.

"Fine," I growled, hanging up the bath towel and putting the Shea butter back in the cabinet. "Next time give me something more substantial to go on than a cryptic message scrawled across my mirror."

I headed back downstairs to finish up my bandages and make my tea. If the relaxing, napping bear tea didn't put me to sleep, perhaps the Southern Comfort I planned to add would.

CHAPTER NINE

THE next morning I woke feeling better than the night before. I hadn't managed to forget anything that happened the previous night, but felt re-energized. Amazing what a good night sleep can do. I showered again, but there were no messages scrawled across the mirror, my phone was a different story. I had two voice messages when I reclaimed my cell phone from were I left it on the kitchen and turned it on.

The first was from Finn, his voice soft and full of worry as he asked me to call him at my first opportunity. He ended the call saying he loved me no matter what, which was his way of apologizing for the implications my lack of fuzziness held over the future longevity of our relationship. I couldn't help but wonder if by some miracle we ever did married, would me being a witch make things easier, or harder for his pack to accept.

The second one was from Kenya LeBosi, the sorcerer elder I'd left a message for last night. She left instructions on where to meet her and a time at which to do it. According to the clock on the stove I had less than an hour to go. Calling Finn back would have to wait.

Retreating to my bedroom I changed from the jeans and t-shirt I originally picked and slipped into a pair of maroon colored khakis, and a white sleeveless shirt. Going to see the elders wasn't a formal affair, but I didn't necessarily want to look like I was heading to the park or a baseball game afterwards either.

Fortunately for me, the address Kenya left was only twenty minutes from home, which meant I had enough time to make a Krispy Kreme run before arriving at the glen.

The meeting was being held in a park recreational area, which I had been to several times before during different events and meetings. Technically the recreational area was city property, but as with most things American, anything can be bought for the right price. It was rumored the previous warlock elder took funds from his present life and traveled back to when a dollar stretched further to purchase the area. I'm not sure if it's true, but like I've said before, most handed down stories are based in reality.

There were already several cars in the area when I arrived. It was impossible to tell which belonged to the witches I was meeting and which belonged to families out to enjoy a lazy Sunday together. Adding my RX-8 to the pile I stepped out and headed down the trail that would take me to the meeting glen.

My ears popping and the fine hair on my arm standing at attention let me know I had just entered a magically protected field. It was a minor spell but an effective one. Simply put anyone that wasn't magically inclined would find the spot unsavory and move elsewhere. I always equated it to stopping at a gas station to use the bathroom, only to find it should be sanctioned as a biological hazard zone.

Three figures sat in the clearing section as I arrived, two women; one Black, one Latina and a man of Asian decent. These were the elders of our paths.

Kenya LeBosi was the sorcerers' elder. I'm not sure of her age, though if I had to guess I'd say around the upper forties to lower fifties, but she wore it well. Her hair was done in thin locks to the tune of a salt and pepper hue. She must have been growing them for a while because they were almost to the small of her back, though she usually wore them pulled back and up with different African style hair accessories. I've only seen them down once. She was a small woman, both in weight and stature. If she was five feet tall it was only by an inch, but she had the presence of someone not to be trifled with.

A large round woman, whose mere presence had a calming effect, took the form of Lupe Mercado, the wizards' elder. Like Kenya she wore her hair long, and like Kenya it was usually all wrapped up into a tight bun at the base of her skull, but her hair still retained the radiant blackness of a crow's wing. She had a pretty face, telling of the beautiful woman she had been in her youth.

I remember when I was ten I met Lupe for the first time; the energy radiating from her reminded me of the earth even then. It was like staring over the edge of the Grand Canyon for the first time. Mom told me it was because she was at one with the earth, and I couldn't help but notice every meeting I encountered her at she had colors of the earth. From the peace signature on the privacy spell I was betting it was Lupe that did the casting.

Lastly there was Ming Wong. Though he was the eldest of the group he looked younger than Kenya. His apparent aged put him somewhere in his early thirties but Ming was easily over a century. Some believed he was alive back in the 1800s when the railroads were still being constructed. Some believed that he actually worked on the railroads. Another rumor had him exiled from China in the early 1900s for sleeping with the wrong woman. There was even a rumor floating around that Bruce Lee faked his death and later assumed the pseudo name of Ming Wong. It's not uncommon for older warlocks to change their name, making up a new identity or even assuming one for someone that's already died. However, not only did Ming Wong look nothing like the pictures of Bruce Lee, it was simply too far fetched to be credible.

Lupe turned to watch me as I approached. She was the first to look towards me even though her back was to me, just another way I knew she had been the one casting. Kenya smiled and patted the ground next to her for me to sit upon.

"Thank you for bringing the others," I began in a low respectful tone. "I hope you realize I would not have contacted you if the need had not been dire."

"Why did you contact us?" Ming questioned. I held his gaze as he spoke, not like he could mesmerize me like the vampires or anything. "Kenya spoke of your request and that you marked it as urgent but nothing else."

"I didn't inform Ms. LeBosi of the details. I thought it best not to leave as detailed a message as would be needed to explain what's going on."

"I trust," Kenya began pressing a hand to my thigh lightly before pulling back. "That this is important as you made it sound?"

For the fourth time in less than a week I recanted the story I had been told of the vampires gone missing, adding the details as they had been picked up along the way. I let my eyes shift from one elder to the other as I laid the details out before them.

Mercifully they didn't interrupt keeping their questions until I had finished. I did leave out the part about my phantom writer. I wasn't sure how or even if it was related to the missing vampires.

"Did you accept the timeline?" Ming questioned at the end.

"Wasn't given a choice."

"What is your next course of action?"

I stared at him, and then let my gaze move around to the other two women. "*This* is my next course of action."

"But you are the ones they turned to for help, that itself is a sign that on some level, they trust you will see this through."

"No, I was the default choice. I already explained the only reason they turned to me was because of my friendship with Sebastian."

"Who must have faith in you to offer your name up," Lupe added.

"I'm not a sentinel, never wanted to be for reasons like this. This is not something that should even be on my plate."

"Whose plate would you have us place it upon?" Ming questioned.

"With all due respect isn't that why you all are the elders? To determine who's equipped to handle something of this magnitude?" they didn't answer right away, just silently exchanged glances between them. "Of all the coven members I know there has to be someone more capable than me. Others who have had success in resolving issues like this before."

"I knew your mother," Kenya spoke softly commanding the attention of all around for a moment. "Before I became and elder, we shared each other's council on many an issues. She was a wise woman, wise beyond her young years, and extremely talented. Had it not been for her death, she would have ascended to the rank of elder, not I. When we lost her, we lost a powerful ally."

I looked away, letting my gaze shift over the glen. If I stood I would have been able to see Alcatraz from our spot, instead I just saw the rising red peaks of the Golden Gate Bridge. I didn't need her to tell me how talented my mother was, or what her death meant to the witch community.

"My mother is dead," I snipped point blank. "So unless you have a spell that will bring her back for this limited engagement I don't see the relevance."

"The relevance is your lack of evolvement," Kenya's voice remained even keeled but took a sharp edge.

I didn't really need the warning, I knew I had just stepped onto a fine line, but it seemed to be my natural reaction when people started comparing me to my mother. She hadn't gone there quite yet, but it was the natural progress of conversations in the past. Last thing I needed to be right now was reminded that I at my age, my mom was twice the witch I was.

"In the time before her death you contributed to the community only when she left you no choice. Since her death your only contribution has been sporadic attendance of caucuses assembled."

"I've never claimed to be interested in the politics of our community when my mother was alive. Her death changed nothing."

"Politics and involvement do not have to walk hand in hand," Ming stated.

I shifted my gaze to him. "They say the same thing about religion, but what is the Pope if not the President of the United States of Catholicism?"

"It is time that you step up and take your place," Kenya stated to Lupe and Ming's agreeing nods. "You have the rare lineage of being born to not one, but two witch parents. It is time you begin to live your life as a full-blooded witch, and not a simple human that occasionally casts when it's beneficial to her. It is time for you to take your place."

"We have decided," Lupe began, her eyes landing on Kenya and Ming before settling on mine. "That this task will be yours to complete."

I just stared at them with my mouth gaping open. Saying I was stunned would have been the understatement of the year. A full minute passed with us sitting there in silence before I spoke, and even then the best I could come up with was, "What?"

"You will never fulfill your potential by remaining on the sidelines, Danika Harlow," Ming stated.

"And you think *this* is the assignment to let me cut my teeth on? Did you miss the part about having ten days to hand over the witch responsible or prove it wasn't us?"

"We heard all that you have spoken here today," Kenya stated. "But the decision was made before your arrival. The details have not swayed our resolution. If anything it solidifies that this is the only road that must be traveled."

I wanted to ask if they were crazy or just on drugs. I wanted to tell them they were outside their minds and to go to hell. Instead I just stood. There was nothing else to say. I could argue to the ground that I was the absolutely wrong choice for this matter but they had taken their listening ears off.

Kenya stood as well, placing a hand on my shoulder. "Remember we are here to provide assistance and council should you need it, Danika."

"Assistance?" I repeated. "You mean like this? If that's what you three call assistance I think there's a misinterpretation of the word somewhere."

"Have faith in your abilities."

Those were her parting words of encouragement. It wasn't even noon yet and already I needed a drink.

* * * * *

I drove around for a couple hours before I called Finn and let him know I was on the way over. I didn't really feel like being around anyone, but I felt like being alone even less. Alone I would just continue to dwell on the ten-day problem and without a solution in sight it was as productive as a dog chasing his tail, and just as dizzying. Besides, mom always said the best way to get my mind off of my problems was to listen to someone else's.

The front gate to his manor was open, but then Finn had said he was barbequing. He hadn't said it, but I knew that meant a part if not all of his pack would be there. I could smell the food almost as soon I came up the way. The circular driveway was littered with cars when I arrived; everything from a second series domesticated Hummer, to a Toyota Prius, and everything in between.

The front door was closed, but I didn't bother entering the house, just walked around the side to the back. Most of the property was left covered in grass, but there was a small section directly behind the house that had been bricked over to create the patio and circle around the in-ground pool.

It looked to be a full house. Lawn chairs had been pulled out and spread across the grass filled with various occupants. Several bodies were already in the pool on those inflatable floating lounge chairs, while others clung to the side talking to people that were lounging on the concrete area. There were even a couple of wolves lying on the grass looking more like over grown German Shepard mixed with something wild and huge. I knew all of the people in his pack on sight, but would be hard pressed to know all their names. There were sixteen people there in total. Twelve werewolves that made up the membership of the Alcatraz Pack, the rest were significant others of the pack.

There was a long picnic style table set up covered with various other items normally found at barbeques: an assortment of chips, potato salad, slaw, spaghetti, plastic utensils, napkins, paper plates and cups, cookies, and a few pies. There were two huge plastic garbage cans near the table that I knew were full of soda and beer without having to walk over and glance inside. A keg sat on the other side of the table. No one could drink like werewolves. Their metabolisms worked so fast, the worse I'd ever seen one was buzzed for thirty minutes and that was after a large consumption of alcohol.

Finn stood on the patio lording over the barbeque grill applying sauce over the meat with a brush as if he were painting a masterpiece on an easel. He was wearing a pair of dark blue basketball shorts that hung to his knees. They covered his thighs but still managed to show the curve of his backside. The tank top was the same color and made of the same material showing off the lean sinewy muscles of his arms. This sort of beach hat that reminded me of something a surfer might wear covered those golden locks of his I loved so much. Of course Finn had been known to surf so I suppose it was appropriate.

I hadn't realized I missed him as much as I did until I saw him standing there. A smile began to creep over my face, only to come to a screeching halt when I saw Simone slide up next to him offering a green Heineken bottle.

I glanced to my right as Finn's second in command of the pack, Luke Harris, strolled over offering me a bottle of Corona, much as Simone had just done. A lime slice was wedged half in, half out the neck of the bottle. Taking the bottle I squeezed the lime past an inch of its life, then shoved the remains down the.

Luke was an attractive looking, well-spoken black man. He was taller than Finn by a good three inches and bigger than Finn in terms of sheer girth and muscle mass.

Finn had the body of a swimmer, but Luke had the body of an NBA all-star. He kept his head completely shaved, but the color of his eyebrows and goatee let me know it would have been black. The description tall, dark, and handsome fit him perfectly. A clear, crisp Benin accent only added to his appeal.

We got along fine for the most part, but there was nothing about his disposition that made me for a second believe he'd be willing to take orders from me. I sometimes wondered why he was second and not alpha but that was a question I never posed to either him or Finn. I didn't really have to, since there were only two things keeping him from it; either he lacked the desire to be Alpha, or he'd already made the bid and lost. Since most physical challenges for the famed title end in the death of the challenger, or the defender it was safe to say a bid probably hadn't been made.

"I know that look," Luke stated, taking a swig of his bottles.

"Yeah?" I turned my eyes back in time to see Simone light her hand on Finn's shoulder. Luke and I bristled simultaneously.

"And I know a great place to hide a body. I can make sure your case never goes to trial even if it's discovered."

That at least got me to relax a bit. The scary part was the words could have as easily been a joke or truth. Luke was a district attorney in the San Francisco court system and one of the best. I think being a werewolf gave him a hell of a leg up in the intimidation department. A good number of his cases were resolved in deals before they even went to trial.

"What?" I turned to regard Luke briefly for a moment. "You don't like the newest member of your pack?"

He gave a shrug, took a drink, looked her over and gave another shrug. "I don't know enough about her to like or dislike her yet, nor do I know her well enough to determine if she will be an asset or liability to the pack. But I do feel her blatant lack of respect for you leaves much to be desired."

Luke's practicality of the first part of his assessment brought a smile to my lips, just as the latter part was touching. I let my eyes move over the people gathered there once more paying special attention to the women of the pack. The coming of Simone bumped the total number up to five, two I got along with, the rest would slash or at least attempt to if we met in a dark alley.

"I hear from Finn that you have problems lately."

"Finn needs to learn to keep his trap shut."

Luke chuckled. "When something troubles you it troubles him. When my Alpha is troubled it's my job to help resolve the issue."

"Privacy isn't high on a werewolf's list is it?"

"Among pack members there's no such thing," he stated chuckling again. "Come; let's take you to your mate."

I nodded, only to turn and find he wasn't at the grill. The basting brush was there, resting back inside the sauce jar and the grill top had been closed, but Finn along with Simone was absent.

"He's in the kitchen," Luke informed.

"Okay that's just creepy," I teased heading into the house through the sliding glass doors with him behind me.

The patio doors actually led into the kitchen, and sure as shooting Finn stood in front of an open refrigerator pulling out fresh corn on the cob already individually wrapped in foil and placing them on a plate Simone held.

"Finn, I don't like corn," I heard her whine.

"Doesn't matter, besides it's not just corn, its grilled corn."

As soon as I stepped into the doorway he turned to face me. A mega watt smile pulled his lips up and dimpled his cheek, but quickly faded after his eyes were able to settle over me for a few seconds. He pulled out the last of the corn, adding that to the plate before kicking the fridge door close and crossing the room to engulf me in his arms.

The embrace was strong, almost to the point of being uncomfortable, but the safety I felt in his arms was like a soothing balm against my nerves. I let my cheek rest against his upper chest, my forehead pressed into the crock of his neck as my own arms found their way around his waist. His spicy scent filled my nose as I relaxed my body into his.

"Simone," Luke called, "Let's put the corn on the grill."

"I was going to help Finn do it."

Her words, more than her voice caused me to stiffen as if I'd been shocked with a stun gun. Finn's embrace tightened, making withdrawal from him impossible.

"And now you will assist me," Luke added. His tone remained civil but it was not a request he was issuing rather a subtle order. Further disobedience would come with a price.

I felt her walk past me, felt her eyes on me but didn't so much as open mine to give her a corresponding glare. She was too smart to attempt anything overt in the presence of both Finn and Luke.

Finn's arms relaxed a bit, letting air return to my lungs, but he seemed in no hurry to let me go, as he pressed his cheek against my head. Worked for me, I was in hurry to rush from his embrace anyway.

"What's the matter?" his voice a soft whisper against my hair.

"I spoke with Juan again last night. He's giving me ten days to get to the bottom of this before going to the Council of Councils."

"Bastard," his right hand began to smooth slowly up and down my back. "Have you gone to the elders?"

I nodded, my head bobbing against his chest. "After getting lectured on how I was nothing like my mom and that I need to start contributing to the community and live up to my potential they're not doing a damn thing."

"You're kidding."

"I wish I was," I dropped my voice to mimic Kenya's. "We are here to provide assistance and council should you need it, Danika." I scoffed lightly, "Which basically means they'll help to a point."

"And if you can't figure it out? Are they really willing to stand by and let their people be slaughtered because they think it's time for you to step up?"

I shrugged.

"If Juan did go to the Council, you think they would really destroy the witches of the area?"

Another shrug.

"Do you think—"

"--Finn I know you mean well, but right now I don't want to think about witches and councils and vampires and…" I sighed turning to press my face into his chest before pulling back so I could see those bright blue eyes of his. "I just want to have a normal afternoon with the love of my life."

He smiled softly, lowering his mouth until I felt the lightest brush of his lips against mine. He parted his lips for me, and I took my time deepening the kiss, allowing our tongues a slow sensuous dance together. Disengaging out lips, I watched the return of the mega watt smile to his face before resting my head against his chest again, this time keeping my eyes open so I could look out onto the patio. Furiously, Simone watched us. I hadn't kissed him like that to rub salt in her eyes… it was just a pleasant side affect.

Before I could give a smug self-satisfying smile to Simone, Finn's finger against my chin distracted my attention as his lips touched against mine again. His strong hands moved down my body, fingers kneading into the muscles along my back on the way to rounding my backside. I should have stopped him, but I found out ages ago it was impossible to concentrate fully while Finn's lips were connected to mine. His kisses were intoxicating, like everything else about him.

"Finn," when his lips left mine in favor of nibbling on the sweet spot of my neck we both enjoyed, I was able to find my voice again. "Finn," it took everything in me not to answer his lips with a soft moan. "You're pack is less than ten feet away."

He chuckled, but he didn't relent. "So?"

"So, I'm not really in the mood to give them a peep show."

I thought he would release me; instead with his hands securely planted on my backside, he hoisted me up against him as if I weighed less than a five pound sack of potatoes. "They'll know anyway."

He took the back stairs, two at a time up to his bedroom, supporting me completely with one arm while he opened the door, then kicking it close behind us. He dropped me onto the bed and blanketed me with his body at the same time. His fingers fumbling with the buttons of my shirt while he continued to nibble and bite down on my neck and shoulders and jaw. He was everywhere, frenzying like a possessed man.

"Finn, I—"

Finn thrust his tongue roughly into my mouth as soon as my lips parted. I could feel the hard length of him straining against his shorts, as he ground his pelvis against my hips.

He got like this around his pack or when my cycle was close to coming on. The two of them together was like catnip for him. He explained it to me once, something to do with the primal urge to reproduce, dominate. No one would ask why we had disappeared or what we were doing; of course being werewolves they could smell the scent of our pheromones through the open window.

The last button wasn't cooperating fast enough and got yanked off for its troubles. Straddling my hips he slid his arms under me, pulling me from the bed as his fingers slid the shirt down my shoulders and off my body. His lips softened as the man struggled to regain control from the beast. Light kisses were pressed to my shoulder, and chest, and lower as his fingers made light work of my bra.

I placed a hand against the mattress for support. Arching against his mouth as lips and tongue lavished languid attention to my breasts. I gave a soft moaning sigh of encouragement as his mouth opened wide, his tongue circling around one dark nipple before biting down hard enough to change the moan to a quick hiss. It didn't hurt; not yet, it would never hurt, unless it was at my request. Finn knew the exact amount of pressure to walk that line that flirted with pain and pleasure without every truly crossing to the abusive side.

Lips planted kisses down my body as he moved lower, his tongue leaving a wet path over the planes of my stomach, teasing my naval, before ranging lower still. Sneaky hands had already unfastening my pants, and fingers trudged them and panties down to discard with the growing pile of clothing on the floor.

He rubbed his cheek against my thigh before pressing his lips there. Looking down my body I saw that ridiculous hat was still securely atop his head, but the eyes that stared back at me suffocated the laughter before it could even bubble from my throat.

The translucent almost iridescent green eyes of his wolf replaced the vibrant blue of the man. He rubbed his cheek against the other thigh before opening his mouth and biting down. Both sets of canine teeth had lengthened, leaving four pointed indentions on my skin. He increased the pressure, those ghostly green eyes focused on me, his teeth unrelenting until he broke the skin and I cried out.

"Shh," he whispered moving up the short distance to my sex.

He rubbed his cheek there as well; the mark of my arousal glistening on his skin.

With his hands under me he shifted my body, lifting me enough to press his chin against my lips, edging it upwards to rub the most sensitive part of me. He didn't stop there; kissing me long and deep. His tongue tasted my essence, drinking me in while reducing me to a withering mass of flesh on the bed. Clutching his sheets and whimpering his name.

The absence of his body against my was acute as he made short work of his clothing, but before I could even sit up and reach for him he was over me again. There was no pause as he covered my body taking one leg around his waist while he guided the other upwards against his chest. There was no hesitation as he sheathed himself snuggly inside my body setting a rhythm for me to match instantaneously.

His knees and arms supported his weight and kept him from pushing the leg pressed against his chest from moving too far back, fortunately I was flexible enough where he wasn't hurting me yet… not that I would have been focused on what my leg was doing. His hips were giving me little cause to focus on anything but their steady movement.

I stated into those eyes of his; even with the wolf staring back at me I could see the emotion built up in them. His gaze piercing, unwavering… unnerving.

A tiny smile turned the corner of his lips up as he shifted his position just a fraction, but enough to allow the new position to nearly unhinge me with pleasure.

Soft cries began to rain from my lips, being pushed out with each thrust. He switched again, this time letting the leg on his chest slide catching the bend of my knee in the crock of his elbow. His lips attacked my mouth, my chin, and throat.

Professions of love whispered against my ear before he claimed my mouth as his own again.

We moved like that, one being; joined at the lips, joined at the pelvis. He responded to me, moving faster when I did, pitching deeper as I lifted my hips against him. He pushed me further than I thought I could go, unrelenting even after the ground was knocked from under me. My explosion was met by his continued unflinching rhythm; ruthlessly creating repeated ebbs and flows, each stronger than the one it preceded. He exhausted me, taking me repeatedly to the precipice and throwing me over the edge. It wasn't until I felt consciousness waning that he finally peaked with me. A primal growl ripped from his lungs.

Sweat drenching both of us, he released my leg before collapsing against me, heaving shuddering breaths wrecking through his body. He tried to move twice before giving up all together and simply burying his face against the crock of my neck. His tongue tickling as he licked the sweat pooling at the bone.

"Did I hurt you?" he whispered, the bass gravel sound of his wolf remained in his voice. It kept me from moving for fear of exciting him again.

"If by hurt you me causing pleasure until I was almost blind, then the answer is yes."

He chuckled, the sound more of a bass vibration in his chest before he bit the nape of my shoulder. I turned my head to the side, offering him the full expanse of my throat as my arms moved around his back to hold him close. On a human, another witch, even a vampire the gesture would have been lost. For Finn it meant more than anything I could have spoken aloud.

CHAPTER TEN

WHEN I woke up, I was groggy. Like coming out of a deep drug or alcohol induced sleep, but I knew where I was almost immediately. The scent of Finn surrounded me in a warm secure blanket, much like his arms held me close to his body. A smile crept across my face as I enjoyed the moment, his arms around me was how I met Finn, though I had far more clothing on at the time, we both did.

I'd been rollerblading, or at least learning how. I found out that day it's never a good idea to learn how to rollerblade in heavily populated areas. Finn and some of his packmates had been on the way to play football when I literally ran into him. We both took a tumble and I ended up sprawled on top of him, his arms wrapped around my waist.

Even then I felt safe in the arms of a perfect stranger. Yes I know, utterly sappy. It had always been like that with him; like nothing bad could touch me as long as I was in his embrace. Part of it was him being alpha and the air of confidence that went with that but mostly it was just Finn.

"What was that?" I questioned, my voice hoarse from the amount of screaming he'd made me do earlier.

"A normal afternoon with the love of your life," he replied, his arms squeezed my body as his lips touched lightly against my forehead.

I stretched as much as possible, wincing a bit when muscles recoiled and attempted to reject movement. "I could learn to enjoy a normal afternoon," I murmured nestling against his chest. Sure I had aches and pains throughout my body but some things were worth it... this was definitely one of them.

Thinking about the intensity of his gaze shot a tingling bolt down through my sex. A bass growl emitted from Finn's throat as he scented the air and caught the smell of my awakening desire for him. His stomach muscles contracted under my fingers as he began repositioning his body, rolling onto his side to face me, his fingers gliding from the nape of my neck into my hair, pressing against my scalp.

"What time is it?" I asked placing my hands against his chest. Instead of staying put my fingers started stroking the tanned skin of his torso.

"Not too late," he whispered before taking my throat between his teeth. "About six or so."

He nudged his head against my jaw, pushing my head back. The feel of his tongue lapping at my neck was enough to send a shiver from there to the root of my spine, rational thought momentarily blocked in the passage. I touched my lips to his shoulder, my tongue trailing my fingers across his smooth skin. The contrast of my dark flesh against his olive complexion wasn't as startling in the absence of light.

The realization that the room was dark finally synched up with the time of night it was, and the two implications began to take a toll on my rising libido.

"Finn," my fingers gently pushed at shoulders they teased and encouraged only a moment ago, "Stop."

He didn't immediately, not that I hadn't expected that to be his response. His body was at the ready, pulsing and stiff against my thigh.

"Finn I have to go."

My announcement was met by him rolling me onto my back, wrists trapped against the mattress in a pair of strong hands. The top of his thighs pressed against the backs of mine, pushing my legs apart so he could poise his need between them. All it took was the slightest push of his hips forward to case himself inside the heat of my body attain.

"Still need to go?" he whispered his voice against my ear.

His hips rotating slowly as he moved his body with languid strokes. It was a contrast to the way we made love earlier. Under normal circumstances I would have been there with him, arching against him. Instead I pushed at the hands holding my wrists prone.

"Finn, please."

He released my hands so he could push himself up to meet my eyes, and stopped moving, but made no attempt to extract himself from my depths. "What's wrong luv? Am I hurting you?"

"No, not in the least, but I have to go."

"Go where?" he chuckled. "I thought you wanted to spend a normal afternoon with your man."

"I do," I agreed. "I did, but it's evening now and I have to get in touch with Sebastian."

All traces of amusement left his face. He shoved his body into me, hard enough to make me gasp but it had nothing to do with pleasure.

"Finnius don't go there."

He placed his palm against my chest when I tried to sit up pushing me back to the bed. When I tried again he pressed the hand against me harder.

"You're thinking about him while I'm making love to you?" he accused.

"You know that's not true."

"They why are you going to him? Why even mention his name right now?"

"Finn, I need his help. My ten days start tonight, and right now I don't have any leads and absolutely nothing to go on. Sebastian and Brenda are the only links to Alexander that I have."

"Let me help you."

"How?"

"You said it was Alexander that broke into your home, right? If I have his scent I might be able to track him."

"You're a werewolf, not a bloodhound. Besides, I have a divination spell that might help locate him."

"Alright say you find him, then what?" his hand moved, but he still made no attempt to disengage our bodies. If anything I'd felt him swell inside me, almost to an uncomfortable point with him remaining motionless.

"I don't know, talk to him? Try to find out what's going on?"

He laughed at that, a deep rumbling laughter that had my eyes narrowing, and my hands shoving against his chest. I wanted to smack him but settled for driving him backwards so I could scamper off the bed; however, extracting his body from mine wasn't as easy as I thought.

Since Sebastian's name was mentioned he had swollen more, moving past uncomfortable to painful. If I hadn't been partially aroused before he would have been stuck. It was only the lubrication that assisted with his withdrawal and even that had me whimpering in pain and him sucking in air on a sharp hiss.

He bent over at the waist to cover up but not before my eyes saw something that didn't look like it should have fit anywhere inside me. Finn was well blessed but the engorged appendage I saw throbbing from the apex of his thighs had moved beyond the blessing stage. With my clothing piled together it was easy to begin to dress. I had my underwear on and was working on my pants when he finally pulled himself together.

"I'm going with you," he stated. It took him a moment to stand and begin dressing and even then, despite the stupid grin still plastered on his face, he seemed in a mild amount of pain.

"I don't need your help," I hissed.

"Sure you do," he replied nonchalantly. "You're not equipped to handle this sort of thing."

"Apparently the elders of my coven don't share your philosophy."

"Dani," he shook his head before he stepped into his underwear and shorts, carefully pulling them up. "This is trial by fire."

"I know that."

"No, baby, I don't think you do," his voice softened as he spoke. "I don't think you realize why they didn't take this from you."

"I get it, Finn. They think I'm wasting my talent and this is supposed to prove if I can hack it or not. It's not a test for them it's a test for me so I can prove that I am my mother's child and take my rightful place. Blah, blah, blah... I'm familiar with the Jedi mind trick."

"That's not what this is about Dani. It's not proving something to yourself; it really is about proving it to them."

"So? What's the big freaking deal? Why is everyone so gung-ho all of a sudden to see what Dani can do?"

"They're thinking about kicking you out, Dani," he finally stated plainly.

"What? H- How do you know that? What do you talk to my elders now? What are you four in league on how to run my life?"

"Because it's what I would be thinking."

"You're an alpha, not an elder. Those are two completely different positions."

"No," he shook his head. "No, you still don't get it. A coven of witches is no different than a pack of werewolves. You're elders are your alphas. Each packmate, each member has a job to do to keep things running smoothly. If one person doesn't do their job the pack doesn't run at optimal energy. They're tired of you not pulling your weight. Why do you think the majority of my wolves have such a hard time accepting you? Sure, part of it is because you aren't a werewolf, but part of it is because you don't contribute anything to your own community so how could you possibly benefit ours."

Anger that just a moment ago blazed in those brown depths was quickly replaced by the regret that comes across the face of someone that knows they've just said too much.

"And what do you say?" I watched him, continuing only when a slight look of confusion clouded his eyes. "When your wolves come to you with that argument what do you say? Do you agree? Do you defend me? What do you say Finn?"

Uncomfortable silence stretched on as we started at each other. I was the one to look away first; I couldn't handle seeing the truth behind those eyes.

"I see." I chuckled; it was either that or cry.

"Dani, I, I didn't mean it like that."

"Come on, Finn, don't back peddle now. You might not have meant it to come out like that, but let's be honest...it's how you see me."

He shook his head. "That's not the only way I see you."

"Right... I'm sure the sex doesn't hurt," the joke fell from my lips flatly to the floor.

"Dani."

I knew I wasn't perfect, I knew Finn and I had our difference of opinions on many topics, I knew he didn't hold me on a pedestal, but I never would have thought he wouldn't defend me to his pack. What hurt even more was I couldn't even be mad at him. A small part of me knew he was right, and that small part was screaming inside.

How do you defend against the truth? I tried to meet his eyes but found I couldn't even hold his gaze, recoiling from his fingers when his hands reached for me.

"Baby—"

"—What?"

"I still want to help,"

"I don't want your help," grabbing my shirt, I walked around him and headed out to my car. I could feel the sting of tears building behind my eyes, and the last thing I wanted to do was cry in front of him. He didn't need to witness me giving into the wound to know how deeply his words had cut.

* * * * *

I left Sebastian a voice message on my way home, arriving there to his car already waiting.

"Everything all right?" the question was out of his mouth as soon as I was out of my car.

"Yeah, why wouldn't it be?"

He hesitated as he watched me, and then gestured with his hand to my front door.

"I suppose after last night I didn't expect to hear from you."

His words reminded me that I was supposed to be angry with him, but after Finn I didn't have the energy, nor did I really feel I had the right to be angry with anyone. I unlocked the door and held it open for Sebastian, who flicked the deadbolt lock closed after entering.

"You sure you're all right?"

"Stop asking if I'm all right."

He held his hands up in surrender before his eyes moved around the foyer landing on the hole in the wall.

"This where you landed Alexander I take it?"

I nodded, watching him inspecting the wall. "You won't find him in there."

"Just admiring your rather handiwork."

I scoffed. "Were you able to bring anything?" I pushed on not wanting to answer the question in his eyes as he turned to regard me.

"Yeah," he dug into his pocket, pulling out something that looked like a sixteenth century high school ring. "According to Brenda, he only took it off when he slept."

I took the ring between my fingers carefully looking it over. It was heavier than I thought, the center stone a large ruby set inside a wide gold band that had two smaller diamonds on either side.

"Is this real gold?" I hefted the ring a few times then tried it on my fingers to see if it would fit. The thumb was as close as I got and it still threatened to slide off if I held my hand down and moved it too much.

"Yes, and no you can't have it afterwards."

"The last thing I want is a link to Alexander."

I motioned for him to follow me, leading him up to the attic where most of my witch supplies were kept. It was the first time Sebastian had been in my attic. Hell it was the first time someone outside of my family had been in my attic. As a child I don't remember either of my parents letting anyone else up there, at least not while I was home.

"So this is what a witch's spell room looks like," Sebastian stated walking the perimeters looking at the walls, ceilings, and floors.

"No, this is what my attic looks like," I corrected.

Moving to a heavy wooden chest, I knelt down, muttering a few words and moving my hand over the lock. Instantly the mechanism clicked and I opened the lid, pulling out a bowl, some frankincense, another bag of herbs, a thin, short iron rod a centimeter in diameter and less than a foot long, a crystal on a long silver chain, a laminated map of the city and a special pedestal.

Clutching my supplies to my chest I took them to the table, leaning over it so everything spilled from my arms. The bowl I set in the middle, placing a couple cones of frankincense in the bottom before sprinkling five pinches from the bag of herbs. Next I took the ring, slid it onto the iron rod and placed that dead center over the bowl. Lastly I set the pedestal over everything, and then secured the map on top of that. Sebastian watched with silent curiosity as I worked standing close enough to see what I was doing, but not get in the way.

"Can I help?" he finally offered after I paused to go over my mental checklist.

"Yeah," I nodded, "There should be four candles in the trunk. Would you get those out and the pack of matches, please?"

He nodded, and as Sebastian turned his attention to getting the matches I moved behind some of the clutter most attics were guilty of having and removed my Grimoire from its hiding place. I trusted Sebastian but I had my limits.

"Set them on the four corners of the circle," I called out still looking over the spell.

It had been a long time since I did a divination spell. The fact that I had to look it up just proved the point that the elders had been making, and Finn so forcefully drove home. At my age, having magic availed to me my entire life; I should have known a simple divination spell like the back of my hand.

Reading over it again I replaced the book, trying to focus my energy and attention back to the task at hand and away from self-pity. There'd be plenty of time to wallow in that later, at least I hoped there would be.

"Alright," I came back taking the matches from him. "Let's seal this puppy in prayer and get the show on the road." As soon as I said the words I stopped, turned and watched Sebastian. "You, can be inside a prayer circle, right?"

"I'm very familiar with the inside of a church if you recall," was his amused answer.

I gave a nod, said a quick prayer, and lit the four candles, before coming back and lighting the herbs and incense. Picking up the crystal I held the tip of the string over the map.

"The bearer of this ring is the one we seek," I spoke.

The incense began to rise from the bowl, and there was a flicker in the candles I didn't think was supposed to happen, but I dismissed it as the pendulum crystal on the end of the chain began to swing. The circles where small at first, swinging in a tight quick clockwise position, but slowly grew larger, and slower until it stopped and swung limply back and forth each one slower than the last until it came to a rest.

"I take it that means it didn't work?" Sebastian queried in a soft voice.

"Maybe I should try…"

I dropped the words when the pendulum began to swing again, this time in a wild erratic fashion. It swung left then right in wild arcs, swinging upwards and around, picking up speed and flying from my fingers into the wall behind us.

"No," I answered before Sebastian could ask. "That's not normal, not by a long shot."

Going to the wall, I expected to see the crystal pendulum sticking out of the wood, what I saw was a hole were it had not only embedded itself into the wall but flown straight through it. Oddly enough the tail end of the chain was the only thing hanging on our side of the wall. Sebastian touched the chain and we watched as it slipped from his fingers, followed by the sounds of the crystal falling to the floor behind the wall.

"Sorry," he offered with a sheepish smile.

With a sigh I let my head sink against the wall, a soft thump resonating at the connection sight.

"This really just hasn't been my day."

We both stood back and examined the wall. It was more paneling than wood like the rest of the walls in the attic. Odd I'd never noticed that before, but then I didn't go around inspecting my walls. It could have been made of paper machete and I wouldn't have noticed.

Our eyes left the hole and met each other at the same time, and I gave a nod to the unvoiced question.

"It won't be pretty."

"And the hole in the foyer is?"

"Point taken."

I moved to retrieve one of the candles while Sebastian went to work on the wall. The sounds of panel splintering and giving way were followed by a gush of air coming from the newly formed larger hole. It was enough to blow out all four candles and send me scrambling for the overhead lights.

"Dani," Sebastian called. "I think you'll want to take a look at this."

Spotting the crystal pendulum lying on the ground, I bent to pick it up, freezing when my eyes caught the darkness beyond.

"Help me tear this away," I urged grabbing one side of the broken panel and pulling it free while Sebastian made light work of the rest.

Facing us from the darkness of the wall was a third fireplace. I hadn't known it was there. And looking at the wall I realized why I hadn't paid attention to it, the damn thing had been enchanted, and masked so that it gave off no resonance.

"Fireplace," I muttered the word that had been scrawled across my mirror last night.

Retrieving one of the candles I relit the wick and returned to the newly uncovered fireplace, holding it in the opening and looking over it carefully.

"Did you know this was here?"

It was larger than the others in the house, bending over I would have been able to walk into the opening and look up the flue to the chimney outside. Kneeling I moved the candle inside the interior of the fireplace, slowly letting my eyes move over every brick stone looking for something I probably wouldn't know when I saw it.

"This is going to sound insane, but last night when I got out of the shower, the word fireplace was fingered on my mirror."

"A ghost?" he leaned into the fireplace. "Perhaps trying to deliver you a message."

"Maybe, I don't know. Ghost encounters aren't exactly my field of study."

"Did you tell the elders of this?"

I gave a sigh. "It's not exactly their field of study either."

"What are we looking for again?"

"I've no idea," we looked at each other, each giving a small chuckle. "I'm guessing we'll know it if and when we see it."

"Something hidden," he reasoned. "Behind a brick perhaps," his eyes cast downward following the path of the candle. "Or perhaps not."

He nudged the log holder with his foot. When it moved he reached down and removed it from the fireplace.

"These stones are loose."

We both started pulling up the black stones on the floor of the fireplace. Each one revealed more of a metal chest that was resting underneath. The more of the chest that was revealed the quick we removed the stones, like two pirates that had found Black Beard's buried treasure. We pulled a miniature black footlocker from the hole, carrying it to the center of the room.

With no lock on the box I expected there to be a spell keeping others from opening it, but other than being slowed by dirt and rust the latch and the top of the chest lifted freely.

The contents could have easily been a replica of the trunk my mother left. There were stout white candles inside, a mirror that's reflective surface seemed to be made of black glass encased in stone, an obsidian bladed ceremonial dagger with the seven Chakra stones in the handle, a black quartz pendulum on a long chain, bowls, and incense and herbs that had long ago dried to dust. Tucked against the sidewall of the chest was something wrapped in dusty cloth, the same size and girth as the Grimoire my mother had left.

"Oh my god," I sat back on my heels, eyes staring into the contents of the box, not daring to touch any of it yet.

"What?" Sebastian looked from me to the box and back. "Whose stuff is this?"

"It's my father's," closing the lid I traced a dust laden pentagram that was carved on the top. "This is my father's Inheritance Chest."

"Inheritance chest?" Sebastian repeated dusting his hands together, then wiping them down the legs of his jeans.

"Yeah, it's the Grimoire and other magical items a witch leaves to their kin, or whoever they want to pass their stuff onto. They call it the witches Inheritance Chest. That's my mom's," I nodded to the wooden box we'd taken supplies out of earlier. "I always assumed when they destroyed my dad they destroyed his chest so it wouldn't fall into the wrong hands."

"It would appear not," Sebastian stated before he stood.

I reached forward tentatively slow to put my hands inside the chest. I didn't feel any magic coming off of it, save the resonance attached to the items, but still I hesitated afraid my fingers would be burned from my hand after breaking some barrier.

Encouraged when my fingers broached the opening and nothing happened I latched onto the covered book, hoisting it out and setting it on the floor, however, a leather bound journal with an aged envelope resting on top caught my eyes.

I felt Sebastian standing over my shoulders as I reached for the letter. The back of the envelope was sealed with black wax, the impression of a skull making up the seal.

On the front my name was printed neatly. I slid my finger under the flap, the wax easily giving way. The paper the letter was written on was old, like ancient parchment old. I found myself holding it at the edges opening it slowly afraid the oil from my fingers would destroy the material. My eyes quickly scanned the neatly printed words until I reached the closing and saw who it was from. I dropped the letter like it had burned my skin, pulling my fingers back and rubbing my hands together.

"Dani?"

"It's from my father," I whispered.

He bent down to pick it up, like me carefully holding it as his eyes went over the words. "You're not going to read it?"

I blinked back tears as I shook my head. Overwhelming and conflicting emotions held my voice hostage; locked in my throat. The man I knew and the man I had heard whispered about at caucus meetings were two different individuals. How could one person be so cruel to some and so loving to others?

"May I read it?" Looking up to Sebastian I gave a confirming nod. His eyes went back to the parchment.

"Dearest Dani," he began walking about the attic. "Let me start by saying how much I love you. You are without a doubt the only thing I've ever created that truly makes my heart swell with pride. I can only image what you have heard about me, and pray that it has not turned your heart against me. I can only hope the love you remembered will guide you through the lies.

"If you're reading this, you've found your inheritance box, and things are indeed in a dire way. I had hoped to shield you from this side of you magic but it would seem things are ominous enough that it is time for you to embrace your necromancy to protect yourself and the ones you love. I am sorry my dear child, I never meant to keep this from you, only shield you from those that would see you harmed simply for the blood in your veins.

"You've probably guessed by now the items in the box were shielded by magic. The Grimoire is no longer safe in the house. Those that are after it or you will have felt the dissolution of the spell and will come for the book. There is a spell under enchantment that will mask the Grimoire. Say this, then hide it, tell none of its new location. Take my journal and keep it with you at all times, read it. I have copied several of the useful spells onto the pages under the text.

"You will need a teacher; alas I cannot trust this task to anyone. There are reasons there are few necromancers about. Say the following words, they will allow me to temporary access the material plane. It will be a poor tutelage but I trust none but myself to guide you in the ways of our magic.

"Lastly once you finish reading this letter burn it. Be strong my child and know that I will always be with you. Sincerely, Your Loving Father."

As he finished the letter, Sebastian knelt beside me, placing it back inside the trunk over the journal.

"Are you all right?"

I shook my head swallowing back the sting of tears. "To be honest I don't know. I feel like all of the air has just been sucked out of the room."

"Your father sounds like he loved you very much."

"He did," I gave a fleeting smile as I glanced to my friend. "He was a violinist with the San Francisco Symphony. I used to sit and watch him play. Instead of bedtime stories I got solo violin concerts. I loved it. It was the most beautiful instrument in the world to me."

Sebastian gave what could actually pass as a fatherly smile as he moved his arm around me for a comforting hug, his hand pressing my head to his shoulders.

"Do you play?"

"I used to," I let myself relax against him for a moment before sitting up. "After he died…" I gave a shrug. "Things change, ya know?"

"Only too well."

"Right," I nodded, looked him over then looked back to the chest. "Listen, I know I'm on a deadline but do you think you can—"

"—Say no more, my dear." He pressed his lips to my temple and stood. "I will see you tomorrow evening, no?"

"Yeah, call me when you're ready to roll."

From the doorway Sebastian turned and gave a deep, noble bow before disappearing down the stairs, leaving me alone with my newly found secrets.

Chapter Eleven

PLACING my father's Inheritance Box inside the much larger Inheritance Box left to me from mom I cast a locking spell over it. The Grimoire, my father's journal and the letter came with me into the car. I cast a quick masking over the Grimoire; it was the weakest of the hiding spells but was the only one I could remember off the top of my head, and I didn't have the right herbs for the hiding spell he recommended in his letter. My spell would break as soon as I opened the book and wouldn't hold up to intense magical scrutiny so the first order of business was to put the book someplace no one would ever look for it, or would think twice before entering.

I drove around the city aimlessly before coming to a stop at the gates of Pine Oaks Cemetery. Though to an outsider it might seem like the most obvious hiding place in the world, it was culturally taboo for a witch to be buried with their Grimoire. Most Grimoires were either handed down to apprentices, or assimilated into the witch's coven to be shared as collective knowledge, or on rare occasions destroyed by the owner. I was also betting if they knew to come to the house to look for it, they'd already searched dad's grave sight.

There were some witches, mostly belonging to the warlock factions that would rather take their secrets to the grave, literally, than share them with others. Countless spells had been lost this way, many which would probably never be discovered again.

The fence was low enough to climb, though I had to toss the Grimoire over the top and shove the journal and letter down the front of my jeans in order to scale it.

Despite the implications of being a witch, it wasn't commonplace for most of us to tip around cemeteries at night. My first time being there after the gate was locked was more than a bit creepy. I kept feeling that any moment a Rottweiler would come charging at me from behind a tombstone.

I couldn't help but notice the irony of me being in a cemetery at night after finding the Grimoire of a necromancer. Of course in fairness to me it wasn't like I was a patron during the day either. Last time I came through the gates was in a limo at my mother's funeral six years ago. She'd requested to be buried in the mausoleum next to my father. I had always figured the last place she wanted her body to spend eternity was next to Dad's. After his death she never talked about him, whenever I asked questions the answer was so vague I eventually stopped. I always assumed she hated him for whatever it is he did.

Had I known my destination would be my parents' mausoleum when I let the house I could have brought the key with me, as it was picking the lock took another ten excruciating minutes. It would have taken thirty seconds or less with the use of quick spell, but I didn't want to leave any sort of magical tracer.

It took me another couple of minutes to work up the nerve to enter the establishment even after I had the door unlocked. I wasn't sure what stopped me from moving forward. It wasn't fear, even though it was so dark inside I could barely see.

After a few trial steps in finally got my feet to work and take me inside.

My eyes adjusted quickly to the darkness, aided by the moonlight shining in from the doorway and the window directly across from it. There where two stone slabs inside the mausoleum, each held the coffin of my mother and father. The plaques on the fronts displayed dates of birth and death and nothing more. Placing everything on top of my father's crypt, I knelt before it, tracing my finger over the brass plate inscription.

I couldn't help but wonder why the spell had worn off. Sure the letter said it was because of some powerful bad, but I'd never heard of a spell that could self-deactivate like that. Not to mention it wasn't coincidence that had my mother's pendent fly through that exact wall. And what about the message on the mirror the night before? Something had led me there; the question was why.

Finding somewhere to actually hide the book proved to be more problematic than I originally thought. There was no way I'd be able to push aside the top to either my dad or mom's tomb, and even if I could that's just a bit too macabre even for me. There was a flower holder in front of each tomb, which of course was completely useless, and a whole lot of empty open space. It took several minutes of me looking around and climbing on top of dad's tomb before I found the ledge over the doorway. It was still rather out in the open, but wrapped in the dark cloth it blended well enough into the shadows.

Climbing down my fingers touched the leather binding of the journal again before extracting the letter I'd tucked inside. I opened it, skimming the page until I reached the passage I was to speak out loud. Would it work all the way out here or did I need to be at home to release him, or whatever affects the spell was supposed to have? The other alternative was to burn the page as he instructed before speaking the passage. For all I knew saying the spell was someway to release dad onto this plane to finish what he started before his death… that or a way to release whatever he was trying to summon before he died.

I was afraid of what I had heard he'd done, but at the same time this was my dad. He'd never used me to his own gains when he was alive, or hurt me. He'd never been anything other than the world's greatest dad. Moving to the window to use the moon as my light source I raised the page and looked over the passage again, reading it over and over until I'd memorized it. Worst case scenario was I unleashed some unholy entity on San Francisco, but hey in nine nights Juan was going to the council anyway.

Taking a deep breath, I read the paper, spoke the words, and waited... and waited, and waited. Nothing happened, no whoosh of air, no clap of thunder, not even the stirring of crickets. I read over the letter again to make sure there wasn't something else I was supposed to do or say. It wasn't until I realized how disappointed I was that nothing happened that I realized I'd really been looking forward to seeing my father again.

My heart stopped when I moved back to collect the journal and saw him standing in the corner. I barely got my hand to my mouth in time to cover the sound traveling from my throat. He looked exactly as he did the last time I saw him heading off to school that morning. Tall, his head shaved clean with a perfectly manicured goatee surrounding his mouth. He was dressed in the black suit mom had picked out for him, the red tie tucked neatly against the front of the shirt.

He didn't look like a ghost, or at least he didn't look to me what I would have though a ghost should look like. Instead of floating his black wing-tipped shoes were placed firmly on the ground. He didn't glow, and was nearly as opaque as any human being.

My involuntary step back to his advance stopped his forward momentum cold.

"Hello little Butterfly," he spoke softly but it was my father's voice, my father's nickname that only he used to call me.

"Dad?"

"Yes, Dani. It's dad."

Had I not been holding onto the side of the tomb I would have been on the floor.

"H-how do I know it's really you?"

"Every night after tucking you in, I would play this for you."

His words faded as he began to hum, his bass sound in the tune to Canon in D by Pachelbel as he used to play in my room every night. My eyes slowly drifted closed, as he continued. I could hear the sound of his violin, picture myself as a young girl curled in bed falling asleep to the notes he coaxed from the strings of his violin. He played it over and over until I feel asleep, the repetition never once bothering him. Tears built behind my closed eyes, wetting the lashes as they rolled down my cheeks. It was a song I imagined would play at my wedding while he walked me down the isle.

"Daddy," the word came out as a choked sob. I lurched forward but this time he retreated.

"Don't," the words seemed to pain him as they came out. "I want to hug you more than anything in the world right now Butterfly, but I don't have the strength to sustain the connection yet."

The words brought me back, brought my hand to my face to wipe the tears from my cheeks.

"How is it possibly you're even here?" I questioned. "Why didn't you come sooner? Why did you wait so long?"

"I've always been here, Dani, keeping an eye on you. When you graduated from college… I was so proud of you baby."

"Well if you've always been here why come out now?"

"It was part of the deal I made."

I shook my head. "Deal? What kind of deal? With who? Dad! Is it true what they said about you? That you were dealing with the dark sides of magic." I could hear the frantic edges creeping into my voice. I knew there were more important things he'd come to discuss but I couldn't get both heart and mind on the same page.

"Shh," he hushed, catching himself before he moved to comfort me. "I don't know why I was killed Dani, I wish I did.

I had hoped I would be able to find out but things work differently in the nether realm."

I had to press my lips together to keep them from shaking. "They said you were raising demons. That you…" I had to stop; my voice broke off as if even the chords in my throat didn't want to verbalize the thoughts.

"Danika, I promise, when I am stronger we will talk about whatever you wish, but you have to listen to me now. It's taking everything I have to maintain my presences on the material plane, and my connection is already slipping."

I sniffed hard, wiping my face with the back of my hand again before refocusing on my father. He slowly began turning transparent, the wall before blocked now visible behind him.

"The journal, there are spells under the text. To reveal and hide them simply say Canon D," I nodded. I wanted to ask questions but even as I watched he was fading from vision. It wasn't an even fade; his torso and head were fading slower than his extremities. "The vampire that came for the Grimoire is being controlled by a necromancer, probably a very powerful one. Find the vampire and you find he who controls him."

"We tried that," I stated in a rush.

"Only necromancy magic can locate that which is already dead. There is a spell in the journal that should help you find him, but you must be careful, Dani. To control zombies are one thing, they have no will of their own and thus are unable to fight. To control a vampire; a being that contains a psyche to fight back and struggle takes very powerful magic."

Each word seemed to take more of his corporal form. By the time he finished his arms and legs had vanished, his torso more of a haze than solid and even his head was slowly fading from sight.

"Daddy please, wait, don't go."

"I can't hold the image any longer Butterfly. I must rest… I will return when I am stronger," he had completely faded by then, only the sound of his voice continued to fill space. "Look after yourself and trust no one, especially Sebastian."

"What? Wait!" I called to the emptiness. "How do you know about Sebastian? Why shouldn't I trust him?" the emptiness didn't answer.

I called for my father several times only to be answered back by silence before I headed back to my car. It took me only two minutes to re-lock the mausoleum, which meant either I was getting better, or locking a lock was easier than opening it.

My hands were shaking as I walked through the cemetery. By the time I reached my car my entire body was trembling. Twice I was almost reduced to a blubbering mess, and twice I was able to pull myself together. I forced my mind to focus on the information I'd been given and not that I'd just seen my father for five seconds for the first time in fifteen years.

A necromancer was at the heart of the problems; that was bad. He was controlling vampires, which apparently meant he had powers out the wazoo; that was worse. Dad told me not to trust anyone but had called Sebastian by name; why? The obvious answer was because he was a vampire thereby possibly subject to being controlled, but there could be other reasons as well. Did he know something about Sebastian that I didn't?

I gave a startled yelp when my phone began ringing, in the silence of the car it sounded like a cannon going off. I hit ignore when Finn's name along with his picture popped up. He was about the last person I wanted to talk to, but the call brought the time sharply to my attention. I probably wouldn't be able to sleep, but if I was I had enough time to get a good five hours if I hurried.

* * * * *

I tossed and turned most of the night occasionally drifting off to sleep only to be awakened by the slightest noise, or what I perceived to be noises. Half of them were genuine originating from somewhere outside by various different creatures, none of which meant any harm to me. The rest were manufactured by my over active imagination. Part of me wanted to call the elders, but they hadn't exactly been a huge help to this point. Besides, they could possibly be on the no trust list.

They claimed it was because it was time for me to answer my destiny, but maybe it was because they didn't want the necromancer found, and figured I'd be the best hope at leaving the mystery unsolved. It seemed a bit like the Chief of Police putting the rookie cadet on a bi-coastal serial killer. Of course this had actually worked in *Silence of the Lamb* but really what were the odds.

By the time I actually did drift off to something resembling a peaceful slumber, the sun crested the horizon, and my alarm went off an hour later. I was emotionally and physically exhausted but at least my head ceased throbbing to my pulse beats.

My father's journal went with me to work. The letter I put through the shredder, burned in one of my mini cauldrons, and scattered the ashes on the way to work. Sure it was overkill, but better overly safe than sorry. Dad's words about Sebastian continued to weigh heavily on my mind as the day stretched on. The morning I concentrated on the responsibilities I had to do within the museum. By the time afternoon arrived I locked myself into my office and pulled my father's journal out.

The first hour was spent reading over his entries, but it wasn't before long I began to feel like I was spying into a private part of his life, which of course I was. The entries were dated back in the seventies and seemed to pick up right after he finished his apprenticeship and was named a master of necromancy.

Pausing from my invasion of his life, I stood, went to my office door, unlocked it, and poked my head out. A quick look to the left and right assured me the halls were cleared, but even so after locking the door I whispered a quick spell that would ensure no key would fit into the lock. Moving back to my desk I sat down, turned to the first page in the journal, and spoke the words my father instructed.

I felt the crackle of magic first; the word of Dad's life slowly faded into the page they were written on, as fresh words bled forward. They were in the same handwriting but these weren't memoirs of a necromancer, unless of course spells can be considered memoirs.

The journal transformed into a mini-Grimoire holding spells, recipes for constructing charms and wards, chants, herbal connotations, and incantations. Some were complete; others had a page number to reference when consulting the Grimoire for alternate ingredients or other uses beyond what was listed. He even had a table of context in the front of the journal that listed what could be found where so I wouldn't have to flip through the entire book.

Going over the table of contents I flipped to the page that contained scrying spells looking over them until I found one that would track a vampire. I'd have to hit the herbal store on the way home, but then I would have had to go anyway for the necessary herbs I needed in the spell to mask Dad's Grimoire properly.

There were simply too many to memorize in one sitting so I went through the book page by page, looking over which seemed to be most effective for what I was going up against. There was even one listed for calling out another witch. It would have been handy against my guy or girl but the witch's name was essential to the spell. Besides, I wasn't sure I was ready to be calling a powerful necromancer out for a showdown. Crazy I was, suicidal not so much.

I stayed locked inside my office well past closing of the museum. Despite Dad's warning I pulled my cell phone out to call Sebastian once the sun had gone down. Whether I was able to trust him or not didn't stop me from having a task to complete, and for that I needed Sebastian.

The phone barely cycled into the third ring before he picked up. His voice was deeper than I was used to hearing it, huskier and dare I say it, sexier. It made me wonder if I had interrupted something interesting.

"Sebastian speaking."

"Hey Bastion, it's Dani."

"Dani," at least he really sounded glad to hear from me. Of course why wouldn't he be? "I was hoping you would call this evening. All is well after last night I trust?"

"About as well as can be expected."

"Good," there was a pause, "Listen after leaving you last night Brenda and I tried to locate Alexander. There is a bond that forms between siblings of the blood. The bond will at times allow for a tracer of sorts."

"Sort of like vampire GPS?"

He chuckled softly. "Yes, very much like that."

"Any luck?"

"Unfortunately no. Either the city is too large, or there is possibly some spell masking his location, or dear Alexander is no longer among the undead."

I paused. That had actually been the first thing I thought of when he said they couldn't find him. "Well, assuming he's still among the living, or undead, I've found another way to possibly locate him."

"We will meet at your house then?"

"We?"

"Brenda has asked to accompany me until Alexander is found or whatever is behind this is destroyed."

"I don't want her in my house," I replied sharply.

"Danika—"

"—She tried to kill me less than a week ago in case you forgot."

"She had no intention of killing you, only persuade you to accompany her."

"She gave me a concussion."

"Her persuasion was a bit too forceful."

It finally dawned on me why Dad said not to trust Sebastian. He was a vampire, and I was the child of a necromancer. Oil; meet vinegar.

"Sebastian did you tell anyone about my father?" There was a long pause; so long I thought he might have hung up. "Sebastian? Did you tell anyone about my father?"

"I will pretend I did not hear you ask that of me."

"If you pretend you didn't hear it, I'll just have to ask again."

"When have I ever betrayed your trust, Danika? Give me the date and time."

"Never," I replied flatly. "Of course it's not like I've asked you to keep a secret that could get me killed before either."

Another long bout of silence filled the air before his very tight voice came back. "No, Danika I have not betrayed your trust in any way shape or form, nor do I intend to either willingly or against."

"Thank you."

"If you will excuse me, there are other matters we need to attend to before meeting with you tonight. Shall we agree upon ten o'clock?"

By the time I opened my mouth to answer the line had already gone dead in my ear. It was the first time he'd hung up on me. Of course it was the first time he'd been that pissed at me. Closing my phone I placed that in my purse, whispered the phrase again, slipped the journal into my bag, and then disengaged the magical lock on my door before heading out.

Sebastian being upset because I didn't trust him was either a very good sign, or a very bad one. Hopefully I would be able to find out which before the answer did me no good.

CHAPTER TWELVE

IN the past forty-eight hours I managed to be pissed off at and piss off the two more important men in my life. All right so technically Finn wasn't pissed off at me but our last words hadn't exactly been about sunshine and roses either. His pack didn't think I was good enough for him; he seemed sketchy on the idea himself, so much so I was starting to wonder what the shelf life our relationship really was. I thought about calling him during the day, but my preoccupation with my father's journal, accompanied by not knowing what I'd say to him kept me from dialing his number.

Then there was Sebastian, though I really wasn't too concern. It wasn't the first time he and I had sharp words with each other and I was fairly certain assuming we both survived the ordeal that it wouldn't be the last. It was the first time he'd hung up on me without saying goodbye. I suppose I offended his moral code as a vampire.

Lastly there was dad's warning about not trusting anyone, especially Sebastian. It occurred to me if I was able to locate Alexander, taking Sebastian might not be the wisest move. If the necromancer had control of Alexander, did they still have control of the other two vampires? Would they be able to take control of Sebastian? For all I knew this guy was trying to mass some sort of vampire army. This could be like leading a lamb to the slaughter. Brenda was the variable. I trusted her like a trusted a crack whore in a crack house.

I pulled into my driveway just as my phone began to ring. I had half a mind not to answer it but instead reached in my back seat searching through my workbag until my fingers closed around the iPhone. I was only mildly surprised to see Finn's number before answering the call.

"Hello?"

"Dani, it's Finn," he greeted softly.

I was quiet for several moments. I really wasn't sure what I should say to him. This wasn't our first argument, not by a long shot, but it was the first time Finn had laid it out in such clear concise way. I wasn't a hundred percent what that meant in terms our future, or if we had one. The good news was I didn't think Finn would break up with me over the phone, of course that didn't mean he wouldn't call to set up a time to kick me to the curb.

My eyes turned towards the house; the interior was completely dark save two lamps in the living room on automatic timers. There were no shadows moving, always a good sign since no one should have been home.

"Dani, you still there?" Finn's soft voice in my ear brought me back from my personal revelry.

"Yeah, can you hold on a moment, please?"

"Sure."

I pressed mute on the phone before closing my eyes and letting my mind move into the house sweeping each floor room by room. When nothing answered back I hoisted the articles from my car and headed towards the back door, quickly stepping inside and locking it behind me before dumping my workbag on the floor, and the herbs on the counter.

"Sorry, I just got home."

"You can call me back if this is a bad time."

"No," I replied quickly. "No if we don't talk now we probably won't for the rest of the night."

"How are things going with that?"

"Slow," I stated before quickly adding. "But we're making progress."

"We?"

I closed my eyes wishing I'd chosen a different word. "Yeah, um, Sebastian is helping out."

The silence on the other end began stretching on but I couldn't claim to be surprised.

"I said I would help you," he finally growled out in a very low, very controlled voice.

"You also said I need to pull my own weight and contribute to my community."

"And leaning on Sebastian for help is your definition of pulling your own weight?"

"Whatever is happening is affecting his community too. If it weren't Sebastian it would be someone else from Juan's party pack. Personally I'd rather it be someone I know so I didn't have to watch my back and my front."

Again the silence before a strained reply. "You're right, I just don't—"

"—Like Sebastian, yeah, I got that Finn. You've made that abundantly clear over and over again. It was one of the few things you didn't bother hiding."

"I'm not going to apologize for what I said last night, Danika."

"No of course not, because that would mean you were wrong."

"Dani I love you," he paused before continuing leaving a pause as pregnant as an elephant in its twenty-first month of gestation.

"But?" I pushed.

"Nothing," he spoke softly.

"Bullshit, what is it Finn? You love me but you can't see yourself with me? You love me but it's in your pack's best interest if we start seeing other people? You love me but what? Just say it. Put it out there so we can stop pretending the five hundred pound gorilla isn't sitting in the corner eating skittles."

"I'm the alpha of my pack, they have no say in who I choose to date."

"That's only half true and you know it."

In the background I could hear someone speaking to him, but I couldn't hear the conversation clearly.

"Dani, I have to go. Can I call you later?"

"I don't know how late I'm going to be working."

"Call me then," he ordered. "When you get in."

"It'll be late."

"It doesn't matter what time, even if it's too late to talk just let me know you made it back home in one piece, all right?"

"All right," I agreed.

"Promise me?"

"I promise I'll call."

He paused, then softly said; "I do love you Dani," before disconnecting the call before I could say it back.

I set my phone on the counter trying not to picture Simone comforting Finn. She was twitching around that house just waiting for the opportunity to sink her claws into him. Could she smell the blood? Would she move in for the kill? Would Finn let her? He was only werewolf after all. I knew better than anyone how sexual they could be, Finn in particular. It was a release for them, and a way to establish dominance and claim, especially over their mates, and especially with the males.

Looking at the herbs, then the time, I tried to clear my head of all things Finn related, which meant putting our problems on the back burner long enough to concentrate on the portions of herbs I needed to mix. I had hoped I'd be able to take the masking spell to the cemetery and work it on the book, but it was already after nine by the time I finished.

Drumming my fingers on the counter, I weighed my option before taking the divination mixture up to the attic. The original game plan was to wait until Sebastian and Brenda arrived and have them wait downstairs while I did my thing, but the closer it approached to ten the more I started to second guess that decision.

I took the white candles from my mother's chest out and set them in the points around the circle. The mini-Grimoire hadn't mentioned anything about specific colored candle, which meant it wasn't relevant to the spell. Making sure I had everything I needed, my father's bowl, a small mirror, Alexander's ring and of course the potion itself, I sealed the circle in pray and began.

I lit the herbs in the bowl; the thick smoke from their burning dried leaves quickly filled the space of the attic thickening the air. "Guide me to the one I seek," I spoke clearly holding Alexander's ring. "Guide me to the wearer of this ring," the words were followed by me dropping the ring into a smaller bowl that sat in the middle of the smoking herbs.

To the average observer the words would have sounded foreign, or possibly even from a made up language, which in a way I suppose it was. It was the language of old and had long become the language of magic, which we are taught originated from elves.

Learning the language was essential for any witch. It was the witches' common language of international communication, the language of spells as most Grimoires, even those considered contemporary were written in Elvish. Above all else whatever power we called upon to work our magic only responded to the ancient language. And whatever power was needed for the spell to work seemed to be responding in spades.

The mirror was set in front of the smoking bowl, and I watched as the reflective surface darkened, blackness creeping in from the sides and spreading until no reflection remained.

Holy shit was on the tip of my tongue, but I managed to hold the phrase back as I watched, images slowly take shape in the mirror. It was like I was looking down from satellite imagery. Traffic moved down different streets I couldn't recognize, the image on the screen gliding over the slow moving cars. Some sort of traffic jam had slowed traffic down to a crawl on the streets.

Ahead I could see the roof lights of police cruisers flashing but the scene never made it that far up. The image veered to the right sweeping down dark deserted streets past buildings under construction by Walsh Construction Company, to buildings that looked like the vibrations alone from the work a few blocks up would cause them to collapse on themselves.

It was into one of these buildings the image swooped, gliding in like a camera strapped to the back of some homing pigeon. It moved down, spiraling through the ground and layers of sub-basement until I was inside a room. Cages sat before me, like some sort of underground zoo or black market exhibit. The panoramic view allowed me to count twelve in total, though that didn't mean there weren't more in another room or behind me.

Three were occupied, though I'm not sure the first two could really be considered occupied. The bodies that were inside were just that, bodies. They looked to be decayed or in various states of decaying. Complete, but in horrible shape; as if the slightest movement of a finger or leg would break that appendage away from the whole. It was an educated guess the two bodies belonged to the two previous vampires taken. A guess that was confirmed when the image zeroed in on the third occupant.

Alexander crouched in the far corner of the cage; snarling. Saliva dripped from his lips, his hair was matted with blood and dirt, and from what I could see there was a wild crazed look in his eyes. This wasn't the regal elegant man that had broken into my home and tried to beat the shit out of me. This was a vampire reduced to its most primal form.

He lunged forward, his arm slashing through the bars of the cage to show hands that were more like shredding talons than fingers. His hissed and spit trying to get to something that was out of my vision.

"Where is it?" the voice whispering against my ear so deep and seductive.

Something hot was touching my throat, so hot it felt like my skin would burn, and just as quickly was gone replaced by a chilling cold as the temperature plunged like I had been transported to the Arctic Circle from my attic.

"Cover the bowl!" dad's unseen voice bellowed.

I didn't have to be told twice, I took the black silk cloth the bowl had been wrapped in and threw it over the opening. Instantly the mirror blacked out before returning to just a reflective surface. The smoke ceased rising from the bowl, as it dissipated quickly like a large fan switch had been flicked to suck it all out.

"Dad?" I called out hesitantly.

Eerie silence answered back.

"Daddy?" still the silence remained.

Raising a shaky hand I looked to my watch. I had fifteen minutes before my guest would arrive. Taking a deep breath I scrubbed my hands down my face, and moved to blow out the candles and head down to my bedroom. A shower would have been nice but it was a luxury I couldn't afford. Instead I turned on the local cable news channel while striping from my work clothes and putting on a pair of black jeans, a black t-shirt, and my black steel-toed boots.

Nothing had looked familiar in the scene displayed but I was betting it was in the San Francisco area. The only other metropolitans in the area it could have been were Oakland or Berkeley. The roof lights on OPD were a different color, and abandoned warehouse just didn't have a Berkeley feel to it.

It took a good ten minutes before I finally got the report I'd been hoping for, enough time for me to boot up my computer and log onto the internet. The pretty blonde new caster told of a jack-knifing truck that caused a five-car pile up. From there it was just a matter of plugging in the street name and doing a search on construction projects by Walsh in the area.

I'd just finished jotting down the address by the time the front door bell rang. It wasn't the building I was in, but if I followed the road down a bit further east I would be in the area. Hopefully I would recognize it when I got there.

"I'll be there in a minute," I called out barreling down the stairs.

My first stop was the kitchen where I emptied the contents of another mixing bowl into five plastic wrap squares I used as make shift baggies. Next I took the two leaves from the small bag I picked up at the herbal store, wrapped them in a napkin and shoved them into my pocket. The last thing I grabbed was the extendable metal baton from workbag. Finn had gotten it for me a couple months after we started dating; self-protection he had called it. Apparently for him self-protection included bludgeoning with a metallic weapon.

I carried it only because it made him feel better, honestly I wasn't sure I would have been able to use it on someone even if it was in my own defense. More than likely I'd just spray them with pepper spray and run like hell. That went in my pocket as well before grabbing my keys and heading outside via the back door.

It's not often you get to surprise a vampire, I have to say it was probably the highlight of my day to see the startled looks on Sebastian and Brenda's face when I stood at the foot of my porch clearing my throat. Sebastian could have been accused casing my house, as he too was dressed for the occasion in black jeans and black t-shirt, though his footwear of choice was black Doc Martens. Brenda was another story entirely.

Stealth for her was a black silk shirt that actually looked better on her complexion than either the red dress or the light blue shirt I'd seen her in before. She strayed a bit away from the black on black on black dress code with her navy blue skintight jeans, but it was her three-inch ankle boots that did it for me. True enough they weren't a stiletto heel but just the thought of her heels and the resounding clunking they would provide had me nearly rolling my eyes. If the going got tough and the tough needed to get the hell out of dodge I hoped girlie could run, because I wasn't living by the Army Ranger code.

"Shall we?" I called out looking from one face to the other before turning away.

"You were able to find Alexander's location?" Brenda questioned coming off the porch first.

It took conscious thought not to step back from her as she walked up looming over me. The three-inch heels just adding to the height advantage she already had over me. Sebastian followed her, discreetly moving in front of her and escorting me to the car.

"That's not how it works," I replied. "I have a general location. I figure I can get us close enough for you to let your blood link hone in on the general findings."

Sebastian held the door open behind him while Brenda rounded the front of the car taking the passenger seat. It was just as well. I don't know how comfortable I would have felt with Brenda at my back.

"How do you know of the link between blood relatives?" she accused whirling to face me once we were all in the car.

"I told her, Brenda," Sebastian confessed.

"You should have kept your mouth shut," she scolded.

"Why? What do you think she will or can do with the information?"

She gave a huff before turning back around, arms crossing over her seat as her face sank into a pout. I gave Sebastian the address I'd gotten for the Walsh construction sight, advising him what street not to take. I also decided against telling them what I'd seen in the mirror. I might not have liked Brenda but it was her brother.

The ride there was in relative silence; I pulled two of the five plastic wrapped powder bags out rolling them around in my fingers. Hopefully I got the ingredients and mixture just right, if I didn't things would get real ugly, real quick.

Sebastian pulled his Beamer in front of the construction sight, killing the lights then the motor. Three sets of eyes looked out the window; scout the area to make sure we were alone.

"Here," I called attention to myself handing each vampire their very own baggie of treats.

"What is this?" Brenda brought it to her nose for a sniff but couldn't get a sent through the plastic. She was at least smart enough not to remove the twist tie.

"If my guess is right and Alexander is under some sort of controlling spell, this should counter the effects. It works best up his nose, but down his throat will get the job done too."

"Thank you," Sebastian looked to bag over before slipping it into his pocket.

"And take this as well," I pulled the napkin out, handing each of them one of the leaves I'd wrapped inside. "Place it under your tongues. If it is a necromancer this will give you some immunity to his effects over you."

Sebastian flicked a button on the mirror to keep the doom light from opening with the doors, but his pale fingers paused as they reached for the handle.

"Perhaps you should wait in the car."

"Oh what, like stay back little lady and let the men handle this? Are you serious?"

"I'm not a man," Brenda pointed out as the analogy got lost on her.

"If we find Alexander we may find the necromancer or entity controlling him. It could be dangerous."

"If it's a necromancer you really think two vampires going in alone stand the best chance of facing him?"

"Good point," he conceded, before following through on his first impulse to climb out of the vehicle.

I climbed out as well, arming myself with pepper spray in one hand, a bag of the concoction in the other, and trying to convince myself this was really a better plan than it seemed in theory. The only thing more fool-hearty than two vampires going in alone to face a necromancer was an inexperienced witch going in alone with two vampires to face a necromancer. I prayed, hard, that if this was a mistake it would be one I'd live through. Sure the leaves I gave would help combat the pull of necromantic magic; but if this guy was as strong as dad made him out to be it was a good chance even the leaves wouldn't slow him down.

Brenda hadn't bothered to secure her hair, so the blonde strands whipped around her face as the wind combed its fingers through. She closed her eyes; a quick shift of my attention to Sebastian saw him place a finger against his lips. I nodded, hands shoved into my jacket pockets, waiting.

"He's this way," Brenda said, the note of hope in her voice was undeniable. "I can feel him. Hurry."

"Together," Sebastian reminded before she took off.

Turns out she could run in three-inch heels as well as I could in my combat boots, if not better. I had to run like I was carrying a football down the field and the entire Chicago Bears defense was on my ass. Everything we passed was familiar. I.D. markers from the glass in my attic stared back at me as we ran past them. Looking ahead, I saw our destination building before we came to a halt in front of it. It looked the same as it had in the mirror; dark, foreboding.

It was a step above walking in darkness inside. The only light was what the broken out windows afforded to shine through. I tried to play rear guard, but I could barely see the two vampires in front of me. If not for Brenda's hair I wouldn't have seen them at all. As it was, I bumped against Sebastian when we came to a halt. I parted my mouth to speak, but found it covered quickly by Sebastian's hand.

He used the hand to hold my face steady as he pressed his lips so close to my ear they literally brushed against the cartilage as he spoke.

"Open your mind to me," his voice was so soft I almost missed it even with his lips so close.

I didn't want to do it. Even for all the years of our friendship, I'd never let Sebastian into my mind; he was after all, still a vampire. Mom had told me, once a vampire was allowed inside your mind; it made it easier for them to return. Like a mental equivalent of inviting a vampire into the home, except vampires didn't need invitation to enter the home. As proven by Alexander, they could pretty much come and go as they pleased.

I clenched my jaw as I went down a silent pros and cons listing. Sebastian's hand still resting on my cheek gave a soft stroke; I'm guessing it was supposed to be reassuring. In the end I opened up a reluctant channel, but only to Sebastian. There was no way Brenda was about to get an all-access pass to my psyche.

"Don't make me kick your ass for this," I shot into his mind.

I heard him chuckle inside my head, *"You have my promise, only on emergencies."*

The hand that was on my cheek moved to my shoulder and traveled down my arm until it reached my wrist. My very own Seeing Eye vampire. We moved down one set of steps. This level didn't seem to be much different than the first other than it was pitch black down here. I've never felt claustrophobic before that moment. I found myself counting the steps from one set of stairs to the other, just in case.

The third level down was lit by small coal mine lanterns strung up against the wall. Down here I heard the steady mechanical sound and felt the vibration from a machine ahead like the heartbeat of a mighty beast. There was also a smell; death and decay so thick and strong I almost gagged twice. The odor didn't seem to affect either vampire, but then neither of them had to breathe. I tried to close my nose off by breathing through my mouth; it was better, but only marginally.

Like a homing pigeon, Brenda led us right to the room I'd seen in the mirror. Everything was the same, from the twelve cages lining the walls; to the decayed bodies inside two of them, to Alexander, like some feral beast hissing at us from the corner. If he recognized his sister he made no acknowledgement.

The smell was infinitely worse in the room, and eventually biological reaction took over and had me puking up remnants of the bagel I scarffed down while making the potions.

Neither vampire wasted time in checking to see that I was all right, both of them heading to the cage with a wild Alexander inside. Tears in my eyes, I turned to watch them when I caught the flicker of the bars.

"Don't touch the cage!" I shouted mentally to Sebastian.

The warning barely left him enough time to take hold of Brenda's arm snatching her back. It was, however, too late for Alexander. One feral-clawed hand tried to reach out to swipe at the creatures approaching. Blue light flared along with a static field. The lights flickers and he jumped back, cradling his injured hand while still hissing at the three of us.

Only Alexander's cage was marked with the seal, which meant whoever had spelled it wasn't worried about the other two. There were two possible reasons a captor wasn't worried about his prisoners escaping; they're so far into Stockholm's Syndrome leaving is the furthest from their mind, or they're dead or dying and can't escape.

I decided to break rank and let my mind push outwards to touch all there. The cat was out the bag anyway. If someone were there, they would be coming to see what had caused Alexander to stir. Nothing answered back from the building so I kept traveling until I reached the main street. So nothing was in the immediate area, that didn't mean something wasn't coming.

"We have to work fast," I stated, speaking aloud for the first time since getting out of the car.

"Get him out of there!" Brenda shrieked staring helplessly at the thing that was her brother.

He simply continued to snarl at her, though experience kept him from reaching through the bars again.

"The other two cages aren't spelled."

I didn't need to say anything else for Sebastian to go to work on the locks. Brenda continued to hover over me as I knelt down in front of the cage concentrating on the lock. Something easier said than done especially with Alexander hissing in the background like a six-foot alley cat.

Hot energy wafted against my hand as if I was holding it next to an open flame, instead of in front of the lock to the cage. The magical resonance was strong; the energy tracer the same as the night Alexander had been in my house.

"We have to leave him," I stated.

"No!" Brenda snatched me to my feet by the collar of my jacket. "You will release him from that cage!"

"Brenda stop!" Sebastian ordered. With both vampires' bodies in his arms from the other two cages, giving her a verbal command was the best he could do.

"I can't deactivate the spell," I tried to explain. "It's too powerful."

"You'll do it now!"

Her arm shoved me against the cage, and it was like landing on a live wire. Bolts of energy shot through my body into hers, like we were moths trapped on a heat lamp. I was trapped against the bars by her body, though I'm not sure I could have moved if I hadn't been. We were both screaming. Sebastian was shouting something, even Alexander was screaming.

Complete chaos broke out in the room. Alexander charged forward again, another snarling play for the bars. His body hit, his talons tried to grab my arm but instead his momentum was enough to dislodge Brenda and me, sending us backwards to the ground in a tangled heap.

Sebastian was calling my name, at least his lips were moving repeatedly and he was looking at me in a very terrified manner. He could have been saying the Pledge of Allegiance;

my ears were ringing so loudly it was impossible for any other sound to make it past. I tried to stand but either my legs weren't functioning or the message wasn't traveling correctly from my brain.

He shifted his grip on the bodies already in his arm as he squatted next to Brenda and me, pulling us up. He couldn't have carried us, not all four of us. It wasn't his strength I doubted but the sheer mechanic of trying to carry four fully-grown adults. He maneuvered my body close to his, cradled between him and Brenda, before pressing the bodies of the other vampires against us.

Movement at the door way caught my attention, the flash of something in a dark hood and cold eyes. I was able to see it only for a second before darkness wrapped around us like a blanket.

CHAPTER THIRTEEN

NOTHING penetrated the darkness that surrounded me, though I could still feel Sebastian's chest against my hands and face. It felt like only a second but one that stretched through infinity. It was disorienting, like spinning in a circle as fast as I could with my arms held out, and as soon as I thought I was finding stability we dropped; grass suddenly under our feet as if I hadn't moved, just jumped in the air and landed.

Having my feet under me, however, and standing proved to be a difficult task. I would have collapsed to the ground with Brenda and the other two bodies if Sebastian hadn't caught me.

"I've got you," he soothed. "You're safe, Dani."

I heard his voice coming from outside my head, which meant at least my ears were working again even if my extremities weren't yet.

I could feel my body still pulsating, still on high alert from the electricity vibrations adding to the spiking adrenaline. I clutched the front of Sebastian's shirt like a life line as I willed my body to relax; deep breaths in through the nose and out through the mouth.

Brenda was shrieking behind me screaming her brother's name over and over. I actually felt sorry for her; I couldn't help it. I couldn't imagine what it must have been like to see someone you love in that condition, be so close to getting them back only to be forced to leave them there.

"Can you stand?" Sebastian questioned, releasing me when I gave a nod.

They were still shaky, but my legs worked. With a kiss to my forehead he moved to help Brenda up, but was attacked for his troubles instead. I watched as they fought each other, though it was more Brenda beating her fist against Sebastian's chest and screaming in frustration.

I knew where I was as soon as I pulled my gaze around the property. The question on my mind was how Sebastian had gotten us from the basement of the warehouse to the Juan's manor. We had touched down somewhere on the grounds; the back of the house about fifty yards in front of us. Brenda's screams had alerted someone in the house as two bodies headed our way. She'd stop pounding on Sebastian's chest at least, and was now crying against it, red tears staining her alabaster face. I moved closer to one of the bodies on the ground.

It looked almost like a mummy without the bandaged wrappings. Clothed in a filthy white polo shirt and a pair of mud stained black slacks was the blackened petrified corpse of one Stanley, or at least what used to be Stanley.

Either he was balding or in the dying process the majority of his hair had fallen out. The few wisps that remained were as white as his shirt had no doubt been before his capture. His eyes were closed, his mouth frozen open as if the last thing he'd done was try to scream for help, or just out of frustration. Teeth gleamed like pearls in his dark mouth, eyeteeth elongated. From the withered condition of his body and the female near him I was guessing he and Matlilda had starved to death. There was a gold chain around his neck with a cross, and a ring on his right ring finger that would have fallen off had his fists not been clenched.

It was the ring that had me kneel down for a closer look. The band was gold and thick, with a coat of arms in the middle made of a gold crown embedded with rubies and emeralds set atop a symmetrical silver cross, with emeralds forming a parenthesis around that. Positioned over the silver cross was a square cut ruby with something that looked like an E with too many prongs in gold embedded into the stone.

I reached out to touch it, turning it more into the moonlight, before turning my attention to Matilda. I couldn't see the design but I saw a gold ring on her finger, and it wasn't the first time I'd seen it.

On Sebastian's finger was the first place I'd seen it, turning my eyes back to him I saw the gold band glittering under the half moon light.

"Sebastian—"

"—Dani get back!"

I turned from Sebastian back to the corpse of Stanley the vampire, eyes riveted to those that were now open. A milky film of death covered the pupils, but it still felt like he was looking at me. I pushed back but he grabbed my wrist in one hand, his torso rising so quickly strings could have pulled him up as he grabbed a handful of hair in the other hand.

He pulled me down against his body so hard the scream leaving turned into a grunt of breath forced from my body. He released my wrist, wrapped his arm around my waist, yanked my head back, and rolled me in one blindingly quick motion. Sebastian yelled his name, but Stanley was beyond hearing; he snarled once and plunged his teeth into my throat.

I screamed. No vampire had ever bitten me before. It was supposed to be orgasmic pleasure personified; all I felt was pain and a sickening feeling as he fed from my throat. There was more power in the frailty of his body than there was in mine, and with each pull of my blood I could feel him thickening as he regained his life while taking mine.

Another scream ripped from my throat as his canines entered my skin again, pulling to make the hole bigger. I could have used my mind to push him, but with his fangs still in my neck it would either work and take a plug of my skin with him, possible severing the artery, or it would piss him off and he would dig his fangs in deeper like a tick determined not to let go.

Sebastian's order to cease did nothing to abate the drinking vampire. Consciousness was still with me, but I was getting light-headed and could feel my body growing cool. He would kill me before he stopped, that much I knew. To make things even more macabre Stanley was becoming aroused.

"Stanley."

It was just the calling of his name, but the vampire at my neck abated his drinking. He snarled as he looked up, my blood staining his lips and dripping from his chin. My heart still hammering so fast I could feel the hot liquid pumping from the gapping wound. The scent called to him and he began to lower his mouth to resume the feast, but hesitated as Juan's soft voice called his name again. Again those eyes, no longer white, but a bright iridescent blue looked up to Juan.

Juan, who was already kneeling close inched forward, Stanley responded by tightening the hand in my hair, ripping another yelp from me as I felt a few strands give way. His eyes snapped back to me with a snarl.

"Stanley, no." Juan's voice was still soft but held a dominant tone to it.

"Danika, it would be wise if you do not make any sudden movements or any at all."

"Get him off of me," I hissed as quietly as possible.

"That, *mi querida*, is what I am endeavoring to do."

If he thought I was going to hold still while some vampire used me as their main course he had another thing coming. Juan continued to speak softly to Stanley, talking him down from the idea of taking my last drop of blood. I didn't need him to get off of me, just release my hair from the vice grip hold it was in, preferable before I bleed out. It was Juan running his nail over his wrist opening a vein to Stanley that eventually got him to let go. He never made it to the wrist.

The blood loss made the push weaker than it had been since I was a kid, but it was enough to heave Stanley backwards off the ground. I stumbled to my feet, heel of my hand pressed against my neck despite the rocketing stab of pain touching it brought. I was running; I had no idea where I was running too, but anywhere seemed better than in the presence of vampires.

The movement only made my blood flow faster, I knew that, could feel the warm, sticky liquid trying to gush past my hand. I made it further than I thought I would, but not as far as I wanted before arms wrapped around my waist and hoisted me from the ground.

"Dani, it's Sebastian," he hissed urgently in my ear, hoping the familiarity we shared would calm me down. It didn't, just having a vampire embracing me sent my body into panicked thrashes. "Dani, please don't make me do this."

Those words only spurred me to fight harder. I shoved him as I had done Stanley; it was enough to push him backwards and for me to take a few steps forward before he did what he only a couple hours ago promised he wouldn't. I felt him in my head; encouraging me in such a tender voice to stop my legs had no choice but to obey. I wanted to push him out but I was too tired. The command was there but lacked force behind it.

Sebastian's arms folded around me, followed by us being once again folded into darkness. The more I struggled the tighter he held me, until I finally stopped. He was speaking softly against my hair; hushed words I almost missed designed to bring me comfort.

It was same as before, it felt like we were flying for a moment, then standing still, then the darkness unfolded into light. Again I felt my legs giving out both from the jarring transport as much as blood loss. Sebastian again caught me, lifting me into his arms as if I didn't weigh a hundred and thirty odd pounds.

"Finnius!" his voice bellowed out as we ran.

My vision normalized enough to recognize we'd dropped down into Finn's back yard. The familiarity of the pool and patio was unmistakable, as was the bass growl that shouted back to Sebastian.

"What the fuck have you done to her?"

"Is that Dani?" Luke questioned.

Knowing he was there was enough to make me try to fight for my own footing even if I would have just crumpled to the ground. Instead Finn literally snatched me from Sebastian, a tight growl rumbled up from his chest.

"You're going pay for this," he snarled.

"I'll explain everything but she's bleeding—"

"—I can fucking see that!" Finn snapped.

"The kitchen counter," Luke stated moving forward back into the house with Finn following.

Containers and dishes cluttered to the floor. Luke swept the raised island then turned the overhead lights on while Finn carefully stretched my body across the surface.

"What's going on in here?" Simone questioned entering the kitchen a banana in one hand, iPod in the other. "What happened to her?"

"Simone get blankets, Luke get my kit from the foyer closet," Finn ordered.

"But I—"

"—Now!" it wasn't just an order this time, but a bass riddled growl in the subordinates direction.

"She's cold," he whispered leaning over me pulling up first one, then the other eyelid to examine my pupils. "Let me see, baby," he cooed softly to me, "Let me see how bad it is." His voice was tight, strained, trying desperately to keep his emotions under control but not winning the battle.

Luke returned with a first-aid kit to rival all first aid kits. He placed it on the counter next to the fridge, ripped open packages and handed Finn's several gauzes. Once they were in Finn's hand he moved forward, grabbing the ends of the blanket and helping Simone place them over me. I moved my hand allowing Finn to see the wound before he placed several of the gauze over it, and then pressed my hand back to it. I had no idea how much damage was done, and Finn's expressionless face gave nothing away. From the look in his eyes it could have very well just been a pinprick. A very painful, blood gushing, pinprick.

"Should I call an ambulance?" Luke questioned.

"No," Finn replied, moving to the case and rummaging through it. "They'll ask questions"

He pulled out one of those glass bottles that had a metal top and rubber stopper in the center, along with a disposable needle he removed from the wrapping. I watched him insert the needle and pull the plunger back feeling the syringe with the contents of the bottle. He moved towards me and I tried to sit, only to meet resistance at the hands of Luke holding my shoulders against the marble countertop.

I struggled as best I could, which didn't equal much resistance for a werewolf. Luke continued to hold me prone while Finn swabbed my arm with an alcohol pad, injected the contents of the little clear bottle into my vein, and then placed the same pad over the wound before covering it with a band-aid.

When he moved back to smooth his hand over my hair it wasn't the emergency flight pilot I was speaking to, but the boyfriend. "You're going to be okay," he whispered softly. "You're gonna feel a little warm then you're going to start feeling sleepy, alright? Just go with it baby, don't fight it."

"Finn, it's not his fault," I muttered softly, my bloody left hand grasping his before he could pull away.

Sebastian took a step towards me but halted at the warning growl that came from both Finn and Luke.

"I didn't harm her," he stated in his own defense.

"No, but you damn sure didn't protect her either."

"I couldn't have predicted this would happen? You honestly think I wanted this?"

"Simone, hold this and apply pressure," he ordered moving my hand away from the gauze covering the wound and letting Simone's take place.

It was just as well, my body was beginning to feel heavy anyway, but the wench squeezed so hard it hurt. Fortunately I was fading in and out of consciousness. I finally blacked out to the sound of Finn and Sebastian arguing.

* * * * *

I didn't wake up on a cold, hard counter in a brightly lit kitchen, but a warm comfortable bed, in Finn's dimly lit bedroom. Finn held me in his arms; my body nestled protectively against his chest but we weren't alone in bed. Two wolves shared the mattress with us.

Luke lay in front of me, curled with head resting on his paws and his nose almost under his tail. His coat was a white and mocha speckled creation; his front left paw was all brown like it had been dipped in milk chocolate and dried that way. The tips of his ears matched that one paw, his snout was a rose hue, and when his eyes were open they were a deep gorgeous chocolate with yellow centers.

The other wolf I assumed was Simone, unless Finn called one of the others from the pack. Her coat was a rich thick gray color with a bib of white fur, and white tipped ears. Her hid quarters rest on my hip, but the majority of her body was resting on top of Finn's.

Both Finn and Luke were born with the werewolf DNA allowing them to shift at will regardless of the phase of the moon or position of sun in the sky. Simone was either born a werewolf, or Finn had forced her change. I was hoping it was the latter, a born werewolf, especially a dominant female fighting for his affections was something I didn't feel like entertaining. One thing was for sure; her heavy ass was cutting off the circulation in my thighs. I wasn't sure why Finn had the wolves in bed with us. I knew there was a healing quality werewolves could pass to injured members of their pack by snuggling together but I'd never heard of that ability working for non-weres.

The lights in the room were off but it wasn't completely dark, day was beginning to break outside and predawn light was filtering in through the sheer covering his balcony door. My neck throbbed like a thousand bees were stinging it simultaneously, I felt a little sick to my stomach and I had to pee like I'd been out drinking all night without a bathroom break. Unfortunately there was no way to get from between and under the bodies without waking anyone. As soon as I tried to stretch, everyone on the bed was awake.

Simone sat up a bit, not into a sitting position but definitely putting more of her weight onto my already numbed hipbone. Luke blinked, gave a good full body stretch then tilted his head back licking my chin, while Finn's arm around my waist tightened, the other hand pushing at Luke's jowls.

"Knock it off, Luke," he warned, though the chuckle that rumbled afterwards put everyone on the bed back at ease.

I raised my hand to the bandage at my neck but never made it. The hand splayed across my stomach caught my wrist, brought my fingers to his lips for a kiss, and then folded my hand back down against the bed, holding it in his embrace.

"On a scale of one to ten how bad?" he murmured.

"Ten being the worse?" I asked and felt his head nodding behind me. "I'd say about an eighteen." As hard as I tried to forget her, I remembered the werewolf on my legs when I tried to stretch them but couldn't move. "You're cutting off my circulation, Simone."

I swear as soon as I said the words the little tramp sat up putting her full weight on me.

"Simone, down," Finn ordered.

But she didn't get down; she got off of me and padded her way up the bed to give Finn a few slow licks to his face, her tongue grazing against his lips.

"Simone don't make me slap your mouth crocked," I warned.

A low rumbling growl emitted from her mouth; her lips pulling back from her teeth in a very aggressive manner. Luke was on his paws giving her an answering growl, a quick warning to mind her place, but when she continued to growl, her tongue snaking out to lick her chops, Finn slammed his forearm against her body. The blow was enough to send her to the floor with a yelping whimper. Rolling onto his back and sitting up, Finn planted his feet on the ground, slowly rising while Luke vaulted over my body landing on the floor in front of Simone. Both of them standing as shields between Simone and me.

The she-wolf whined, pressing her self against the floor in front of the two males, her tail curling around her backside while Luke continued to give off low rumbling warning growls.

"It's time you go to your own bed, Simone."

When she continued to whimper and not move, Luke snapped his teeth at her, the powerful jaws closing just inches from one of those vanilla tipped ears. She yelped, before jumping up and scampering out of the open door; her tail hung low to the ground between her legs, her retreat quietly masked against the thick carpet in the room. Both males followed, Luke heading out the door behind her, Finn shutting the door behind both of them. I used the opportunity to climb from the bed and head to the bathroom, though as soon as I was vertical I had to hold onto the furniture or wall to make sure I was stable.

I kept my eyes down from the mirror as I washed my hands, I didn't want to see how ashen the blood loss made my skin, or the bandage that wrapped around my throat, feeling it was more than enough. Finn had removed my blood stained clothing replacing them with a pair of his boxers and a wife-beater. Judging from the spring mountain smell in the fibers he'd pulled the articles straight from his drawer.

One of the bedside lamps had been turned on by the time I made my slow moving return. Rubber tubing, alcohol package, and another syringe, or perhaps the same from earlier sat filled on the table ready to deliver the liquid into my vein. Finn leaned against the wall between the bathroom door and the bedside table the lamp sat on dressed only in a pair of pajama bottoms. His arms were folded over his naked chest, rope like muscles flexed and straining against his skin. If there was any fat on that body I'd have been hard pressed to find it. Crisp blue eyes watched as I slowly made my way from the door to the bed.

As soon as I sat down he moved forward, arms unfurling as his fingers reached for the alcohol square. I was at the perfect eye level to focus on those rippling muscles of his abs before the thin trail of fine dark blonde hair under his navel pulled my gaze lower.

Finn's nostrils flared, a smile tugged the corner of his lips up. He placed a finger under my chin, gently turning my face up to his as he lowered his lips to mine. A soft meeting of flesh against flesh, my bottom lip momentarily taken between his before he pulled back. I leaned forward, my cheek resting against his stomach as his fingers slowing combed their way through my hair. He bent down, from the waist, placing a kiss on top of my head before kneeling in front of me.

"Give me your arm," he instructed.

Carefully removing the band-aid covering the early needle prick, he tore open the foil package, removing and rubbing the alcohol filled gauze over the entire crock of my elbow. Placing that back on the table he took the tube and wrapped it around the upper part of my arm.

"Make a fist for me."

I did as he asked, watching him pick up and uncap the syringe and watch my arm and veins.

"What's that?"

"Morphine," he replied softly.

"Is that necessary?"

Finding the vein he was looking for, he untied the band and he slid the needle into my skin. His other hand gripping my forearm in case I decided to move on him. Once the plunger was pushed all the way in and the entire contents in my vein he quickly removed the needle and set everything on the table.

"It's for the pain, darling. It'll help you sleep too."

Turning off the light, he helped me scoot under the covers before joining me, his arms once again pulling my body snug against his. I rested my cheek and palm against his chest, breathing in the warm musky scent of him; enjoying the feel of his fingers stroking my back.

"I'll call work for you, tell them you were attacked by a dog or something and won't be in for a few days," he stated softly, his lips brushing against my forehead as he spoke. "I want you to stay here for a while," he continued. "I'll go to your house later, pick up some of your things."

"There are a few things I need you to bring back."

"I'll wait until you're awake again so you can make a list, okay?"

I nodded my head against his chest, my fingers finding one erect nipple and idly toying with it. I should have stopped when I felt the muscles in his arm and stomach contract; instead I continued to tease him lightly until his other hand closed around my fingers.

"You really need to stop doing that," he chastised with a soft chuckle.

"Finn, don't go all primal possessive on me, but what happened with Sebastian? He's not a pile of ash in your fireplace is he?"

He gave a sigh, brought my fingers to his lips for a quick kiss then released them, pillowing his head on that arm. "Yeah he's still alive, or undead, or whatever you want to call it," he snorted out another breath. "Bastard had the nerve to say it wasn't his fault."

"It wasn't," I agreed, knowing he might not take the words the way they were meant. "I thought Stanley was dead-dead, I didn't know he was in some blood deprived stasis."

"No, but you can't tell me Sebastian didn't know. He should have been watching you."

"I'm not a child; I don't need someone watching me like I'm going to wander into traffic."

The hand on my back stopped rubbing for a moment. I felt his head shift, knew as soon as I looked up it would be into those eyes.

"That's not what I was trying to imply, Dani. Sebastian went there to help *and* protect you."

"He did help."

"Yeah but he fucked up the protection part. Dropping in the back yard with my woman in his arms bloody? Bastard is lucky Luke was there or I would have taken his throat out."

"You don't mean that," I murmured.

I tried to keep my eyes open but they were so damn heavy it was like lead weights were tied to the lashes.

"Like hell I don't."

"You'd start a war," I reminded.

"He almost started one himself, bringing you in like that."

He said something else, probably saying what else he had planned to do to Sebastian, but the words were lost, like waves against my ears as the drug clouded my brain and again pulled me under.

CHAPTER FOURTEEN

IT was somewhere right before or right after noon when I woke up the second time. Finn had called off work for both of us and was on stand by with a pad for me to list the items I needed him to retrieve, and another shot of morphine. A shot I was able to postpone until I returned from my house with him.

Some of the herbs I needed I knew by sight not by a label in their containers; if he brought the wrong one thinking it was the same the effects could be tragically dire. I also wanted to get my father's journal, and despite our relationship's duration having him pawing around in my underwear drawer still seemed taboo.

He let me stay awake long enough to eat. I wasn't hungry, but that didn't stop him from threatening to sit on me and force-feed me if I didn't eat. I was also able to mix the ingredients for the paste to go over my throat wound, before he again gave me a dose of morphine and tucked me into bed.

When I woke again I was alone in his bedroom, the bedside lamp was once again employed, this time to keep the darkness outside at bay. I was feeling better, but in the grand scheme of things that wasn't saying much. The pain had gone from blinding to throbbing; from an eighteen to about a nine but it was still registering. Pulling out a pair of jeans, t-shirt and socks I made my way into the bathroom taking care of the necessities before running myself a nice hot bath, complete with mounds of bubbles.

The heated waters felt like heaven to my muscles. It felt so good instead of climbing out when the water turned lukewarm I drained some and turned the hot tap on, filling the tub up again. I could have lounged in the tub all night, but I had heard the voices downstairs.

By the time I was dressed there was a message for me on my cell from Sebastian. In light of the injuries I suffered at the hands of one of his vampires, Juan was giving me a grace period of a week to recover before the resumption of the now nine remaining nights. He asked me to give him a call when I could, he wanted verbal confirmation I was all right, and to share information about the warehouse that couldn't be left on the phone.

Through the complete duration of the three-minute message he apologized about a dozen times. I would have called back, but I was sure by now Finn knew I was up. If I didn't head downstairs soon he'd be up to check on me.

The last thing I needed was for Finn to enter the room while I was on the phone with Sebastian. The man knew it was harmless, but the wolf would rebel at his mate talking to another dominant creature in his bedroom no less. No one would ever accuse a dominant male werewolf of rational thought involving his mate.

My progress to the door paused when I felt a drastic lowering of temperature in the. My breath frosted the air with each exhalation, and I had to fight the urge to run my hands up and down my arms to conserve the heat inside. It lasted a good fifteen seconds, leaving just as quickly and abruptly as it had arrived.

"Dad?" my voice was soft, his name tentatively leaving my lips as I called him.

"You are learning, Little Butterfly," my dad's voice came back disembodied.

I smirked. "Even lay people know cold spots equal a ghostly presence, dad."

"That's correct, but more to the point, cold spots illustrate a ghost's presence when they can't or choose not to manifest fully into the material plane, but want to get your attention."

"Daddy, I know you're probably here on some serious boogety, boogety business but I've a question that's not related to the peril at hand."

"That being?"

"How does the whole material/twilight realm thing work? Are you always there, like my shadow or something? I mean... do you see *everything*?"

It had been something bothering me after dad confessed he'd been watching me since his death. Having my dad watching me in the bathroom was creepy enough in and of itself, but knowing he was in the room while I was having sex could potentially send me to therapy... or the nearest nunnery.

"Think of the material plane as an interrogation room, and the twilight realm as the room behind the one-way mirror," he began softly. "As long as there is a tether there can be a ghost in any given area, at any given point in time. We can hear and see everything that happens, if we chose. There is always the option to leave the immediate area if something happens that we do not wish to see, or if nothing is happening and we choose to seek entertainment elsewhere."

I heaved a sigh of relief a bright smile on my lips as I nodded. "Aw'ight, cool."

"So, you were able to track the necromancer to his layer," he stated.

"Yeah, or at least where he was keeping the vampires. What was that spell he had over the cage?"

"A simple warding spell."

"Wait," I paused. "How can it be a simple spell? I have a ward-breaking spell, a pretty strong one. Heck it's one of the main ones I know by heart and it didn't do jack."

"You're breaking spell was not woven with elements of the dead arts."

"Wait, are you saying death magic can only be broken by death magic?"

"What has experience proven? You've had two instances now where your mother's spells have failed. The first when you attempted to track a vampire that had the dead arts cast over him; the second when you attempted to break the ward."

"Why?" he was right, I could see he was right but it still didn't make sense. "My spells work on the other witches' casting, what makes necromancy so special?"

"Because it is the art of the dead, Babygirl," he replied. "What makes it so different is the same thing that makes if feared. Death is the one thing people are never apathetic about. They may hate it, be in love with it, embrace it, fear it, be intrigued by it, the list goes on and on, but the one thing people never are is indifferent about it. Those that claim otherwise are either lying to you or themselves."

"So basically what you're telling me is I'm fucked."

"Watch you language, Danika."

I wanted to ask was he serious, but ghost entity or not he was still my father. "Fine, in over my head."

"You're my daughter; of course you're not in over your head. But you need to start thinking like a necromancer, Dani," he warned. "Because you were able to find him he knows you have the book, and he knows who you are. He's going to come after you, and you need to be."

"How?"

"Read," he stated simply. "Don't go back to the Grimoire now, it's too risky.   Study the one in my journal. Memorize the spells and incantations. Your enemies aren't going to give you a time out to flip through a book and come up with the right spell."

"What if that's not enough?"

"You're smart, Dani. Remember when you were sixteen and you went on that weekend ski trip?"

"I sorta fail to see the connection between skiing and vanquishing a necromancer."

"What did that girl, Tasha say to you?"

I sighed as I took a seat on the end of the bed, "She said I'd never learn how to side shuttle in three days."

"And come Sunday morning what were you doing?"

That actually brought a smile to my lips, albeit a hesitant one. "This isn't exactly the same thing, dad. If I don't learn how to side shuttle this time people are going to die."

"It's the same principle, Babygirl. Don't ever let someone tell you what you can and can't do. Don't let the doubts others have about you become your own. You do that and you might as well go to that fool's lair and present your throat to him right now."

"Alright," I conceded pushing my fingers through my hair. "Alright I see…"

I fell silent when I saw the shadow of feet under the small rise on the bedroom door. A tentative knock followed closely after the arrival.

"Come in," I called, still sitting on the bed.

The door opened and a petite brunette by the name of Sarah Miller stuck her head inside. There was nothing about Sarah that really stood out, most of the time someone could be in the room with her and completely forget she was there. Her hair ranged from light brown during the winter and fall months, to a dark blonde during summer, and spring. She hid her crystal blue eyes behind non-prescription glass frames even around the pack. It wouldn't have been an oddity if werewolves weren't renowned for having the keenest vision of all the preternatural beings.

I've tried to hold a conversation with her on the times when we've been in the same vicinity but she literally doesn't speak unless spoken to and then it's only to answer the question asked. Talking to her is like talking to a leprechaun only duller.

She's definitely the weakest link in Finn's pack. Sure she's a werewolf and has the super strength, but strength is only part of the mixture needed to fight. I've seen strong humans get their asses kicked by individuals that were weaker than them but knew what they were doing. What good is throwing a punch that never connects to anything?

"I'm sorry to interrupt," she began looking curiously around the room. Her eyes met mine and immediately looked down in a submissive gesture. "Finn wanted me to see if you felt like joining us in the family room?"

"Sure," I stated softly, "Tell him I'll be right down, okay?"

She gave a slight nod, but paused as her eyes flickered up and around the room again before looking down the hallway.

"Was there something else?"

"Oh, oh no," she gave a shake of her head, closing the door quietly behind her.

I moved to the door and listened to her retreating footsteps on the carpet before speaking again.

"Dad?" I called cautiously but there was no answer. "Dad you still there?"

The answering silence pulled a sigh from my lips. I'd have to ask dad what the rules were for his coming and going.

I checked the mirror before heading down; surprised I didn't look quite the hot mess I had expected. If Sarah were there, chances are the rest of the pack would be too.

I really didn't feel like dealing with the questions and the stares and the unvoiced question in the eyes of the other dominant females wondering if they could take me. However, Finn had asked me to join, and though he made it sound like I had the option to refuse, to decline the invitation would have been a subtle insult. Like I said, everything for werewolves meant something. There was no such thing as an empty gesture. Finn wouldn't have made the request if he didn't think I'd be up to putting in an appearance.

Some called it a family room, others called it a den but it was basically the same thing; one huge room. A large flat screen television was mounted on the far wall complete with a combination DVD/VCR and of course those glorious surround sound speakers that gave the illusion of being in a theater. There were eight black leather chairs, and three black leather couches with small tables near by or for the chairs actual cup holders, set in front the television and on cascading levels to further the illusion of being in a milder version of stadium seating.

Against the wall was Finn's collection of DVDs and videocassettes that would rival the local blockbusters. Finn was a big movie buff. I'd say seventy percent of our evening dates were spent going to movies. Not that I objected; I was a sucker for movie popcorn, and Finn's running commentary through the movies made it worth the trip.

The other half of the room was more conducive to actually conversing with other people and contributing to share time. Three couches were arranged against the walls, still in the theme of black, but with a scrubbed suede covering, a couple of matching chairs to the couch, a couple of wicker chairs with thick black comfortable pillows, a bean bag chair that was set on some sort of pedestal and a few scattered pillows comfortable enough to sit or lay on. All the furniture made that end of the room seem a bit cluttered but it hadn't been done to be aesthetically pleasing, it had been done so everyone would have a place to sit, and congregate.

I'm not sure if it had been purposely left open or recently vacated, but there was an empty seat on the couch next to Finn. My desire was to just keep my eyes down, make my way to the couch and sit in the safety of Finn's warmth. What I did was pause in the doorway meeting the eyes of all the women in the room.

Sarah was easy; the girl barely met my gaze before quickly looking down. Simone didn't bother looking at me at all, but then she'd already been beaten once today.

Katrina Rodgers met my gaze and held it for a long time. She sat on the arm of the chair Luke occupied. Though they'd both been in the pack for quite a while, the two of them had only been dating for the past six months. They'd spent most of their time competing against each other.

Katrina wanted to be second in command, and though she might have been the strongest female in the pack, she wasn't stronger than Luke. Sometimes I wondered if she wasn't dating Luke simple as a way of automatically getting recognition. Just as my being mated to Finn meant I was automatically Alpha female, her being mated to Luke meant she was second in command.

We got along so long as the topic didn't relate to the pack. She like many others didn't think I could hold the spot as Alpha female, but she'd always maintained a level of respect. She broke eye contact first, but was careful to simply slant her gaze to the side.

Padma Zafar was tougher. She didn't think she should be Alpha, she knew it. Knew she could do a better job at protecting the pack than a witch. When Nancy and I talk about her I call her the Hindu princess. She was far thinner than me, having the body and build of the typical anorexic catalogue model, but she was a werewolf, which meant she could physically kick my ass. Unlike Simone, Padma wasn't interested in Finn, being his lover would have just been part of the job, this woman wanted the title.

Large eyes with irises the color of honey glared at me. I watched her nostrils flaring as she breathed in deep, probably debating her options; charge, or don't charge.

"Every battle has its time, Padma," came the gentle voice of one of the dominant males in the pack, Joseph Kano.

Joseph Kano was one of the dominant males of Alcatraz Pack, and probably the one I trusted least of all. Something about the guy just didn't sit right with me from the peach fuzz on top of his beanie little head; to the way those beady eyes of his would stare into people; to the way his too thin lips would press together and all but disappear.

The same qualities that made him a savage stoke broker and an aggressive werewolf made him distrustful in my eyes, even if he had shown loyalty to the pack. Momma had an expression she used to say when a person gave off that vibe, that their skin just felt wrong. Well, Joseph's skin definitely felt wrong.

She finally looked away, her eyes pivoting to Joseph before dropping down to examine her manicured nails, leaving me free to make my way from the door to the seat next to Finn. The leather was still warm with the body heat of the person who'd sat there before me. His mouth immediately found mine as I sat, for a very quick press of lips to lips.

One of the other two dominant males in the room, Colton Bargas, watched me intently as I moved from the doorway to the couch. There was a question in those dark eyes but he held his tongue. He gave a slight inclination of his head to me when I cast my gaze in his direction. I looked away first; there was no way I was about to try to start some shit with a man that for all intents and purpose was the Black-Latino version of a brick house.

Marco Cruz shared the couch with us sitting to my immediate left. He gave a warm smile as I sat, a perpetual lock of curl rested against his forehead no matter how many times he moved it. Marco wasn't dominant by nature or choice but necessity. A blessing of his Portuguese lineage, he was by far the best-looking member of Alcatraz Pack regardless of gender, even Padma for all her beauty. Marco, however, was gay; to have been submissive in a testosterone based family like werewolves would have made him the proverbial sitting duck.

The last three members of the pack, the three submissive males; Vincent Baldwin, who's fair complexion, strawberry blonde hair, and light blue eyes was belied by a muscular physique. Louis Harper, an art history major that had more limbs than he knew to do with in both physical and wolf form. And Anthony Gambini, who would have been more attractive if his human form wasn't as hairy as his wolf form all occupied the same couch to the left of Finn.

They all watched me closely as if at any given moment I was going to break out into an entertaining dance jig.

"Heard you took on a vampire and lived," Marco stated giving me a playful nudge.

"If by live you mean survived after nearly getting my throat ripped out, then yeah."

I couldn't help but to return his smile, though it made me wonder how bad a scar the encounter would leave. I'd never used Nancy's remedy for such a serious injury before.

He shrugged dismissively. "I heard the vamp was in the throws of a blood rage. It couldn't have been easy to get away from that."

I found myself looking to Finn, wondering exactly what it was he told them. His reply was to give a mysterious smirk.

"Perhaps we can save the wonders of Danika's ability to run away from danger for after we've dealt with the problems at hand," Padma stated. Maybe it was her accent that had the words dripping with spite. Maybe that's just how they were intended to sound.

"I'm sure I can set up a time for you to go toe to toe against a corpse that's been starved for days maybe weeks and see how much better you fair," I replied. Not a challenge, at least not yet.

Her retort was put on hold by Finn holding his hand up to silent both of us, though it was her, his eyes bore into, and her that looked to the floor, successfully cowed.

"Perhaps we were wrong in thinking with time, Padma's words would become as graceful as her movements," Luke stated.

Another warning.

She didn't like it, I could tell by the way her body tensed and her glaring gaze narrowed on the floor, but she had the good sense to not look up and meet either the Alpha's or Beta's challenging eyes.

"But," Luke continued, "Her point, however ill phrased has merit. We still have a very serious problem and no solution."

I looked from Luke, to Katrina sitting on the arm of the chair, to Finn who was nodding his head in agreement.

"What's the problem?"

"We may have gargoyles encroaching in our territory," he stated calmly. "It hasn't been confirmed yet."

"Has someone seen them?" I questioned.

"No," Marco answered beating Padma to whatever smart mouthed comment she was about to make. "But I've smelled them around the orchestra building, which is actually worse than seeing them."

"Gargoyles don't have pheromones, which means they don't have a natural scent," Finn began before I could even ask the question.

"Then what's Marco smelling?"

"There feces," Luke informed.

"They're playing shadow games," Katrina took over, leaning forward on her armrest perch just a bit. "They're eating and shitting in our territory without announcing their presence or asking permission to set up camp is their way of say they don't think we're strong enough to kick them out. It's a challenge."

I nodded pretending I understood when I hadn't a clue what was going on. Why would the gargoyles specifically single out Finn's wolves to throw down the gauntlet? I understood why other were-creature needed to inform Finn when they wanted to settle into his territory, but gargoyles weren't were-creatures. So why did it matter if they got permission or not?

"How do we find them?"

There was a collective pause in the room at my question, as glances circles around the room to end on their Alpha.

"Gargoyles are very good at not being found when they don't want to. I think right now they're testing us, trying to see how strong we are, and how smart we are. Gargoyles are renowned to be excellent tacticians," though his eyes went around the room, I was fairly certain the last sentence had been for my benefit.

"And when we find them?" Louis asked.

"We convince them San Francisco is not the city for them. It's been gargoyle free since 1945 and I intend to keep it that way."

I frowned a bit; a habitual movement I didn't realize I was making until it was too late.

"Something is wrong?" Simone challenged, arms folding over her chest.

"No," I growled between teeth, glaring at Simone who quickly looked away. "But I always thought gargoyles where benign creatures. What's wrong with having a few on your territory?" I turned my attention to Finn.

"Generally speaking they are benign in small quantities," Finn began. "But they're like rats. All they need is a foothold in the city, and next thing you know they're sending out the signal to every gargoyle in the country to take up residence in San Francisco."

"But," I began. "I thought gargoyles were protectors."

"That," Luke commented, "Is what they would have society believe."

"Then what's the truth?"

Luke opened his mouth, but a look from Finn silenced his words. Despite me giving Finn the eye he wasn't about to go into detail and I knew better than to press the matter in an open meeting. The question on the table; was he keeping the truth from me, or from others in his pack.

"So we find the dirty bastards and beat them down with the welcome mat," Simone stated with a satisfied grin.

"First thing is first," Finn stated. "We have to find them before we can do anything." He fell silent for a moment, thinking as he leaned forward, letting his forearms rest on his thighs. "Marco you said you smelled them around the orchestra building." Knowing it was a statement and not a question Marco remained silent. "Tomorrow I want you to take Vincent and see if you can find a trace of them. You're looking for what the droppings consist of, and how old they are. If we can figure out what they're eating we might be able to narrow where they are hiding."

"You got it boss," Marco stated with a nod.

"Anyone have any question?" Finn asked letting his gaze move around his wolves gathered.

"I got a question," Colton stated. "When's the food going to get here, I'm starved?"

As if on cue the doorbell rang, and werewolves sprang from their seat trying to beat each other to the front door. I waited for the others to clear out before attempting to brave the hall to the dining room to avoid accidental trampling. Never get between a hungry werewolf and food, though they wouldn't start to eat until Finn and I had chosen what we wanted. Bonus of being Alpha.

"Finn?" my voice was enough to stop him but I laid my fingers against his arm just in case. "What was Luke going to say about the gargoyles?"

He shook his head, a finger touching my cheek and moving down my face. He tried to give a smile but it never touched his eyes. He wasn't scared but he was worried, for Finn that was almost as bad.

"It's not important," he finally replied in a soft voice.

"Finn, you've never lied to me before, please don't start now because you think you're protecting my delicate sensibility from something."

He closed his eyes, pressing those perfect lips of his together before opening them and moving to the door. I was ready to protest his departure, but instead of leaving he called down the hall and told the others to start eating, before closing the door and turning to face me.

"I don't want you to talk to the other women about this," he began, taking my hand and leading me back to the couch we occupied.

"You say that like I have much of an option to do otherwise."

"I'm serious, Dani," his hand squeezed mine in gentle insistence. "It's why I stopped Luke from continuing. Katrina knows but she's the only female in the pack that does, and I don't want to freak the others out."

"Okay, but you're starting to freak me out."

"I'm sorry baby, I don't mean to," he spoke softly taking both my hands between his.

"Just tell me."

"Gargoyles don't eat people, but they're not exactly the champions of people as legend and fables depict. Female gargoyles are born sterile, which means in order for the males to reproduce, they have to seek females outside of their race to mother their children."

I opened my mouth and closed it just as quick. I could already see were the story was going.

"Back in the fifteenth and sixteenth centuries when there was still mystery in the world and people believed in other sentient beings, believed in werewolves and witches and vampires and dragons as more than just folklore gargoyles were able to use extortion as their trade. They would keep villages safe from us, and in exchange they had their pick of women in the village to impregnate."

I nodded and Finn stood, heading to the bookcase. He ran his fingers over the spines of the collection until finding the right one, an older looking book, and thick like a dictionary without a name on the cover. He stood there, flipping through the pages until he found the one he wanted, only then did he move back to the couch.

"Here," he placed the book on my lap open to a picture. "This is what your typical gargoyle looks like."

The creature looked very much like that of traditional gargoyles in movies and throughout history. It was perched on the edge of a building, its fingers and toes ending in long claw like talons, huge leathery bat wings sprouting from its shoulders and open to an impressive span. Its face was like a short snout dog, with rows of razor sharp teeth gleaming, a pair of beady eyes, and two pointed ears sticking up from the side of his head. There was no fur or scales on its body, but thick leathery skin like that of its wings.

Finn took the book back before I could begin flipping through it. "Imagine being given to a creature like that and forced to have sex," the thought was enough to make me cringe. "Most of their minds were broken, which was just as well, though born the same size as human babies babies gargoyles don't travel through the birth canal. They claw their way from their mother's wombs."

I winced, covering my mouth with my hand. My stomach was uneasy to start with but now it was doing flips. "Tell me the villages decided it wasn't worth the price."

"No one really knows how it is gargoyles bled to the shadows with the rest of us. They don't have the ability to shift into anything else, but I guess if trolls can survive…" he gave a vague shrug as he stood and re-shelved the book. "It's like the age of enlightenment came along and everyone forget of the existence of other creatures. There's been a rumor circulating for hundreds of years that the elder witches around the world came together and cast a spell removing the knowledge of existence of paranormal creatures from the collective cogency of human consciousness."

I lifted my eyebrow, arms folding over my chest. "I've heard that rumor. Do you believe that's what happened?"

He gave an impish smile accompanied by a slight shrug. "Why not? It definitely could be a possibility, especially when the world went to bed knowing about these things and woke believing they were just folklore and fairy tales. Anyway, back on subject." I nodded, he returned to the couch. "Despite people no longer believing in them, they still needed to procreate."

"So instead of extorting for their women they just started pulling snatch and grabs, right?"

He nodded, "Exactly, and somewhere along the line they discovered women of the were-species make much better breeding stock that humans. There bodies are stronger and thanks to the accelerated healing abilities they are able to survive the traumatic birth. Their minds are just as fragile but you don't have to be lucid to get pregnant and give birth."

I whistled softly averting my gaze from his as he slowly returned to the couch. No wonder he didn't want the others to know.

"If there's a confrontation I'm not even sure I want the females there. And I know that's going to cause a lot of contention and bad feelings but if any of them are carried off... they'll go for the submissive ones, Sarah, Simone—"

"—Hold up, you're telling me Simone is submissive?"

"Yeah."

"You're kidding."

"No, I'm not kidding. Simone is submissive."

I blinked, lifted an eyebrow, and then leaned back against the couch as I folded my arms over my chest. "Never would have guessed that the way she's always strutting around here growling, tossing looks and her snatch at you in front of me."

"She's borderline," he amended. "But I think if you were 'were' her attitude would be different. Not to mention not all submissives are as submissive as Sarah. She's an extreme case, even for us."

"Then I guess that means I'll just have to kick her ass one good time."

"Or two," he corrected, with a slight smile. "Simone's hard headed, it might take more than once."

Opening his arms, Finn moved them around my shoulders and waist as he pulled me against his chest. His lips pressed against my forehead as he smoothed his hand up and down my back.

"I don't want you to worry about this too much, alright?" he whispered into my hair. "We won't know anything until Marco and Vincent get back to me with their recon findings so there's no use in getting your self worked up about this. You've got enough on your plate already."

"I have a bit of a reprieve on that," I stated tilting my face up to his. "A week to heal up."

"Awfully generous of them," he muttered, his arms squeezing me for a hug then relaxing as he pulled us both to our feet. "Hungry?"

"Not really."

"Try to eat something for me, please?"

I knew he tacked that please on the end in hopes of appealing to my more amicable natures. Werewolf alpha or not he was still subjected to the rules of courtesy and etiquette.

"What did you order?"

"Are you kidding? What didn't I order," he grinned, opening the door so the aroma smacked into our faces as we emerged from the room. "Pizza, Chinese, barbeque, and chicken wings from that place you like."

That brought a slight smirk to my lips, my arm moving around his waist as we walked. "From that place I like huh?"

"Just for you."

"Well in that case, I guess I'll eat something."

CHAPTER FIFTEEN

HAVING good work ethics comes in handy at the oddest of times. I hadn't called off sick in over two years, so my boss was more than happy to give me any time off I needed. The week was spent in the pack house; Finn made it clear though the request for me to stay had been poised as just that, a request, it wasn't really up for discussion. It would have been nice to not have to deal with Simone, but for the most part she found things to do during the day that removed her from the house. On the days she remained it was large enough for us not to come in contact with each other.

I spent every waking hour going over the mini-Grimoire and committing the spells, incantations, and chants to memory. I also gave my domestic skills a dusting off by cooking every night. It wasn't that I didn't know how to cook; I just rarely did unless it was for company; cooking for one just seemed to be a waste of time. Finn enjoyed himself, giving a hearty 'Honey I'm home,' as soon as he walked through the door every day.

Sebastian and I hadn't talked much other than to find out after my attack by Stanley they returned to the building. Unfortunately Alexander had already been removed. A body had been found in the area badly mutilated with her throat ripped out.

The lack of the blood on the scene led investigators to believe they had found the dump sight; and the victim had been killed elsewhere. I didn't bother trying to convince myself she hadn't died at Alexander's hands, but then I'd never been good at lying to myself. I just used it as fuel to continue my studying.

Despite utilizing various outside locations on the property to continue my studying by the fifth day I was suffering from cabin fever. That was how I ended up at a quaint hole in the wall restaurant along the Wharf with Finn. It was a very cozy place, with limited seating and no reservations.

Every time I ate there all the tables were full yet, there was never a line waiting to be seated. A group of people would come to dine as another group was leaving. Just like Magic. Which is exactly what it was. More than likely the restaurant was either owned or managed by a warlock.

I looked across the table watching Finn polish off the remains of the sushi. An order that would have been a challenge for three people to finish was nothing for a werewolf to consume entirely, especially with the full moon only four days away. In four more hours he would be in his kitchen making a sandwich if not an entire meal again. Of course I could hardly talk about his eating habits as a plate of empty crab leg shells sat in front of me.

We had placed our dessert order with the meal, so as one waiter came to bus the empty plates away, another brought out a slice of pie. Key lime pie for me and French silk for Finn, both heaping with whipped cream.

Dinner out was Finn's way of giving me the night off from kitchen detail. He hadn't said it, but I knew the way his mind worked. It was his quiet way of showing how much he appreciated me. That it separated me and Simone for a few hours was just an added bonus.

I sat quietly watching Finn demolish the pie one massive forkful at a time. He'd shaved for the occasion; his smooth face void of the typical five o'clock shadow. A pale gauzy type shirt with buttons up the center covered his chest. Though the sleeves were long he'd unbuttoned them and rolled them just past his forearms. He looked up in time to catch me staring at him, the smile on his lips touching his chocolate colored eyes.

"You're beautiful, you know that?" he spoke softly, holding my gaze with such intensity I wanted to look away.

"So are you," I teased softly.

"I'm beautiful?" he chuckled softly.

"What, guys can't be beautiful?"

"Personally I prefer, ruggedly handsome, or hot," he continued, grinning. "Beautiful makes me sound like a punk."

"I don't think you're manhood is in any danger of being questioned."

Each of us finished our dessert. I ducked into the ladies room while Finn covered the check and tip. Just like clock work as we left, they cleaned the table and a family of three entered. If Finn suspected anything he remained silent, just held the door open for everyone then draped his arm around my shoulder as mine went around his waist.

We silently fell into step together, strolling arm in arm along the pier. It seemed like months since we got to do something as mundane and normal as enjoying a quiet evening out as a couple. My throat was healing nicely if not slowly. I still wore a bandage around it; more to keep the ugly, still angry looking scar from catching attention.

I wanted to ask Finn about the search for gargoyle intelligence, but I wasn't quite ready to shatter the peaceful feel of the evening just yet.

"Did you want to catch a movie?" Finn asked. His hand moved to squeeze my shoulder and pull me close enough so our hips bumped each other as we walked.

I chuckled peering up at him. "Is that your subtle way of telling me there something in the theaters you want to see?"

"No, surprisingly there's nothing out right now I haven't seen or am interested in seeing."

"Oh my God," I stopped walking pulling away from him for a moment. "Who are you and what have you done to Finnius Macleod?"

My remark earned me a swat to my backside and a mumbled, "Smart ass," before we resumed our entangled walk.

I felt his nose pressing against the crown of my head, inhaling the scent of my hair and the shampoo used that morning to wash it, before he placed a kiss to my temple.

"Doesn't Kailani live near here?" he questioned looking up at the apartments as if he would see her leaning out waving at us.

"Five blocks down and one block in," I lifted an eyebrow smirking. "Why, you wanna go say hi?"

"No, just making conversation," he replied softly before he halted our process again. "What do you think?" he stated.

"About Kailani?"

"No," he gave a nodding gesture, "About that? You up for it?"

I looked from his face to the building, to the name on the moniker that read Historical Torture Museum. The doors were open inviting the public inside, and on either side in glass cases were pictures of different torture devices assumedly one would find after stepping inside.

"I'm a witch, Finn, what do you think?"

"You realize torture devices were used on more than just witches."

"Yes, Finn, I know that," I replied a bit tersely.

"And they're even having a lecture tonight," he stated pulling me closer to the box office.

"Maybe they'll even have a demonstration," I muttered.

"Don't worry, I'll protect you, baby," he turned to face me, his hands capturing my face so his thumbs could stroke my cheeks. "Please."

I frowned. The hair on my arms and the back of my neck were standing on end. There was something not right that generated from the building and flowed over my skin like dirty rain water. And it was beyond simply being a torture museum. I could taste it on the back of my tongue, bitter and thick.

Everything inside me screamed this was not a place I wanted to be.

"Finn, you really want to patron a place that glorifies the inhumane treatment of humans?"

"That's not what they're doing," he took my hand, leading me to one of the displays. "See... their mission is to reveal the inhumanity behind it not promote it. Besides, aren't archeologist supposed to be into this kind of stuff?"

"It's not that..." I paused, rubbing my fingers against my forehead. "Alright," I finally caved. "Let's go look at all the disgusting ways they used to make people conform to their beliefs."

He kissed me as he plucked his wallet from his pocket, paid our admission and recaptured my hand leading me inside. As soon as we entered I wanted to run back out the door. It felt like stepping inside my own coffin. My stomach revolted sending salty saliva to my mouth in waves so thick I thought for sure I would vomit, before it settled back down. My insides felt cold, but my skin was hot and clammy. Finn was talking but I couldn't concentrate on him, I could barely hear him.

The sound of waves roaring in my ears, were replaced by quiet sobbing, and pain-filled moans. Standing in front of the device aptly named the rack I could hear the clicking of the cogs being turned, the anguished cries of an invisible soul stretched across it, and the unrelenting demands of the torturer to confess. The smells were next in line, assailing my senses. Feces, urine, blood, sweat, rotten eggs, and other vile orders worked into the cavity of my nose, as the heat grew more oppressive.

By the time we rounded the first corner I felt like I was on the verge of passing out. Finn had released my hand long ago, but then it normal for us to set our own pace in a museum, moving ahead or lingering behind the other. Meeting up later only to drift apart again.

He was a couple of displays ahead of me, talking to a man in a dark suit. His skin was the color of rich earth, his hair a thick rug of curls, and eyes so empty and hollow it was like staring into the eyes of a corpse.

I pressed my fingers to the hollow of my throat were sweat was pooling, but when I pulled away it wasn't the clear liquid of sweat but beads of red blood that clung to my fingers. Straw covered the floor beneath my feet instead of the faux cobblestone design, chains rattled to the left, but they weren't empty as they had been before.

The displays were no longer displays, but active devices. Each with an unfortunate soul strapped and bleeding. Each with a demon in the guise of a human at the helm of the torture. Their eyes met mine, skulls covered with muscles, lipless mouths grinning at me as their victims screamed in pain.

"Finn!"

I shrieked his name, as I watched black blood flowing from the mouth of the man he spoke with. He turned to me; a look of utter confusion replaced quickly by concern in his eyes as the sockets went empty and began to bleed. I stumbled back down the pathway; legs wobbling, threatening to give out with each step closer to the entrance.

My skin felt like it was melting off my bones by the time I made it outside, gasping down lungful after lungful of cool night air. The gentle breeze a balm against my raw flesh. The further away I moved from the building the more stable my steps grew until I was able to slump my body against the chains at the edge of the boardwalk.

The smell of fish was strong by the water's edge, but even that odor was preferable to the smells of decaying flesh. Finn's voice rained against my ears as he moved quickly to join me, palm resting on my back as I continued to gulp down air like I'd been hyperventilating. We moved to a bench so I could sit.

Whatever had happened was limited to inside the museum. Now that I was outside my senses were returning to normal, though this heaviness continued to weigh upon me.

"Dani? Baby, what happened?"

I touched Finn's face as he sat next to me; thankful his beautiful blue eyes had returned. It wasn't enough though, not until my arms were around his shoulders holding him tight against my body.

"I don't know," I shook my head. I pulled slowly away, eyes still searching his face to make sure everything was intact. "It was like... I could see images, people being tortured, people torturing... and the smell."

I closed my eyes as the memory alone made me gag. Shivering slightly, I vigorous rubbed my hands up and down my arms, trying to work heat back into my skin.

"How about we call it a night, baby."

I nodded, giving a weary smile. "Yeah, I've actually managed to tire myself out."

The feeling like I was being followed or watched never really left. It stayed with me on the walk back to Finn's car, and during the ride home. It continued inside when I went up to his bedroom to shower and change into a pair of his boxers and one of my t-shirt.

And it lingered as I rested in the warmth of his arms, adding a weight to the darkness of the room. His bedroom felt like a tomb, drafty with a chill that penetrated the bones. Despite the preternatural warmth of Finn's body I was tucked against, and the weight of the winter blankets still on the bed, I felt myself shivering.

"Cold?" he asked softly, nuzzling my hair. "I can turn the heat if you want."

I shook my head, curling my fingers into fist so they cold digits didn't press against his chest. As usual Finn's torso was naked; his body clothed only in cotton pajama pants. "Finn?"

"Yeah?" another pressing nuzzle of his nose to my hair.

"Who was that guy?"

His fingers brushed against the hair at my temple while he nuzzled lower, his nose tracing the cartilage of my ear before nuzzling behind it. "What guy, baby?"

"The one you were talking to at the museum?"

"Oh, no one," he murmured, petting his hands down my sides and hips before running them back up, his fingers edging up the hem of the shirt. "Just a tourist visiting from Africa."

His hands felt exquisite against my body, oddly it had nothing to do with the skillful way he touched me but just the heat from his fingers. He continued to nuzzle my jaw, light kisses placed on the underside of my chin while he slowly caressed my breasts, cupping them in the palm while his fingers passed over the already tight nipples causing them to constrict even more.

"Am I turning you on?" he trailed kisses against my collarbone through the cotton shirt.

"No," I teased.

"Really? Then why are your nipples so hard?"

A sharp gasp came instead of an answer as his fingers latched on and squeezed so hard it was almost painful.

"I'm cold," I was finally able to answer once my brain was able to pass a coherent thought to my mouth.

He chuckled softly; a deep bass-riddled sound that made my stomach quiver.

"Let's see if I can warm you up."

His mouth took my nipple, the cotton still between us soon saturated as his tongue and lips lavished attention, suckling away the pain he attempted to create a moment prior. I could feel his body moving as his other hand first worked to remove his pants, then the boxers I wore.

I wanted to wrap my fingers around his biceps as his arms worked to de-cloth us but was more afraid now that the frigid digits would ruin the moment and shock him back into reality. His fingers continued to leave a fiery path against my skin; igniting every inch they connected with.

"You feel so good," he whispered, once his lips finally disengaged from my breasts and moved back up to place kisses against my ear.

I thought he was going to push me onto my back, but as his arms moved around my body he rolled onto his side, facing me. His left hand skimmed down my hip and thigh, raising my right leg to rest against his hip. The other hand pushed my body against his.

"I like you being here," he trading off whispers for kisses so deep it made me forget about the oppressive darkness. "Sure the circumstances that brought you were fucked up, but I liked it. I liked coming home knowing I'd find you here."

"Mm-hmm," I giggled softly, combing my fingers through his hair to keep from pressing them against his skin. "I think you just liked coming home to a ready meal."

"I liked having you here to do this," his fingers found me then; rubbing against my lips before pushing into the heat.

He massaged them against my muscles, dragging them out and smoothing them over my lips. His thumb collected my own essences as it slowly leaked out then rubbing the moist pad in a circular motion against the sensitive flesh until I was caught between moving away and getting closer to him.

"Finn," his name left my lips in a strangled moan. My fingers finally unfurling to clasp his arm.

I tried to hold my hips still, but his fingers set up an unrelenting pattern and it wasn't long before I was moving with him, rolling into his fingers and against his thumb.

"Move in with me," he requested softly.

"I can't," I moaned.

"Why?"

His fingers moved faster, shifting angles, the thumb now accompanied with the forefinger as he pinched and manipulated me into near frenzy.

"Oh, God, Finn, please!"

"Do you love me?"

"Yes!"

"Tell me you want me," his lips whispered against mine.

"I want you, Finn," I cried out as his fingers created a slow burn that started in my core and threaten ever increasingly to over take ever part of my body.

This man knew exactly how to touch me, and exactly how to produce a deep aching torment that caused my body to tremble with expectation. The darkness was forgotten as his all-consuming heat engulfed me. Exploring fingers extracted, grabbed my waist and held me prone as he buried himself inside on a deep grunt of exhalation.

His lips touched my neck above the bandage as he set his strokes to a deep, slow, rhythmic pacing. My thigh captured between his, his captured between mine, our bodies twined together. We moved as one, holding the other so tight it was impossible to believe we were two separate entities. His lips burned against my face, my throat my shoulders, my nose buried against his hair, nibbling his ear.

We moved faster, need taking the place of gentleness. Declaration of love and my name became one chanted mantra, split into sections of twos and threes before joining together again as one long word. I felt his muscles contracting; new he was waiting for me as English gave way to gentle foreign guttural speech.

I arched my leg up wrapping around his waist, each following thrust simultaneously satisfying a stoking the fire that built and coiled and twisted until my body relented and caved to his demand.

His name exploded from my mouth before I buried my lips into the crock of his shoulder. Each orgasm crested by the wave of the next as he continued to plunge his body into mine. His hand gripping my thigh, pulling my leg up higher until movement stilled; my name stuttering from his lips before transforming into howl of release.

His body quivered as he rolled me under him, pressing me into the mattress. I could feel the change in his back, the vertebras beginning to separate in a shift then forced back into place as he fought to control his beast.

"Don't move," he begged softly, his voice hitting a bass level I'd never heard from his. One that shot tiny bolts of fear dancing along my spine. "God, please… don't do that," the words came out of his mouth in a heated rush against my skin. "Don't scent the air with your fear, Dani, please."

I could feel his muscles quivering under his skin with the need to shift, yet unable. He continued to hold his beast in check but he was struggling, and from the way his spine trembled under my fingers the man was losing.

"Finn?"

His answer was a long low growl as his teeth gently began to nibble my shoulder. I could feel the elongated fangs, biting against the skin without breaking it; his tongue moving to lick the sweat from the hollow of my throat was wider, thinner than it should have been.

"Dani…" my name didn't sound like anything I'd heard from him, somewhere between a moan and a growl, spoken through a throat that wasn't quite made for human speech.

He scrambled from the bed so fast he almost did a back flip, landing on the ground with a thud. I pulled my legs up to my chest listening to the sounds of his labored breath, not sure what the hell my next move should be. I'd seen Finn change before, but never like this. I knew the wolf was harder to resist the closer it got to the full moon, but even still he'd never lost control like that.

Shifting for a natural werewolf is flawless, like removing a coat made of skin and trading it for fur. I'd seen Finn shift before; he made me watch the night I told him I knew what he was. Wanted to make sure it was something I'd be able to handle. It had been easy; almost magical, but there was nothing magical or easy about this shift. It was like something was ripping his wolf out, forcing it to change with him fighting every step of the way.

I was moving to peak over the side of the bed when the startling sound of a wolf howl came from downstairs.

"Aw… hell no!"

It was all the encouragement I needed to leap from the bed throwing clothing on so quick I didn't realize or care that I had put Finn's pajama pants on instead of the boxers I'd been wearing. He'd managed to push himself up, balancing on his arms his body still shaking violently as his muscles visibly convulsed under his flesh.

"Finn?" I questioned, cautiously moving towards him.

"Bathroom," he growled.

He lifted his head so I could meet his eyes, the translucent green of his wolf stared back at me, the canines on top and bottom already lengthened to that of a wolf.

Scratching and growls at the other side of the bedroom door momentarily drew my attention. Simone had be out when we returned home, unfortunately it sounded as if she'd made it back.

"Now!" he yelled.

I didn't see what the protection the wooden door would offer save maybe produce a weapon when splintered but I didn't stay to argue. Arguing with a werewolf in the middle of fighting a change is a good way to end up on a morgue slab.

I leapfrogged over the bed, crashed into the wall and did a vertical roll into the bathroom kicking the door shut behind me. The space between the bottom of the door and the floor was too narrow for me to see anything, and there was no keyhole, so I was forced to try to make out the meaning of the sounds with my ear pressed against the wood. The end result was like playing charades but not being able to watch the clues.

I heard the bedroom door open followed by snarls and growls at different pitches. There was a whimper thrown in, a couple of thumping sounds, and then silence. I continued to listen, ear pressed so hard against the wood I'm surprised my head didn't pop out on the other side. I stood and waited; wrapped my hand against the doorknob and waited. It wasn't until after I heard the distant howl that I opened the door.

The patio door was open, the window blowing the curtains back into the room. I moved to the wall that my gym shoes sat in front of, slipping the sneakers onto my feet before moving out onto the balcony. Two howls came this time from somewhere on the property past the tree line. So Finn and Simone were out there running around somewhere. The thought alone infuriated me. Sure I knew in a few days he would have been running with her anyway, but running with a full pack wasn't the same as running solo.

Turning back to the room I inhaled and promptly crinkled my nose at the stench. I don't know how I missed it when I came out of the bathroom. It reeked of burnt matches and rotten eggs strong enough to make me place my hand over my nose and turn the light on to make sure there wasn't a cartoon shoved under the bed.

Looking to the bed there was one thing I was sure of, sleep was not going to happen to night, and if it did, it would be a long time coming. Simone and Finn were outside in the woods doing who knows what. I trusted Finn as a man, as a wolf I wasn't so sure.

Grabbing a throw from the footlocker, and fishing dad's journal out of my bag I headed downstairs to the den. I wasn't sure I'd feel like reading but at least there was probably a good movie I could watch.

CHAPTER SIXTEEN

"**GOOD** morning, Dr. Harlow. What are you doing here?"

Her name was Greta, or Gretchen, or Gretel, or something German along those lines, and though she had meant no ill will with the harmless question I found myself almost biting her head off.

"Just trying to catch up on some work," the reply was tossed over my shoulder, my steps not faltering in the least on the way to my office.

Gret/a/chen/el was the seventh person to ask what I was doing there, or inform me they heard I had been sick, or some variation of the two. Heading to the museum on a Sunday in the guise of working had actually seemed like a good idea when I left Finn's house in the morning. Clearly it wasn't well thought out. Neither Finn nor Simone had made it back from whatever they were doing last night. Going tramping around in the grounds behind the manor didn't seem to rank up there with brilliant ideas, and sitting around twiddling my thumbs hadn't been an option.

Closing and locking my office door behind me, I wished I had stopped to pick up a sandwich; lunching in the cafeteria would only mean fending off more of the same questions.

The smell of rotten eggs was still in my nose causing my stomach to rebel. It had greatly faded, but it was as if it was clinging to my clothing, just strong enough to convince me anything eaten had a fifty-fifty chance of staying down.

I had left a message for Finn taped to his mirror asking him to call my cell when he got home. I wanted to know what happened, but at the same time I wasn't sure if I was ready for the truth; if the truth was anything short of nothing happening. So to keep my mind distracted from forming various scenarios I continued in my father's journal where I had left off.

The bad, potentially dangers part of being a master-less apprentice: not knowing the limitations of casting ability. Magic pulled on the casters energy and power, some simpler spells seemed to have no affect, others left the caster a bit drained of energy, while others still left the caster unconscious. Then there were the spells that were more powerful than the witch attempting them. Among the witches of any given sect those were often referred to as apprentice killers. Sometimes spell nicknames are misnomers; this wasn't one of those times.

Problem was, only master witches from that particular sect knew which spells were apprentice killers. Sure some could be reasoned through common sense. I'd run across a few different spells that robbed the target of life, some of souls, those were easy to skip over for the time being. But there were ambiguous ones. These were questions I'd have to ask dad next time he popped up. Hopefully he'd hang around longer than ten minutes. He said it would take time for him to get stronger, unfortunately that was something I didn't have in great abundance.

It was easy for me to become absorbed into studying once I began the process; ignoring things became habit to the exclusion of everything. This included the knock that came on my door hours later. I must have missed more than a couple successions of them; the pounding is what finally snapped my head out of the book.

"Who is it?" I called, pulling the glasses down the bridge of my nose in an attempt to discern who was on the other side of the clouded glass pane in the door frame.

"Dani, it's Finn."

I almost told him to come in until I remembered I'd locked the door, "Just a minute." I whispered the words that would switch out the text from spells to journal then tucked the book into my workbag. I hadn't told Finn about finding my dad's inheritance box. I hadn't told Finn about any of it; the ghostly visits, the Grimoire, hell I hadn't even told him my father was a necromancer, just that he died when I was twelve.

At the time it had been because I didn't want the sympathy from him that comes when people find out a person lost a parent young, no matter their current age. Then it was because him knowing dad was a necromancer was pointless. Now I tried to chalk it up to timing, but my conscious wasn't buying it.

Crossing to the door, I flipped the lock and opened it, making a sweeping gesture with my free hand for Finn to come inside before shutting the door behind him. He looked to the door, pausing a moment before following me to my desk and taking a seat in one of the chairs on the non-business side.

"What's that about?"

"What?"

"Locking your office door."

I shrugged. "I didn't want to be disturbed." I was hoping the statement had enough elements of truth that he wouldn't be able to scent the lie.

He watched me silently for a few minutes. I'm pretty sure he knew I wasn't telling him something, but I guess in the face of last night he was willing to leave well enough alone for the time being.

I had envisioned this conversation in my head since leaving the house in the morning. There were multiple versions of how it would start, progress and end, some with me flat out accusing him, others with me telling him I didn't want to know. I liked the ones where I let him start first; it was what I had ultimately decided to do... let him begin. Of course with him sitting across from me rational thought flew out the window.

"So what happened last night?" at least I didn't jump straight to accusation, like I'd outlined in one of my scenarios.

He met my eyes, which I told myself was a good thing. If he slept with her he wouldn't have been able to look me in the eyes. For a moment I tried to pretend he wasn't an Alpha and that rule didn't apply to him. For a moment I was successful in the deception.

"I love you."

Those three words that always settled me down in the past had the exact opposite effect and sent me bolting from my chair. Finn moved quicker than I could, one arm snagging around my waist from behind, while the other wrapped around my torso effectively pinning my arms to my sides.

"No," he whispered against my hair. "Baby, that didn't happen," there was an urgency in his voice as he spoke. "I swear to you that didn't happen between us."

"Then what did happen, Finn?"

Despite the fact that I wasn't struggling against him, Finn made no attempt to release me. He continued to nuzzle my hair, rubbing his cheek against me, saturating his scent into the strands. I was tense in his arms, my body like my mind waiting for the shoe to not only drop, but kick me in the side of the head. He was trembling slightly, but I wasn't sure if it was fear of my reaction or something else.

"I don't know," his words were still a soft whispered against my hair. "I don't know how to describe it without scaring you."

"Try."

"It's natural for us to want to mate in wolf form," he began, softly. "It's as natural as having sex in this skin, maybe even more so," I noticed his words held a cautionary note to them. "It's a concerted effort to control it, you've seen slippages of that control when my eyes change to my wolf, or my canines grow. It's why on the full moon, in addition to needing to be with my pack, I purposely stay away from you. I want to give you all of me, but I can't do that with you not being 'were', and I'm afraid during the full moon that desire will override my control—"

"—Finn," I tried to pull away to face him but his arms constricted around me like a boa.

"Last night my wolf was fighting me, Dani. The howl, the shifting... my wolf wanted you last night. It wanted to mate you, it wanted ravage you and make you like him, and for the first time since I was a kid I didn't have control over it."

"Isn't that normal? The full moon is only what two or three nights away, isn't your wolf supposed to be stronger around then?"

"You don't understand, baby, or maybe I'm not explaining it right. I'm dominant, I'm a born wolf, and I'm Alpha. No one is supposed to be able to force a change on me except maybe an Alpha more dominant than me, yet last night that's exactly what it felt like was happening... like something was pulling my wolf out against my command."

"That's what happened to Simone too, isn't it?"

I felt him nodding, his cheek moving against my hair. "Except she never stood a chance. She contracted lycanthropy through an attack and she's submissive. She just assumed I had forced the turn, which for her translated into I was in danger. From there, instincts kicked in."

"Okay," I soothed forcing my body to relax.

Finn was feeding off of the responses my body was throwing out. If I didn't calm down he wouldn't either. Once my muscles came down from Defcon 3, his grip visibly relaxed, though he made no attempt to release me.

"Do you still feel that way?"

He sighed, one long exhale of breath against my neck as he nuzzled it. "I didn't, until I walked in here with you. Last night, once I was out of the room, the desire never left but the need weakened enough to fight it, chasing Simone all night helped... No."

The word was spoken as a command and was followed by a nip to the nape of my shoulder. It instantly collapsed the muscles that were tensing so I melted against his back.

"This morning it was gone, like it never happened, all the way until I walked into this office."

"And now?"

"Now I can feel your pulse in the back of my throat; your heart beating in the same rhythm as mine," he groaned softly.

His hold became less comforting and more possessive as his fingers curved against my body. He dragged his canines against my throat, holding my body against him. It felt like a steel pipe had been shoved down the front of his pants and was pressing against my backside.

"I want to taste your blood, Dani," his voice dropped several decibels. It scared the shit out of me; that it was turning me on scared me even more, because I knew the rumblings of that voice meant his wolf was close to the surface.

He pushed me forward pinning me between his body and the wall; hands moving so one pressed against the wall in front of me, the other stroking my throat under my chin. He craned my head back so our lips could meet; his colliding against mine. I smelled it again, that slight tinge of sulfuric stench in the air like someone had just lit an entire book of matches. If it hadn't been for the scent…

"Baby… stop… You have to stop." he didn't and I couldn't blame him, my voice lacked any kind of conviction.

"I can't," he purred, grinding his hips against mine to drive his intentions home. "I want you. Baby, I need you. Can't you feel it? The heat? My body, burning for you?"

He turned me around with the intent to have a better access to my body, but it also gave me a better access to his. My voice was betraying me, and though I couldn't smell it I know my scent was betraying me, but my body at least was still willing to listen to my brain.

I grabbed his ear as he leaned in to bite my throat, gripping hard enough to yank his head back and have him snarl in pain. His instincts had him shove his body against mine, but I felt him go still, watched the war of wolf against man happening behind his eyes before he sealed them closed.

Pulling away from me, he stalked to the other side of · my office. I watched him struggle to regain his composure, balling his hands into tight fists, opening them so he could press the palms flat against the top of the steel file cabinet. I watched as Finn's legs buckled leaving only the hands on the file cabinet to keep him upright.

"Finn," I took a tentative step towards him but stopped at the sound of his growling voice.

"Don't, baby I'm barely holding on as it is."

"What should I do?"

"Stay away from me, stay away from the house, at least for a few days. At least until after the full moon."

"Finn we can get through this together."

Again I tried to approach him and again his voice stopped me. "Don't!" he yelled. "Dani all I want to do right now is to maul you so you'll become infected with my DNA and become my true mate. Except I'm not sure I'd be able to stop attacking you once I start."

Finn's wolf stared back at me with luminance pale green eyes, as he spoke I could see both sets of canines had indeed lengthened, but also the other teeth were sharper, pointier. He was sweating buckets, creating a deep V in both the front and back of his shirt along his spine and breastbone. Every muscle in his body was wound so tight it was a miracle nothing had popped out of place.

"Go," he growled. When I didn't move fast enough he barked, "Baby, please just go! Get out of here! Go!"

The last words chased me from my office and sent me quickly down the hallway towards the stairs that would lead behind the scenes of some exhibits. I didn't have a destination but anywhere was preferable to a room with a changing werewolf.

* * * * *

With it being Sunday the museum closed at five as opposed to six, giving me virtually free reign of the exhibits without worry of running into anyone. I wandered for a good forty-five minutes before returning to my office. I would have stayed away longer but remembered my father's journal was left unattended in my workbag. I entered, making a beeline to the bag; my breath only exhaled when I opened it and saw the journal lying at the bottom. Finn was gone, but he'd left a nice sized dent in the top of my file cabinet.

I jumped back with a startled yelp as something scurried from under my desk across the room. I was on my desk in a minute, not because of what I thought it was, but what I knew it wasn't. Too big for a mouse I tried to tell myself it was a rat, but damn it the last time I checked rats weren't bipedal. If I were prone to believe they existed I would have sworn Stripes just ran across my floor, but gremlins were just a creation in a Spielberg movie.

Climbing back down, I cautiously moved to the where I'd seen it run behind the file cabinet. It was a quick check to reveal whatever I saw wasn't behind there, or the bookcase, or any of the other furniture in the room. Getting on my knees I checked the floor but there was nothing lurking under my desk or anywhere else.

I was about to give up when I caught a nose full of that stench. My brain finally put an ID on the smell, sulfur. I'd only had one chemistry class so the scent wasn't easily recognized, but once I'd made the connection there was no denying it. It burned my nostrils, but I inhaled deeply trying to get a bead on the source of the odor. It was so obvious I couldn't believe I'd overlooked moving my door from where it still rest open against the wall.

A gremlin was about the closest description my mind could wrap around, that or a hairless version of the Tiki doll from *Trilogy of Terror*. It was tiny, a foot, maybe eighteen inches at the most from the floor to the top of its baldhead. Its body was the color of charcoal and actually looked like it had been burnt. It was malnourished, its burnt skin sunken in to reveal the perfect outline of a four pair ribcage. Thin arms that led to clawed little fingers, and legs that led to clawed little toes, and a bulbous head containing sickly yellow eyes, pointy ears sticking out of the side and a mouth full of razor sharp teeth.

I jumped back, hand covering my mouth literally too stunned to do anything. The creature, who wasn't as surprised to see me, hissed letting a trail of thick saliva spittle from its teeth and took hopping leaps towards my desk. It took me a second to realize it was going for my father's journal, and half of that time for the necessary phrase to fly from my mouth.

The first time I said the phrase the book disappeared and reappeared in my hand, the second time it was my bag. I bolted out the door as if I'd just been tasered in the hind parts, slipping my bag over my head and the book inside as I ran down the hall to the stairs. I didn't waste time looking back, I could hear the claws of its feet, hell maybe its hands too, on the tiled floor behind me.

I bypassed the elevator, taking the stairs two at a time until I reached the main landing, legs pumping towards the back employee entrance only to skid to a halt before reaching it. Standing between the only working exit and me was Alexander.

This wasn't the feral creature from the cage that wanted to rip my arms off, but the debonair vampire that had broken into my house the other night. He was healthy again; skin glowing, hair thick and lustrous, which meant he was being feed regularly or recently.

A smile started to spread across his lips, but I didn't hang around to watch it grow fully; I couldn't double back either so I headed into the exhibits. Hunched over I ran low between the displays.

It occurred to me to cast a protection spell over myself, or a shield of darkness that I had learned from my father's book. It also occurred to me that if I guessed correctly the necromancer was controlling Alexander. Casting might be the very thing he was hoping I'd do… all the quicker to find me. Not to mention there was still some imp, demon thing. On the carpeted floor of the exhibits I couldn't hear the tale-tell clicking of his claws.

"Come out, come out, wherever you are," Alexander called, giving his position away.

I inched further back into the exhibit, following the path that would eventually lead back around to the main hall.

"We just want the book, little one," he continued. "We know you've found your father's Grimoire. My little pet has seen it with his own eyes. All you need do is slide it on the floor to me, and we shall let you go."

I rolled my eyes, I couldn't help it. If he thought I was going to fall for old we'll let you go trick he was sorely mistaken. I could tell where Alexander was, but I still had no idea where the little demon creature was lurking. I wasn't too worried about it. Hopefully he didn't have any real power or he would have used it in my office instead of chasing me down the hallway.

I decided to make a run for it, hoping he was too far away for his speed to be a factor. He hissed as soon as he spotted me rising. He was coming for me, and just as predicted the bastard creature was standing in the doorway. It didn't move, just stood there hissing, its teeth bared, claws raised threateningly. It honestly thought it would intimidate me. Right up until I stepped on it.

It shrieked before falling silent as I felt the sickening crunch of its bones giving way under my shoe. I didn't have time to be sick or disgusted; I could feel Alexander at my back. I dropped to the ground twisting my body; eyes glued to him as he first lunged at me on his own accord, and then went sailing with the aid of my magic into the wall. More solidly built than the walls of my home the concrete didn't give way as he crumpled to the floor.

Something inside me made me stop. I wasn't running anymore. I raised my hand; fingers open, twisting it at the wrist as Alexander's body left the ground. He struggled in my grip almost forcing me to drop him. I pushed my hand forward and his body followed the movement slamming, pinned to the wall.

He was strong; the fact that he was struggling like King Kong against steel chains didn't help. I could feel the blood dripping down from my nose onto the front of my blouse. I knew I wouldn't be able to hold him long, I could already feel it slipping. My mind raced with what to do with him before it hit me.

Re-doubling my efforts I slammed him back immobile against the wall with everything I had in me. The vampire hissed, fangs lengthening past feed length. These weren't fangs to pierce the jugular, they were meant to rip it out of the throat. He lunged forward and I shoved him back, my mind was screaming in pain, blood flowing from a steady stream out both nostrils. The scent couldn't have been helping but I didn't need to hold him much longer.

I shoved my hand inside the side zipper on my bag; coming back with one of the baggies filled with the powder I'd mixed to break the spell back in the warehouse. This was either going to be the best idea I had all week, or it was going to be my ass. Every ounce of strength I had was focused into holding him, if this didn't work I wouldn't have the energy to run from him or hold him back.

With one hand I shoved the baggie into his mouth as he opened it to hiss at me, with the other shoved his jaw closed forcing his teeth to rip through the thin plastic sending the powder down his throat and up into his sinuses. He shrieked his struggles increased until I was unable to hold him anymore.

My hold dropped and we both hit the floor. Him shrieking and kicking against the faux stones of the hall; me back peddling and stumbling trying to get my feet to work in a forward motion. It was when he let out a shriek that threatened to rupture my eardrums that I stopped moving and just assumed the fetal position, then all dropped into a deafening silence.

I might have thought I lost my hearing had I not heard my own breathing. Slowly I uncurled my body, my eyes fixed to the spot where Alexander had dropped. He wasn't lying on the ground; he was standing, staring right at me with those electric blue eyes, while his hands brushed down the sleeves of his shirt.

Had it worked? Even if it did there was a chance he still saw me as a threat. I began to edge my way backwards when he spoke.

"Easy," his voice was softer than it had been before, the tone was the same but there was something different about it. When he took a step forward and I continued to move backwards he paused, holding his hands palms up in a sign of surrender. "Easy," he softened his voice like he was talking down a jumper. "Easy girl."

"Fuck easy," I mustered up enough energy to push him backward about two feet before another gush of blood erupted from my nose.

"You keep that up and you're going to pass out right there on the floor."

How the Sam Hell he knew that?

"You spend time with a witch in your head and things rub off. I'm not going to hurt you."

"This time," I pointed out pushing myself against the wall and using it to stand.

Too bad I wasn't sure my legs would support my weight. I could feel the blood still flowing rather freely. Putting my fingers to my nose would do little to stop it, but if felt like I should be doing something other than letting it bleed all over the place.

"Last times I wasn't in control of my body."

"How do I know you are now?"

"You made a remedy without knowing what the outcome would be?"

I noticed he was inching closer to me but I decided not to cat and mouse it. If he wanted to catch me he'd be able to. "I've never tried it before tonight, maybe I didn't get the quantities right."

He smiled at that, paused, and took a few more steps. "You should trust your instincts more."

When he was six feet from me I held my hand up to pause him. "Just… just give me a moment."

"Unfortunately we don't have a moment," he countered and gestured to where the demon imp had been. His body was no longer there. Alexander held a hand up to stave off my questions. "I will explain what I can later, but we must leave, now."

"Where?"

"Anywhere would be preferable to here. By now he knows you've broken his spell over me, and his pet has undoubtedly run back to tell him you have your father's book. I have no desire to be under his spell again, and you are currently not strong enough to fight him."

"My car—"

"—He will be able to track your car though the scent the demon left."

"Then how—"

"—You'll have to trust me."

"Not gonna happen."

"You don't have a choice."

His lips parted into a devious smile, and I knew letting my guard down had just cost my life. Quick as a snake his hand circled my wrist, while his arm wrapped around my waist. I tried to push him back but only succeeded in moving both of us and forcing more blood in a spurting stream from my nose. Then just as Sebastian had done in the warehouse and on the lawn, Alexander folded us away into the night.

CHAPTER SEVENTEEN

WE dropped onto the ground, or I should say when he pulled the darkness away to reveal reality again he remained standing but released me letting me drop to the grass. It might not have been the gentlemanly thing to do but at least I was free so that gave me some hope. Of course it probably just meant he wasn't concerned with me running.

"You shouldn't have struggled so much," he chastised staring down at me. "You almost made me drop you… twice."

"News flash, Bright Eyes, you did drop me."

"I meant in transit," he corrected. "Dropping a few feet I assure you is preferable than me losing my grip while in the middle of transport between space."

"Because the road here was paved with your good intentions, right?" I shot back slowly climbing to my feet.

I began looking around, taking in as much of the new location while not losing sight of Alexander; still half expecting the necromancer to materialize. He never did.

Even more surprising still was the choice of landing or opening was a cemetery. It didn't look familiar, but then it wasn't like I hung out in the local cemeteries either.

"Where are we?" I questioned.

"Does it matter?"

"You brought me to a cemetery."

He gave a shrug, arms folding across his chest as he watched me like he found me greatly amusing. "Very observant. I thought you would feel safest here."

"You thought I'd feel safe in a cemetery?"

"You're a necromancer are you not?"

I paused. Vampires were very good at sensing lies from mortals, at least mortals that weren't trained in lying to vampires. Turns out I didn't need to bother.

"Don't bother denying it, I already know you are. I can sense it in your blood; a side effect I am assuming from my duration of being possessed by that... witch."

"You know one could argue being in a cemetery when you are being chased by a necromancer borders on idiocy."

I felt his eyes on me; saw one slender red eyebrow arch slightly over a dazzling blue eye. "Sebastian said you were charming. I doubt he would think to look for us in a cemetery, after all who in their right mind would hide from a necromancer in a cemetery?"

He had a point there. I relaxed a bit, and seated myself at the base of an angel statue over a grave. It felt odd, trusting someone that had tried to kill me but casting over him I didn't feel that other presence as I had when he was in my house and in the museum earlier tonight. I touched the top of my lip and came back with red tacky fingers. The free flowing blood had stopped but I still looked a mess.

I heard a rip and looked up as Alexander approached me, offering a section of the shirt he had torn.

"Perhaps this will do until you can clean yourself up properly."

"Thanks," I took the cloth, it wasn't in the best of conditions but it was better than walking around with dried blood above my lips.

I wiped as much of the blood away as I could before folding and shoving the cloth into my pocket. Alexander knelt slowly in front of me, his eyes focused on my nose.

"I must leave you for a few minutes," he stated.

"What? Why?" It was funny a few moments ago I just wanted to get the hell away from him, now I didn't want him to leave.

"He only allowed me enough blood to function. I believe had you not arrived at the warehouse when you did he would have let me reduce to a husking shell as the others. I need to feed, and you have already given enough blood for one night."

Silently I nodded to that.

"Unless of course you would like for me—"

"—I'll wait for you here."

He smirked as he rose. "As you wish."

And just like that he was gone, disappearing from the edges inward until there was nothing left. I heaved a sigh before stretching out on the ground, clutching my bag to my stomach, my hand resting over the lump created by my journal. Physically I was okay, but mentally I was exhausted. My head didn't just hurt, it felt like my brain had just doubled in size and was being crushed by the confines of my skull.

"Too much too soon," I muttered softly to the night. "But at least I made it out alive."

"More than alive," my father's voice came back.

Opening my eyes I sat up to see him leaning against the statue I sat on a moment ago.

"You did well, Babygirl."

"It's not over."

"No, but you've just proven you're capable of anything."

"Breaking a root is one thing, killing or disabling or destroying this guy or whatever it is I have to do to get him to stop is something else entirely."

"True, but if you can do one, you can do the other. Everything is a step on the ladder leading to the next level, Dani. You can't run until you walk. I'm sorry I couldn't warn you about the demon."

"You knew about that?"

He nodded. "His energy prevented me from crossing to this plane completely to contact you, but I was able distract it enough to keep it from harming you."

"Thanks... it didn't hurt you, did it?"

He chuckled at that. "Sweetheart it would take more than a minion of Largos to hurt me, even in this form."

"Minion of Largos?" I repeated. "What's that?"

"Something conjured up from the dark realm, from the chaos realm to be exact," he began. "Largos is one of the six demon gods, his specialty is chaos; creating and by doing so birthing the essence of many different negative emotions the other demon lords need to feed, anger, rage lust... all of these can be by-products. What you saw was a lesser demon, one of his workers. Finnius' inability to maintain any level of control around you..."

My mouth dropped open. "That was because of that little gremlin looking thing?"

"Yes, the more base a nature the easier it is to provoke. The only thing that saved your boyfriend was because he was a dominant alpha werewolf. I doubt he would have been able to resist if he weren't."

I narrowed my eyes, sitting up completely now. "So that thing made Finn... why summon a minion why not just summon this Largos?"

"Because no one witch has the ability to summon a demon god. Not if he wishes to control and not be controlled by it. It would be like trying to summon Ares, or Athena."

"Then why summon this thing at all?"

"Who are you talking to?"

Just as he disappeared, Alexander materialized next to me.

"I—" I had just shifted my gaze from dad to Alexander for a heartbeat, but by the time I looked back dad was gone.

I gave a frustrating sigh as I shifted my attention back to Alexander. His cheeks and lips had a healthy pink tinge to them almost looking down right rosy, his eyes were already alive and dancing but there was a different light behind them now. Even his hair had a healthy sheen to it. I didn't realize just how corpse like he looked before until I took in the sight of him after the blood infusion.

"Is she still alive?"

That earned me a smile. "What makes you think my donor was female?"

On that I just gave him a pointed look. Fiction seemed to enjoy depicting vampires as gay or bisexual but unless I missed my guess this guy was from the Viking era. Sex with women was the standard procedure I was betting man flesh wasn't on his radar.

"Yes," he finally conceded. "She is very much alive, they both are." He dropped to the balls of his feet squatting in front of me, his eyes boring into mine. "And might I add it was quite the enjoyable experience for them. I could always go for dessert, if you've changed you mind."

"Why here?" I stated choosing to ignore the offer. "Why not take us to the Bat Cave?"

"The Bat Cave?"

"Juan's manor."

"Ah," he stood and offered his hand, only dropping it after I climbed unassisted to my feet. "You were already apprehensive and you were... drained," he stated after carefully choosing the word. "I thought you would feel more at ease gathering your wits on neutral ground than surrounded by vampires."

I nodded and took a step only to find his body blocking my path.

"How is it you've managed to live as a necromancer all these years and remain undetected?"

"I wasn't a necromancer until recently."

"Come now, Danika. I know you must be born into necromancy."

"It's complicated alright, lets just leave it at that," I tried to move again but this time he grabbed my arm.

"The one that possessed me, that bound me into his services, he spoke of a Daniel

Harlow. It was his Grimoire he sent me looking for. Sent me inside your home to look for."

"He was my father? What of it?"

"And it is his Grimoire you carry with you?"

He reached a hand out to my bag and found himself struck in the chest but it wasn't from me. Something moved through me then materialized between Alexander and me. It took me a second to realize it was dad.

"Hurt my daughter, vampire. And I promise you'll beg for the sun," his voice was low and threatening.

I had no idea what it was dad did, but Alexander was on the ground in front of him, clutching a hand to his chest as if he were suffering a heart attack. His eyes went wide as he stared up. His mouth twisted in a silent scream.

"Not…my…intent," he was finally able to choke out, before gasping in a breath as dad released whatever hold he had. "I meant her no harm," he finally panted slowly pulling himself to his feet. "But that book puts her life in danger."

Dad glanced over his shoulder at me but didn't move, he did fade a bit. His mass thinning out and becoming more transparent.

"He wants your Grimoire; it is why I was sent to her house. When he couldn't find it he was ready to move on until he felt the call. He kept saying it was calling him."

"Who is he?" Dad demanded.

"I do not know his name, only that his origins are rooted in Africa."

"What would a necromancer from Africa want with my Grimoire?"

Alexander straightened his clothing, and then ran a hand over his hair. "It is not just yours; he already has the Grimoire of three elders."

"Which elders?"

"That I do not know, nor do I know why he is collecting them, whose he is collecting, how many more he needs, or what his intentions are once he has gathered all those he desires."

"Maybe the other elders will know," I stated.

"No," dad stopped short of shouting but barely. "You must not tell the other witches what you know. They will want to know how you came by this information. Once they find out you are a necromancer you life, may not be safe."

"What? Why?"

"Dani, focus, one major catastrophe at a time," dad chastised.

"He will stop at nothing to obtain your Grimoire, that much I know," Alexander stated. "It is like an obsession. The little beast has seen it and has told him you carry it. He was trying to take it from you tonight at the museum. When he failed, I was sent to retrieve it and you."

Dad began to fade more until only the faint outline of his head and torso remained.

"Daddy what do I do?"

"You cannot let him get the book."

They were his final words on the subject before he disappeared completely.

"Where did he go?" Alexander answered glancing around, then up, then finally back to me. "Is he gone?"

"Sort of, you get used to it after a while."

I paused for a few moments my mind racing at trying to come up with a game plan. It obviously thought dad's journal was the Grimoire, which was good, but only because it kept him from looking for the real thing. Unfortunately there were still some potent spells inside the mini-Grimoire. Why was he going around snatching up other Grimoires? I didn't bother wondering what happened to the witches. No witch just gives up their Grimoire. He would've had to pry it from their cold dead hands, and I was guessing that hadn't been an issue for him.

One thought pushed through that had nothing to do with Grimoires, witches or the like. Finn. He was beating himself up because he thought he was losing control, when it was really just the residual effect of some damn chaos demon god's imp.

"I need to talk to Finn"

"Your werewolf lover?"

I narrowed my eyes. "That minion was screwing with his control. I need to let him know what he's dealing with in case there are any residual side effects."

"Very well, but first we need to go to the Bat Cave, as you call it. I need to let my sister know that with your assistance, I have been freed."

"With my assistance?" I raised an eyebrow on that. "Is that vampire for; *my ass would still be a necromancer's bitch boy if it weren't for you?*"

"So very enchanting," he stated tilting his head to the side and watching me with a very amused expression like I was some precocious child. "I see why Sebastian is so fond of you."

I ran my tongue over my front top teeth before sucking on them, just watching the vampire in front of me. Sure he was fine, didn't mean I trusted him any further than I could throw him. He was still a vampire.

"Come," he held his arms out. "We shall go to the Manor, and then we shall reassure your wolf of his masculinity."

"Keep it up and you're going to have to add me kicking your ass for being a pretentious jerk to the itinerary."

"That just might be worth it," he chuckled.

I didn't want to be that close to him, but space, or lack there of seemed to be a requirement for journeying through the space/time continuum. My muscles tensed as soon as his arms moved around my body. I watched the darkness fold around us, it was the first time I was aware enough to really experience what the traveling felt like. I was aware of us moving, even though the rate was so fast it felt like we were stationary. I felt his arms tight, catching me in a hug; my own hands curled into fists and pressed against his chest. And just like that; darkness gave way and we stood on the lawn of Juan's Manor.

"You can let go now," I stated after we were prone for a good five seconds and his arms were still around me.

"You mean to tell me you're not enjoying yourself?" even as he spoke he released me, flashed a quick wink and began to head to the house calling, "Come along," as he moved.

I hated being treated like a child or an afterthought but I followed anyway. The other option would have been to stand out there refusing to go… like a child.

Brenda came barreling out of the front door before we even made it to the porch; hitting Alexander with a force so strong it almost knocked him back. They spoke to each other in a language that was foreign to my ears though it sounded German or perhaps Dutch. Juan and Sebastian followed Brenda's charge at a much slower dignified gait. Behind them the rest of the vampires were gathering in the doorway including good ol' Stanley. I felt him watching me; his eyes turning away when I looked up to meet his gaze.

Brenda's beady little eyes turned to me when I heard Alexander mention my name. Her expression was something akin to appreciation but the words thank you never left her mouth.

"*Senorita* Harlow," Juan stated finally moving forward. He stepped down off the porch, hands raised as he gave a soft golf clap. "I see you have performed a miracle, just as Sebastian said you would."

"So you'll call off your hounds, right? No going to CoC?"

The statement brought a confused look to his face. "Why on earth would I do that?"

"Why? Hello, take a look around. I got your people back; none of them are any worse for wear."

"Stanley and Matilda were mere husks when you returned them if memory serves."

"And Stanley nearly ripped out my goddamn throat; more than even there," I tossed back.

He paused at that as if he were actually considering the statement. "Perhaps we should discuss this further inside, *sí*?"

"Actually I'm fine right here."

"You don't trust me," he chuckled. "That is flattering but hardly necessary."

"Perhaps we should accommodate her," Sebastian began. "Dani has brought three of our own back to the fold and has twice suffered at the hands of two here. If she weren't mistrustful surely that would mean something was amiss."

Juan seemed to concede as he gave a nod. "Will you at least join us in the gazebo behind the house?"

I nodded. "I can do gazebo."

They were humoring me, I knew it, and they knew it. My protesting was a moot point. It wasn't like I'd really be able to get away from a brood of vampires if they decided to kick something off, but illusion was everything.

Brenda and Alexander led the walk around the back of the house followed by Juan. Sebastian fell into step next to me, an encouraging smile on his lips meant to put me at ease with the twins from the garage at my back. The rest of the vampires stayed inside.

"You are feeling better?" Sebastian asked softly.

"Yeah."

"Dani, I'm sorry about what happened last week."

There was more he was ready to say but I lifted my hand waving the words away. "It wasn't your fault Sebastian. Being all up in a vampire's grill ranked up there with the all time dumbest things I've ever done."

"Still, you were under my protection."

The gazebo looked like any other, save it was larger than average. The benches running along the inside of the railing could have easily accommodated a dozen people. I sat next to the doorway, grateful when Sebastian took a seat next to me. Juan sat across the way with Peter seated on his right.

He leered at me, lifting his lip in a sneer of disdain as he folded his arms over his chest.

Once the others were seated Alexander conveyed to them the same thing he had conveyed to me in the cemetery. Unfortunately it turned out there were more holes in his memory than he originally let on.

"You have no recollection of how the necromancer came into your home or your sanctuary?" Juan repeated. I could hear the surprise in his voice accompanied by anger.

"No," Alexander answered. "I have no memories of that night."

"Maybe he learned to teleport," I stated.

"He's a necromancer," Peter spat. "Only warlocks have the ability to teleport as we do."

"Well first off I didn't say he teleported as you do. Secondly he's collecting Grimoires? What you think necromancers are the only witches that keep them?"

"And your father's book is the one he currently searches for. That makes you a necromancer. Witch," he stated the word as an accusation, his eyes daring me to deny it.

"I wasn't a practicing one," I pointed out.

"Interesting choice of tenses," Juan stated casually. "Even more interesting is what you plan to do with your father's Grimoire."

"I don't plan on handing it over to him," I stated. "Or you."

"What would I do with a necromancer's Grimoire?"

"You're right," I began, "Why would a vampire possibly want a book that would allow him the ability to summon and control entities from other planes and realms?"

I looked away as his eyes narrowed. No way in hell I was going to meet that gaze. I felt the weight of his eyes lift from mine and chanced a glance upwards to watch him cleaning his nails.

"You know, there was a time a century or so ago, when vampires were sanctioned to kill necromancers on sight, even those that could not call their power to heel."

"There was a time when vampires were necromancers' slaves too. Do you really want to continue this trip down memory lane?"

"Tell me why I shouldn't kill you right where you sit?" his voice dropped to a dangerous whisper. My glance in Sebastian's direction made him release a sinister chuckle that had my flesh crawling. "He cannot save you."

"You're not going to kill me," I tried to keep my voice as even toned as possible. Easier said than done when my heart was hammering in my chest like Flo Jo during an Olympic hurdle event.

"Enlighten me, why is that?"

"Because you need me to destroy this necromancer and save your asses. And because with the proof of Alexander's statement the CoC would never sanction a witch hunt on San Francisco's coven because of the actions of an outsider. The fact that he didn't announce his presence gives us a loop-hole, but having killed other necromancers takes us clean off the revenge billing you're trying to shove down my throat."

He sat across from me, silent. Waves of anger emitted from him reaching all the way to where I sat, but I had him. So long as there was no proof that the witch was working under orders for the local Elders we were in danger, but if he went to the CoC now, with the truth in Alexander's head and now his story retold to all present there was no way they could justifiable destroy us.

"It would seem that you have managed to exceed my expectations," Juan stated in that suave voice again. "Congratulations, *senorita*, it is not often I am surprised anymore."

"Happy I could shock the shit out of you."

"You are wrong about one thing," he stood walking slowly towards me.

He waved his hand to Sebastian to move. When he didn't immediately oblige, Juan trained his eyes on him. The vampire eventually stood changing his position of sitting next to me, to leaning against the doorway across from me.

"It is not our asses that need saving, but yours," he leaned back stretching his arm across the back of the bench and putting him entirely too close to me for my liking. "According to Alexander, now that he knows what blood flows in your veins it is no longer simply your father's Grimoire he is after, but your blood as well."

I felt his fingers playing with my hair; it took everything in me not to recoil from him. Or maybe that was my body trying to get closer. I didn't like Juan, I sure as hell didn't trust him, but as with the first time I met him, there was this air about him. This vampire didn't have to hunt for food, food came to him.

"How do you know he wants my blood, Alexander didn't even know that?"

"Because I've been around for centuries. Blood is more than just nourishment for vampires it is also the driving force behind many necromancer spells. The caster either takes it from themselves, or others. The more powerful the necromancer, the more powerful the blood, the better the spell works."

"Danika is not a powerful necromancer," Sebastian pointed out.

"Correction, Danika has not tapped into the power of her blood. Blood that is very, very potent," his eyes left me and went to Sebastian. "There is a difference between inexperience and inability. Why do you think it is you crave her company? Necromancer's blood is a siren's song to a vampire."

I bolted up moving out of the gazebo and onto the lawn. I could feel him trying to creep into my head. He stood, bouncing down the stairs but keeping his distance from me.

"You see, *senorita*, tracking this witch and destroying him is as much in your best interest as our own. If he has the power to conjure minions to do his bidding you are not safe until he is found and destroyed. I offer you room and board here, for a fee, of course."

"Juan," Sebastian spoke softly, but Juan raised his hand in a silencing motion.

"I was willing to allow her to stay under your protection when I thought she was merely a sorcerer. Now that the truth of her linage has been revealed as part necromancer… well…" he gave a slight shrug and an almost wistful sigh. "It has been many, many decades since I have drunk from that intoxicating label. I suspect, my son, if you had any idea you would have sampled her years ago, perhaps even claimed her for yourself before that wolf ever came into her life."

"You're disturbed, you know that?" I stated, finally pushed beyond the pale for the night.

"Nevertheless, sanctuary remains open for you here. You will be safe; all you need offer me is your blood."

"I already have someplace safe to go, and surprise, surprise I don't have to give him my blood."

"Blood, body," he waved his hand dismissively. "It's all the same, and if this little minion was tracking your movements while you were there, how safe do you really think it is? If the necromancer has not already looked for you there, it's only a matter of time before he does."

I silently cursed myself for allowing Juan to distract me. I pulled out my cell hitting Finn's number on speed dial. When his cell phone went to voicemail I dialed his home phone, getting the same response. When the third attempt to reach Finn's cell ended in voicemail yet again I dialed another number.

"Hello?"

"Luke, it's Dani, have you heard from Finn tonight?"

"We spoke earlier this evening but that was around six," he paused. "Is everything alright?"

"I don't know. Meet me at his house, as soon as you can."

"Do you need me to pick you up?"

"No," I replied looking to Sebastian. "I'll be there before you."

"What is going on? Is Finn alright?"

"The more questions you ask the longer it's going to take for you to get there."

Sebastian was already moving forward as I ended the call and shoved my phone into my pocket.

"My car is out front," he stated.

"I need faster than wheels."

With a nod his arms moved around my body; the enveloping darkness was almost instantaneous.

CHAPTER EIGHTEEN

WE stepped out of the fold in Finn's backyard almost in the exact same area when he brought me after Stanley's attack. What greeted us wasn't the calm of his property, but what could have passed for a war zone; the very least a crime scene. The back yard was littered with broken glass from the patio door. The furniture was smashed, tangled in different pieces and scattered across the lawn, while some of if floated in the pool. The worse part was the bodies.

Some looked like they'd been mauled, bites taken out of them, claws that had opened vicious wounds... wounds that as I inspected them closer hadn't bled. There was no sign of blood on or around them, and the bodies were cold as ice, as if they hadn't just died but had been dead for hours, hell maybe even days. Looking around just showed more sighs of struggle, but it was looking back to the patio door that finally got my legs moving inside. There was dried blood clinging to the jagged edges of the patio door still connected to the frame.

"Finn?" I called his name once softly; before I knew it my feet were moving at an accelerated pace towards the house. The soles of my shoes crunched over broken glass as I took the patio entrance into the kitchen.

"Dani wait, it might not be safe."

I heard Sebastian voice but his words didn't register against my ears. I wasn't even sure if he was following me or not, though it didn't matter. Attila the Hun and all his Barbarians could have been waiting inside for me, and I still would have charged into the house.

"Finn! Finn!"

The more I saw the more frantic my cries for him became. The inside of the house far worse than the outside; furniture smashed, blood splattered and smeared everywhere. What items hadn't been broken were toppled over or thrown about as if they were either used as projectile in a fight or knocked over during the course of it. Lamps on the floor with skewed shades threw odd patterns against the wall. Toppled over couches and chairs with cushions displaced and ripped on the floor.

"Finnius! Simone?"

Upstairs was no better. There was blood black and red smeared on the walls, holes punched and dented in different places throughout. Only silence answered me back as I ran from one room to another looking for either of the two occupants and finding nothing but more signs of a fight and struggle. I didn't even realize Sebastian was with me until I arrived back in the living room to see his balancing on the balls of his feet investigating the body that lay in the middles of the living room.

"I can't find Finn," I told myself I wouldn't get hysterical. Never mind the fact that the house looked like the latest venue for the UFC cage match.

"My guess is he is no longer here."

"What is that thing?"

"A zombie. As are the others in the back yard."

"What are zombies doing in Finn's house?"

My phone rang, interrupting the silence and whatever words were about to fall from Sebastian's lips. I pulled the phone from my pocket so fast I almost dropped it.

Finn's name showing up on the caller ID along with the picture of the both of us I'd assigned to his number. Relief flooded my body as I snapped the phone open pressing it against my ear.

"Finn? Finn? Are you okay? Where are you? What happened at the house?"

"So many questions," came back a voice that was definitely not Finn's. It was deeper, darker, and held such a heavy African accent it was hard to catch all the words. "Such concern for Mr. Macleod, it is most touching."

"Who is this?" even as I asked the question I knew the answer.

"I believe you know who this is, yes?" his words switched to Elvish, but I kept mine in English so I wouldn't have to repeat the entire conversation to Sebastian.

"Mama always said it was polite to introduce yourself," I was thankful my voice didn't betray the way my insides were shaking.

"If you believe I will introduce myself you are in for a long wait indeed, and I'm afraid the luxury of time is something your wolf friends cannot enjoy."

"Where's Finn?"

"He is here."

"I want to speak with him."

"I'm afraid that is not one of the options."

"You want something from me, I want to speak to him or you can go straight to hell you son of a—"

"I hardly think you are in the position to be making demands. I tell you he is alive, you may believe it or you may not, but how long he and the girl remain alive is entirely up to you," his voice had taken on a darker edge to it, threatening. It made me want to shiver and I wasn't even standing in front of him.

"What do you want?"

"You know what I want."

A thousand responses went through my head. I needed time but that was something I didn't have the luxury of either.

"This has nothing to do with him. This is between you and me."

He must have found my words amusing, because he erupted with such a laugh it took him several minutes to compose himself enough so he could talk. "Dear child what makes you think I care anything about that?"

Well, appealing to his human nature was out. "Fine," I ground out through my teeth. "I can't get the book tonight," I stated silently thanking my brain for kicking into high gear.

"I know you have the book on you."

"Correction I had the book on me. You really think after that stunt you pulled at the museum with your little minion I'd continue to run around with my father's Grimoire on me?"

"Where is the book?"

"Someplace where you can't get it, and I can't retrieve it until morning."

There was extended silence on the other end of the phone. "You are sorely trying my patience, girl," he finally hissed out. "You will retrieve the book tomorrow, and you will await my call, but know this. Each hour of delay adds to the torment the wolves will experience, and I have many ways of tormenting wolves."

On cue I heard distinctly female shrieks in the background and the howl of a very angry male. Sebastian must have heard it to as he moved closer to the phone. I cringed, the emptiness in my stomach threatened to erupt and send me into drive heaves. I didn't like Simone, but that didn't mean I wanted her tortured. Assuming of course it was Simone.

"You sick bastard," the words slipped from my mouth without me even realizing I uttered them.

"Flattery will not save your friends," he chuckled. "I feel the slightest pull of you trying to track my location; I will remove something very precious from your male wolf and salve the wound with silver so he cannot grow it back."

Before I could say anything the line went dead. I could feel the anger building up inside me, causing my entire body to shake with the need to destroy something. I drew my hand back but Sebastian caught it before the phone could fly. I turned punching him hard in the stomach, only for him to catch that arm too before the hit.

"Control your anger," he whispered holding me tight enough to keep me from moving. "Save your rage for the one that deserves it."

A growl filled with all the pain, anger, and frustration raging through my body. It had been a long time since I felt so utterly and completely helpless before. I'd forgotten how much I hated the feeling. If I tracked his location or even tracked Finn with necromancy he'd know it, and I couldn't track him with the blood magic my mother gave me.

I felt Sebastian forcing his way into my mind, past the barrier I'd constructed to keep all vampires out. Each time a vampire was able to gain access to the mind the next time was always easier until they could come and go as they pleased. My mistake had been letting him in period, valid reasoning or not.

Had I not already been drained I might have been able to keep him out, but now my barrier was equivalent to an unlocked screen door.

"_Calm yourself,_" as he spoke to me inside my head I could feel a cool breeze moving over my body, extinguishing the fire and forcing my body to relax. "_You won't be able to help him if you cannot think clearly._"

I wanted to fight against it, but it would just tire me out more, so I gave in to his control. It wasn't until my body slumped in his arms completely relaxed that he released his grip, and backed out of my psyche.

"I want you to know something," I stated, my voice holding a reserve not of calm.

"Do that again, and I promise I'll kick your ass."

"Fair enough."

Sebastian released me, backing away as I picked my way to the couch, righted it, and then sat down. Head held in my hands I wanted to cry, but I couldn't afford to waste my time with tears. Finn was counting on me, Simone was counting on me, I had to think of a way to find them tonight without the

Necromancer knowing, because if I waited until tomorrow I'd be dead.

"I have to find him," I stated.

"Perhaps, Alexander would be able to help. He is able to recall much of his time under the necromancer's possession, I'm sure…"

His words stopped when I began shaking my head. "He's smarter than that. Remember what happened when we rescued Stanley and Matilda? Either Alexander was never at his central location and thusly would be no help, or he moved his central location as soon as I broke his hold over Alexander."

Sebastian turned his attention to the front window and began moving to the door. "I believe Luke has arrived."

"You might not want to get that," I stood moving to the door. "You're not exactly on their favorite people list."

Sebastian opted to lean against the archway leading from the foyer to the living room while I opened the door. I wasn't the least bit surprised to see Katrina and Sarah climbing out of Luke's car, nor was it a shocker that other cars joined his in the driveway until the rest of the pack was walking towards the entrance. Having the entire pack assembled would mean I'd only have to explain things once. It also meant it might be a very short night for me. No matter how I told the story there were going to be some that saw this as my fault. Hell maybe it was.

"What's he doing here?" Padma demanded when she stepped inside and saw Sebastian.

"What the fuck happened in here?" was Joseph's greeting.

"Where's Finn?" Sarah asked in a high strung panic laced voice.

"That blood. That Finn's blood!" Colton's voice rang out.

"What the hell is that?" I turned finding Marco standing over the zombie.

One after the other onslaught of questions kaleidoscoped together until my ears vibrated with their voices. The anger from early that Sebastian had worked so hard to calm returned so quickly my body broke out in a sweat from the sudden raise in temperature. I didn't have enough time to wonder why I was having such a physical reaction to being pissed off. Maybe, if I was lucky enough to survive this I could address the question then.

"Enough!" I shouted snapping back a growl. "Shut the hell up and take a seat so I can tell you what the fuck is going on."

Dead silence followed my outburst. The males in the room, even Luke glared at me, they didn't like being told what to do by a woman but none of them said a word. Sarah actually whimpered, cowering behind Luke, while both Katrina and Padma looked at me as if I'd grown a second and third head. Katrina's stare was more one of quiet admiration while Padma looked like she was deciding which of my arms she would rip off and beat me with first.

I growled a soft warning in the back of my throat as I took a step towards Padma. "I said sit down," my voice had dropped to a low soft sound.

She moved first, picking her way through the living room to right one of the chairs that were knocked over. With the seat cushion shredded and half the stuffing yanked out she decided to perch on the arm of the chair. One by one the werewolves entered the room and either sat on remnants of furniture of the floor, or leaned against the wall in various places.

"That," I pointed to the dead body on the floor. "Is a zombie, there are more of them out back. They were probably sent here along with something else to attack me and get this," I pulled my father's Grimoire from the bag still around my shoulder. "I'm guessing when they didn't find me; they decided to take Finn and Simone."

I saw Vincent frowning, but before I could ask him to hold questions words were flying out of his mouth. "Why would gargoyles want a book?"

"It's not a book," Luke corrected his eyes never leaving mine. "It's a Grimoire."

"Okay, why would they want—"

"—It wasn't the gargoyles, Vincent," I said with a sigh. This time when Joe opened his mouth I was able to beat him. "Look everyone just shut up until I'm done."

He growled, but he held his tongue.

"I'm sure Finn or Luke or both have told you about this witch that was been possessing vampires," when I looked around and saw various heads nodding I continued. "I don't know why but this necromancer is collecting other necromancers' Grimoires like they're trading cards; this," I tapped the book, "...is the next one on his hit list. Now tonight, I was able to break the hold he had on the last vampire in this city, that's what he's doing here," I gestured to Sebastian. "Sebastian was with me when I realized Finn might be in danger."

I looked around the room, my eyes hitting each werewolf before moving to the next. I purposely saved Sebastian for last so I'd be able to look away from someone that wouldn't see it as a direct challenge.

"By the time we made it here, Finn and Simone were already taken. From the looks of things they put up a hell of a struggle. A few moments ago I got a call from the one that's taken them."

"What did he want?" Luke stated.

"He wants me and the book," I stated calmly.

"You?" Katrina finally interjected. "Why would a necromancer want you?"

"Because she's obviously a necromancer," Joseph snorted his eyes burning into me daring me to deny it. "Why else would she have a Grimoire?"

I could feel all their eyes on me now waiting for either a confirmation or denial.

"If it makes you feel better he's not inviting me over to have tea, he wants my blood."

"Why?" Marco asked.

"I don't know."

"Where are Finn and Simone?" Padma demanded.

I shook my head. "I don't know."

I hated those words but it was all I could tell them.

"So what are you doing to get our Alpha back?" she demanded. "Or was your big plan to dump this in our lap?"

I glared out her; I could feel the anger welling up again. "You know, you might want to pretend that you're not a raving bitch, and act like you give a damn about finding your pack mate and Alpha, for just... I don't know... a minute. What do you say?"

"You bitch!" she hissed, as she rose to her feet.

She said something in Hindu before spitting to the floor. Katrina was on her feet standing in between both of us. I hadn't realized I'd pushed away from the wall until I felt fingers pulling back on my arm.

"This is not helping your Alpha," Sebastian stated. "Danika was able to buy at least a few hours. She told this necromancer she wouldn't be able to get the Grimoire until morning, I suggest you all use that time coming up with a plan to find Finn and Simone, or what you will do when it comes time to make the trade, as I doubt he will agree to Danika arrive at any designated point with one member of the pack at her back, let alone the entire cast of characters."

"Sebastian is right," Luke stated then looked to me. "Is there any way you can track this necromancer?"

"Sure, but he's already threatened to make Finn a permanent eunuch if he feels me casting on him."

"Do you believe he would keep his word and exchange Finn and Simone for you?" Sebastian questioned.

Katrina glared at the vampire. "You say that like we have a choice. Rather he relinquishes Finn or not he will kill the both of them if we do not make the trade or at least attempt to."

"Can we wait until tomorrow and, I don't know, have the exchange in a public place?" Sarah whispered.

"Finn will not agree to leave without Danika," Luke stated plainly. "She will either leave when he leaves or we all stay."

"Finn may not have a choice," I stated. I didn't want to tell him Finn might be in no condition to realize if I was leaving with them or not. Hell he might not know he was leaving.

"Can you at least beat this necromancer in a fair fight?" Joseph stated in a weary voice as if he already knew the answer.

"He's stronger than me," I stated. "I won't be able to take him with a frontal assault. He's older than me and he has access to several more Grimoires than I do," I added after his noise of disgust. I don't know why I felt I had to justify myself to him, or any of them.

"Age," he replied in a snotty tone. "Does not dictate who is more powerful among werewolves."

"Well I'm a goddamn witch, alright?" pushing my hands through my hair I let out a loud primal scream. "You think I'm not beating myself up over this? That I don't realize this is somehow my fault? I love Finn, not knowing where he is or what's happening to him has me sick to my goddamn stomach, so I don't need any of you reminding me what I am, and what I'm not or how things would be so much fucking better if I weren't in his life."

"That is not what he meant," Luke stated softly.

"Oh that's exactly what he meant…"

I would have said more but I felt a chill flooding over my arms and face. I looked to Sebastian but he seemed more focus on the werewolves in front of him than me. It took seeing Sarah shiver for me to realize what was going on.

"I need a few minutes alone," I muttered.

I headed up the stairs to Finn's bedroom, shutting and locking the door, and then continued to the bathroom where I turned the shower on. I might have revealed a good deal of myself to Finn's pack tonight but I wasn't ready to reveal my ghost dad to them. From the way he let me know he was there without taking form he felt the same.

"Calm down, Dani."

His words were meant to comfort but just succeeded in pissing me off.

"Everyone keeps telling me to calm down; I don't need to calm down I need to find Finn."

"And being enraged is going to help you accomplish that?"

I knew he was right but reasoning and emotions weren't trying to sync up right now. I was so pissed it took me a while to realize I couldn't see him.

"Dad why—"

"—I'm too weak. It takes more than a week to build up enough strength to cross to your side and interact with the living. My confrontation in the graveyard with Alexander took most of my strength."

"Great," I muttered, "This is perfect. I might as well just wait for him to call and hand myself and the book over on a silver platter."

"You're not giving up," dad said, his voice not one to be negotiated with.

"I can't use my magic to find him, that doesn't leave me a lot of options."

"You might not be able to use your magic, but you can use your brain, girl."

I had to ball my hands into tight fists and count the frustration building up back down. "How is that going to help me find him?"

"He had to have left clues behind. There has to be some way to track him or the beings that took Finn back to their point of origin. All we have to do is find the clues."

I breathed out and breathed in again, scrubbing my hands down my face. "Alright, alright, we know we're dealing with zombies, or at least they are part of the equation, but... I thought zombies were weak."

When nothing but silence answered me back I knew I was again on my own. Frustration returned thick on my tongue, taking everything in me to push it back down. Dad and Sebastian were right, there was no way I'd be able to come up with anything while steam was rising from the top of my head.

Shutting off the shower I walked back into the bedroom. The fight hadn't made it in here yet, but that faint scent of sulfur remained in the air. That caught my attention, enough to have me unlock the door and head back downstairs. I walked the perimeter of the house on the inside, before doing the same outside. There were a total of six zombie bodies, but there was something else next to the bodies outside that I originally missed.

Kneeling, I dipped my finger into the burnt circular pattern on the grass, tossing what turned out to be ashes and bringing it to my nose. The sulfuric smell was so strong I gagged.

"Zombies *and* minions," I muttered allowed.

I wiped my hands on the seat of my pants as I stood letting my eyes move over the expanse of the backyard. It was only a few hours earlier that I was concerned Finn and Simone had sex while he chased her, or at least after he caught her. That had been the first time I had smelled the sulfur, last night in his bedroom. Of course then I didn't realize what it was I smelled, or what it meant.

"You've found something?"

Luke's voice was soft announcing his presence as he stepped into the back yard. Katrina walked with him, Sebastian just a bit behind the pair.

"Maybe, there are sulfuric traces here."

"What does that mean?" Katrina questioned.

"Sulfur is associated with demons or their minions," Luke stated.

"Earlier this evening I killed one, or dispelled it or whatever you do to get rid of minions."

"Which brings me to a question I've been wondering," Sebastian stated moving closer to observe the scorched ground. "How is it the little creature knew to find you at the museum?"

I shrugged. "It's not like I'm in the witness protection program Sebastian," I stated. "This necromancer knew where to find my dad. It's not unthinkable that he found out who I was and where I worked."

"Yes, but do you usually work on Sundays?"

"No," I stated slowly watching him, wondering where he was going, when it hit me. "Son of a bitch."

"What?" it was a chorus of three voices.

"Last night, after..." I paused glancing around the faces. "Finn and Simone started to lose control, shifting."

Luke nodded. "Yes I heard his howl last night."

"Right well, see, later today he comes to the museum trying to explain what happened. He said it felt like something was making him shift, making him lose control."

"That doesn't make any sense," Katrina stated. "Nothing but a stronger Alpha could force a change on him."

"Right," I said again pointing at her, "But a minion of Largos can."

"Who or what is Largos?" Luke questioned.

I waved my hands dismissively at that, my mind working faster than my mouth could keep up with. "I'll explain that later, the gist is Largos is a Demon Lord of Chaos, and what better chaos to thrive on than a rampaging werewolf. I mean think of the destruction and chaos it would cause." I continued walking a bit, gesturing as I spoke.

"For a minute I thought maybe the minion knew I was at the museum because if followed Finn there, but I remember the smell of sulfur as I was driving and walking into my office, and Finn stated he only felt like he was losing control when he was around me, which means the minion had to have been attached to me."

"When did Finn start losing control?" Luke questioned.

"Last night, after we… um… had sex," I don't know why it embarrassed me to say.

It wasn't like the pack thought we hadn't consummated our relationship. Hell chances were they'd heard the consummation happening once or twice.

"So it is safe to assume this demon attached itself to you some time last night?" Luke continued.

"What difference does it make when the damn thing started following them?" Katrina ranted. "It's not like finding this demon, minion, whatever is going to help us find Finnius."

"No," Sebastian injected. "But if we are able to find where it was picked up from, perhaps that will put us one step closer to locating this necromancer."

I listened to the three of them going back and forth for a while before eventually closing my eyes and blocking them out all together. My mind racing trying to remember the first time I noticed the slightest change in Finn, the first time I noticed the slightest change in anything. It didn't take long to retrace our steps back from last night.

"Guys," I stated softly the louder when they continued to go back and forth. "The Historical Torture Museum," that got their attention.

"What about it?" Luke questioned.

"That's where I first noticed the smell of rotten eggs. At the time I didn't know it was sulfur, I thought, I don't know it didn't even register through all the other things happening."

"What do you mean?" Sebastian asked. "What other things?"

"Last night we had dinner on the Wharf and afterwards walking pass, Finn had this urge to go to the Torture Museum. They were having a topic on witch hunts," I shook my head. "Anyway we ended up going in and I swear not twenty seconds after I stepped inside it felt like," I pressed my lips together frustrated. "Like I was actually in a dungeon, not just walking through displays. Everything was real, and the smell, the feel, even..." I stopped my hands covering my mouth. "Oh my god."

"What? Danika what is it?" Luke stopped himself before he grabbed my arms.

"They guy, the guy Finn was talking to last night. The way he looked at me, the way I felt when he... like he was drinking my soul." I cut my eyes to Sebastian.

"Alexander said the necromancer was from Africa, or at least he had an African accent. The guy that was talking to Finn last night spoke with an African accent."

"That doesn't mean it's him," Katrina stated.

"It's too much of a coincidence not to check out," I replied.

"How do you suggest we handle this?" Luke turned his attention to me fully.

"This time of night I'm sure the museum will be closed."

"I don't see as we have any other choice," I looked to the faces present. "If he's not there, maybe there's some tracer that was left. Calling a minion uses serious magic, and I can guarantee he summoned from there. And if he summoned from there, he has left some sort of spell residue that may be able to track back to him."

"I thought you said he would be able to tell if you cast a spell to track him."

I nodded. "He can, but I'm not going to be tracking him."

"Then...?" she looked from me to Luke, who looked just as confused as her.

"Come on," I turned heading back inside the house, and pulling out my cell. "I'll explain on the way."

CHAPTER NINETEEN

BETWEEN Luke's second generation Hummer and Marco's Durango we were able to fit everyone into the two vehicles. Speakerphone allowed us to make the plan between the two cars. Team A would be entering the Museum; Team B would maintain position in the cars. It was no accident that the majority of the werewolves on Team B were submissive.

If the necromancer was in the area they would be the easiest target. Once his little minions managed to pollute them into changing there was no telling what chaos would break loose. Padma remaining with them was also no accident.

I told her it was because they needed a dominant werewolf in the event something spilled over and affected them, which was partially true. That I didn't trust her to not take the opportunity to wipe me out and blame it on a minion's influence played heavily into the equation as well.

Kailani stood waiting for us when we arrived. I told everyone I was calling in backup, I just didn't tell them who or what that backup was. Climbing out of the Hummer I knew there'd be an onslaught of questions. Beyond the fact that no one knew I had called her, she didn't look like she would be able to lend anything to the group, except maybe distract the necromancer with her beauty.

She was dressed more conservatively than usual, which for Kailani meant the tan cargo shorts she wore were long enough to cover her entire butt instead of offering snatching peeks of the lower swells, while the t-shirt only gave a flash of her flat belly instead of the full on view. I was surprised to see a pair of gym shoes on her feet. I didn't think she owned anything but sandals and high heels.

Kailani waved erratically and came bouncing over to us as Team A piled out of the vehicles and Team B rearranged into just Luke's Hummer, though all eyes were on us. She had a huge smile on her face as if she were going to meet Orlando Bloom for the first time and not fight a very powerful necromancer.

"Is she a demon?" Luke leaned in to whisper.

"No I'm not a demon silly," she hit his arm playfully. "Do I look like a demon?"

She placed her hands on her hip for emphasis, squaring her shoulders so her modest chest was more pronounced.

"No," I assured her no wanting Luke's words to offend her. "But we might be facing some demons… well, technically minions but same smell… literally."

She started at me then with eyes that quickly doubled in size. I thought she was going to pass out instead she leapt onto me; arms locking around my neck in a tight hug.

"Thank you, thank you, thank you," she squeezed me tight then placed a kiss on my cheek before releasing me. "It's been a long time since I battled a demon, or even a minion."

"Who are you?" Katrina finally asked with an edge of annoyance in her voice.

"Kailani, this is part of Finn's pack," I began gesturing as I spoke. "This is Finn's second Luke, my second Katrina, and Marco, Colton, and Joseph. Guys this is Kailani… she's, um, a friend I think can help."

No one said anything. Kailani grinned at the group and the group stared at me.

"What?" I stated a little more testily then intended as I looked from one to the other. "I'm not about to explain why I think Kailani can help, you're just going to have to trust that I know what I'm doing, alright?"

Luke continued to stare at me with the oddest expression before lowering his eyes and inclining his head. "As you command."

The submissive gesture of him lowering his eyes made me stare at him for a moment. Of all the things Luke was submissive to me wasn't one of them. I wasn't the only one that caught it; Joseph looked so piss the only thing that was missing was steam radiating from his ears. Sebastian looked amused; Katrina looked awe struck, while Colton and Marco just looked confused.

"You need to know," I began turning to Kailani, "That we're dealing with a very powerful necromancer as well. Wait… I'm getting ahead of myself; we might be dealing with a very powerful necromancer if we can find him before tomorrow morning."

"He's here," Sebastian stated plainly, all the amusement gone from his face. "Where? How do you know that, vampire?" Joseph demanded.

"There," Sebastian raised a hand and pointed to the museum. "I can sense his presence inside."

"Does that mean he can feel you as well?" I asked.

He nodded.

"Can't you shield him or something?" Colton questioned.

"I could, but to do so would alert him that I knew he was near, which could tip him off that we are coming for him. As it stands there is a good chance he believes this is just a fortuitous moment."

"You wanna explain that in English?" Colton continued annoyed now.

"Deserted place, hungry vampire looking for food," I supplied quickly then looked to Sebastian. "I'm thinking maybe you want to sit this one out."

"And let you have all the fun?" he chuckled at that. "Besides, he can't control me yet. If he thought he could he would have been out here already."

"What makes you so sure?" Joseph turned to face Sebastian, arms folded over his chest.

"I'm too old," he informed flatly. "He doesn't have the power or ability to control me yet. Trying would only kill him, and his own death isn't what he wants."

Joseph growled, I'm not sure which he protested more the answer or the glib way Sebastian delivered it. Personally I found it amusing and reassuring.

"Well then why don't you call some of your other undead friends to join the fight," Joseph snapped. "Why the hell should we risk our necks alone?"

"What assistance did your pack provide when it was three of ours that were missing?" first it was just his head, but as he spoke Sebastian turned his entire body to face Joseph. "I think the number topped out somewhere around zero."

"Joseph," Katrina began. "Do you really want a bunch of vampires that may or may not be susceptible watching your back while you're going to fight a necromancer that's possessed some of them before?"

Joseph remained silent; deciding glaring was preferable to answering Katrina.

"We need to find a way inside," I began heading towards the building. "I'm blocking right now, but the minute I use magic of any kind he'll know we're here."

"Leave getting inside to me," Marco grinned and jogged ahead of us before disappearing around back.

Under normal circumstances the seven people standing in front of a closed building would have looked like we were casing the joint. Come to think of it, it probably still would have looked that way, had anyone been around to take notice. Fortunately with it being two in the morning the other shops along the Wharf had closed hours ago and with it being early Tuesday morning the residential foot traffic was blessedly absent.

Luke opened his hand and pressed his palm to the glass of the front door. "I can feel Finn. He's inside there somewhere… Simone as well."

"How?" the one word slipped soundless from my lips.

"It is a gift of the blood," he answered with a slight smile. "Once accepted into the pack our spirits are linked by blood. It doesn't work over great distances but when close enough some of us can feel when others of our family are near."

I looked to Katrina but she shook her head. "It's an ability only some werewolves possess. You either know it, or you don't."

I wanted to ask if the ability allowed him to tell the condition of the packmates or only their location. I wanted to know if Finn was alright, but I was too scared. I knew I wouldn't be able to handle it if Luke told me Finn was dead or dying so I hoped for the best, not letting my mind travel down the 'what-if' road.

Marco came back around the front, that bright grin still in place as he removed a small leather case from the inside of his jacket pocket, extracted some tools and began to work on the lock. "Alarm's been disabled. I suspect since he's inside its not armed, but just in case I disconnected the wires."

"What's the plan once we get inside?" Katrina asked on a low whisper.

"We find them," I leaned back looking at the building. "This place can't be that big, two stories up, a basement maybe a sub-basement. Once inside, Luke you take the pack, find Finn and get the hell out of dodge. Sebastian, me, and Kailani will find the necromancer."

"I'll go with you," Katrina stated. "Four are better odds than three."

"The important thing is to get Finn and Simone out of here."

"The important thing," she corrected, "Is to get Finn, you, and Simone out."

"Got it!" Marco whispered triumphantly, replacing his tools back in their pouch and that in his jacket.

It was creepier than when Finn and I visited the place last night. The cobblestone walkway was dark, the only lights coming from the exhibits themselves. I could feel the heat, same as before building around me until it was an oppressive force pushing against my skin. There was no other way to go, save the pathway that was in front of us. To the left and right instruments designed solely to bring upon pain and death surrounded us.

"He knows we are here," I stated on a soft whisper, letting my shielding drop.

"Yes," came a heavily accented disembodies voice. "I know you are here, I have known you were outside for quite some time."

Everyone in the group froze. I took hold of Kailani's hand as I chanted a few words, feeling her energy rush through my body as I called on the spell of protection learned years ago from my mother. It was why I had asked her to come. I wouldn't have involved her at all but I needed more energy than what was left in my body.

The spell wouldn't work against anything the necromancer through at us directly, but it would shield the others from the minions or other nastiness he might have lurking about.

That eerie disembodied voice laughed, though cackle is more effective a description. The sound went through my body, dropping my temperature just as surely as the heat before had pressed down against it. I wanted to throw up. I could feel the bile trying to rise as I forced it back down.

"Come, hurry, we are waiting for you."

The words were followed by the laugh again; then a sound much shriller and close as Sebastian dropped to the ground. He cried out in pain, his hands pressed to either side of his head as if he were trying to press the ends together.

"Sebastian!"

My movement to my friend was placed on hold as a female screamed just ahead of me followed by a growling howl.

"Go!" Sebastian roared, teeth bared, fangs extending well past feeding to full on battle mode.

I wanted to help Sebastian but I knew I'd never be able to without dipping my already dwindling energy even lower. Kailani could charge me like a back-up generator but there was only so much the body could take before collapsing. Leaving Sebastian to his fate and praying he came out on the other side, we moved as a group around bend after bend in the walkway. It was what awaited us around the corner that my stomach won its rebellion and sent dry heaves mixed with acid to the cobblestone.

Simone sat in some sort of chairs, but this was no normal chair. Long pointed spikes covered the back, seat, arms, and legs. Even the foot rest that extended from the wooden device had spikes sticking up, and they were all embedded into Simone's body.

A silver band around her chest and lap pushed the majority of her body back onto the contraption and prevented her from struggling. There were similar bands of silver on her ankles, arms and feet holding them prone as well.

She continued to scream long howls of pain as dark minion little creatures intensified the pain by tightening the bands. Her struggles increased when she saw us, which only served to assist in torturing herself further.

Finn sat near her on a simple iron chair. His hands were bound behind his back, I couldn't see with what but I was guessing it was silver cuffs or something equivalent, since his ankles were chained to the chair with silver shackles. A silver band circled his neck, on it were two forks set against each other. Constructed into three silver prongs on each setting one was rammed down into his chest, while the other was shoved into his chin forcing his head back into a painful degree.

Like Simone, he had his own set of minions, pushing the back of his head and forcing his jaw to impale further on the device. The wolves growled collectively; the anger and rage surging through their bodies intensified by the minions, who gleefully continued to torture Finn and Simone.

Each snarl from the five brought more pain to the two until they were playing off of each other, using their own packmates to dictate the torture.

"Show yourself!" I could feel my own rage building inside like a squatting beast in the pit of my stomach that was struggling to its feet.

"Show me the book," the voice instructed.

Either my fingers stopped working or the straps were purposely becoming more difficult, but I had to struggle with the flap for a good ten seconds before I was able to undo them and pull the book out. As soon as the book was out arms circled around me as Sebastian grabbed me from behind.

"No!"

We were all so focused on the minions in front of us none realized Sebastian was no longer howling on the floor, or that he was now under the control of the necromancer.

Katrina was the first to lose it, dropping to the floor I watched as she effortlessly shifted into a large wolf with thick auburn hued fur. She would have lunged at Sebastian had Luke not managed to get a hold of her.

Sebastian gripped a handful of my hair, yanking my head back and to the side. I felt his tongue followed by his teeth dragging against my skin. I wanted to struggle but I didn't want to excite him or the werewolves more than everyone already was.

Katrina was furry, Colton, and Joseph, eyes and teeth had already made the transfer to beast, Marco's teeth were extended but he continued to struggle as his eyes transitioned back and forth. Only Luke seemed to still have a tenuous restraint on his wolf.

Kailani seemed torn between pulling Sebastian off of me, confronting the minions that continued to torment Finn and Simone, or possible changing form herself. Her eyes were no longer deep brown but bright amber, the pupils flattening from round spheres vertical slits. Finn was also fighting a losing battle.

His eyes had been glued to me since we entered and he seemed to have been drawing calmness from that, until of course Sebastian grabbed me. Now his eyes were a bright translucent green. I watched as he fought his body's instinct to bulk up.

"No," I tried to keep my voice calmer this time, aimed at the werewolves dying to rip Sebastian apart.

"Soon enough, vampire," the necromancer crooned. "Soon enough you will have her blood but not yet."

He decided to show himself, stepping from the shadows of the corridor ahead of us, flanked by a zombie on either side. As soon as he appeared the minions ceased their torments, hopping to swarm around his legs like pets greeting their master's return.

He was shorter than I remembered, of course that meant nothing in terms of power. Even a midget could have done what he was doing if they were strong enough. His head wasn't shaved, but the hairline had retreated further back on his head causing the front to shine with the lights from the exhibits. He had a mouth full of bright white teeth, which surprised me. For some reason I thought they would be black like he was suffering from scurvy and needed a good dose of vitamin C. He was stocky; what his body lacked in height he made up for in girth, and those dark beady eyes bore into me as if he could see right through me.

"*Dani, it's alright*," Sebastian's voice resonated in my head.

I grabbed onto Kailani's hand, the connection of flesh against flesh not only allowing me to draw from her power but connect the three minds.

"*Sebastian?*" I continued to struggle a bit, keeping up the pretense as I projected my thoughts. "*He's not controlling you?*"

"*No,*" he answered, his fingers flexed as if tightening but no pain ever came.

"*How?*"

"*You're father is assisting me, but you must work quickly. He grows weaker with each second and this necromancer is stronger than I thought, strong enough where he may be able to possess me without your father's aid.*"

"*We must lead him away from here,*" Kailani stated. "*Distract him so that his attention is not focused on Sebastian.*"

"*There's only one thing that will do that.*"

I cast my eyes desperately around the area; mind racing. Forward was out, there was no way I'd make it past him and the zombies, and all those little minions even with using magic to push them out of the way. Back was out; we'd only be able to run down the path so far until we reached the front door. We'd been lucky there were no people passing earlier but that luck might not hold out forever. He'd already proven civilian casualties was not something he cared about.

Out of options that only left one, ducking through the door on the right. It was marked employees only, which meant it could have just led to a broom closet. But the release bar going across the middle made me think there was something beyond than just a small room.

"*The door,*" I whispered it to both of them. "*On my go, Sebastian release me and move back. Kailani and me will go through there.*"

"*I should go with you.*"

"*No, you already said he's stronger than you thought. If dad burns out before we can take him down... besides Finn and Simone are being held by silver, if the others touch it, it'll burn their fingers. You'll need to help free them.*"

Sebastian's tensing body pulled my hair more, producing a hiss from my lips.

"*Very well, Be. Careful.*"

"*You say that like I have a choice.*"

"*Don't worry, Sebastian,*" Kailani cooed softly to him. "*She is precious to me too; I will take care of her.*"

Finn continued to snarl as the necromancer approached, his hand held up for a moment to signal the minions and zombies to hold their position.

"This was too easy," he stated with a chuckle. "Here you thought you would surprise me and instead walked right into my trap. And you bring me," he gestured around, "So many presents."

He snatched the book from my hands that proud smile spreading his lips. It made me sick to watch his fingers pawing over dad's book. The only thing that kept me from lunging for it was knowing it would be back in my hands soon.

"I don't mind telling you, I find myself disappointed. I thought for sure the daughter of the infamous Daniel Harlow would prove a challenge. You put on such a magnificent display at the museum, breaking my hold over Alexander, only to concede to me so easily."

"You said you would release Finn and Simone if I brought you my father's Grimoire."

"I remember making no, such arrangement."

As he focused on leafing through his spoils I watched the smile fading; watched the rage seeping into his eyes as he realized what he was holding wasn't a Grimoire but just a journal of his history.

"Still disappointed?"

I spoke the same phrase I had back at work early; the book vanishing from his hands and rematerializing in mine. As soon as I began speaking, Sebastian released me, moving at record speed back down the path we'd come. Kailani and I took off, the necromancers enraged howls chasing behind us as we flew through the door.

Behind the door was a set of stairs heading down. I took lead; I had no idea where we were going but I had been right in my prediction. The door banged against the wall as the necromancer threw it open and pursued us.

"Where are we going?" Kailani asked.

"I have no idea. Let's just keep running until we can't anymore."

"Why are we not fighting him?"

"To give the others a chance."

We held hands and ran, I didn't want to chance some horror movie slip up and have one of us go down. The stairs dropped us in the basement level in front of another door that was blessedly unlocked. The hallway beyond was like a maze. Doors to the left and the right held dark rooms on the other side. We had just turned the corner when again the boom of the door being yanked open followed behind us.

I heard him behind us, but felt the energy chasing us, moving faster than he was. I dove to the ground yanking Kailani down with me as the dark matter whizzed over us.

We stayed there for a moment; one hand held up fingers pointed at the corner we just rounded, the other tightly fastened around Kailani. As soon as he was around the bend we spoke the words softly together.

The necromancer hit the corner of the wall hard enough were his spine should have snapped in the other direction. When it didn't, I pulled Kailani up with me and began running again. Sebastian was right.

"He's too strong," I yelled as we moved.

"We can take him."

"He should be lying there dead not chasing us."

My only hope was that we had given the group upstairs enough time to dispense with the zombies and minions and free the others. But plans on escaping evaporated when the hallway lead to a room with large flappable double doors. I was positive there was an exit beyond the room but what I thought would be our salvation became our cell.

The room led nowhere, at least not to any discernible exit. It looked to be the store room for items in the gift store, and maybe some that we taken off of exhibit or waiting their turn to be ogled by many. There was no where to go save back the way we came, but as I turned around still clutching Kailani's hand I watched him push open the double doors. That malicious smile back on his face. I moved in front of Kailani edging her backwards to the sound of his cackling voice.

"Ah, now *that* is the spirit I was looking for in Harlow's daughter."

"It ain't over until the fat lady sings."

"Then let us finish this, in an old-fashion duel, winner takes soul."

"You mean all," I corrected as we slowly began to circle each other.

"For a necromancer my dear child, soul equals all."

We continued to circle each other; I continued to use my body to block Kailani from any direct shots he might throw at her. I wasn't sure what effect necromancy magic had when used against a sea dragon; now didn't seem like the right time to find out.

"I would take you on as my apprentice, had circumstances been different," he continued.

I cracked a smile at that, "Guess I'm lucky after all."

He reacted quicker than I thought but my chant was still only a half second behind his. I released Kailani's hand not wanting to risk the pull of necromancy through her body. I knew I wouldn't last long like this, but again, all I needed was to buy the others enough time to get out.

Two sets of hands raised towards each other, dark matter left both in long serpentine tendrils. They tangled and twined together as the magic and energy from him entered me and my power entered him. He laughed at the first feeling of my magic washing over him.

"This? This is all you have?"

The laughter flowed over me like acid, pissing me off, but my body wasn't able to supply my demands. I felt his energy cutting into me, opening wounds on my flesh and burning into my skin. Blood was running down my forehead and arms, I felt it trickling down my spine under my shirt. For every tiny cut I opened on him black blood oozed a moment before sealing the gash. For ever tiny cut I opened on him he exacted five and six more on my flesh.

I dropped to my knees, my energy eking out while his continued to pour against and consume me. If this had been a contemporary duel it would be over now, ending when one part was no longer able to keep their footing. If I ended it now he'd kill me all the sooner.

"Give me your hand!" Kailani shouted kneeling next to me.

I tried to talk but blood bubbled and spilled over my lips. All I could do was shake my head.

"*Let me help you,*" she repeated this time directly into my mind, her voice blocking out the cackling of the necromancer.

Without waiting for an answer I felt her hand wrap around the back of my neck.

Where her palm touched my skin instantly cooled; like jumping into a cold pool on a ninety degree day. I gasped; my back bowing as the dark energy flowing from my fingers changed to a brilliant blinding light. It blasted through the necromancer's tendrils slamming full force into his body so hard it carried him back against the wall and continued to pour out through me.

We were both screaming as multiple cuts opened on his body like a psychopathic surgeon was slicing into him relentlessly with a scalpel. I tried to stop, I didn't want him dead. There were too many questions that only he had the answers. Death was too easy, yet I couldn't control the power, the flood gate had been opened and I had no way to pull it back.

The necromancer dropped to the ground more seeping flesh than man. The energy flared through the room then doubled back entering my body like a heat seeking missile. I heard myself scream, heard an explosion; I saw my father, a horrified look on his face, and then I saw nothing.

CHAPTER TWENTY

Two weeks later...

SOMETHING about the soft rhythmic beeping was comforting instead of annoying, even though I'm pretty sure that was what woke me up. My body hurt with an ache I felt in my body down to my bones. It's like I'd been tore apart and sewn back together by Dr. Frankenstein.

What had happened? And where the hell was I? I was definitely lying down; I could feel a bed soft and uncomfortable under my body. I tried to swallow, but my esophagus refused to constrict around a tube shoved inside.

I opened my eyes carefully, still not completely sure what I would find on the other side of my lids, surprised to see it was a hospital room. The beeping was from a heartbeat monitoring machine stationed next to my bed.

I had a tube up my nose delivering pure oxygen, an IV in one arm and another in my hand. The tube that didn't seem to be connected to anything, just shoved down my throat, my guess was used for feeding, and of course the catheter completed everything.

My eyes stung. Opening them hurt, but closing them hurt even more, they were so dried out my lids felt like sandpaper sliding over them. Various parts of my flesh that was visible were covered by square gauze held in place by tape. I released a soft, low groan; with the tube shoved down my throat it was the only sound I could make. I tried to remember what happened to get me here, but the last solid thing my mind would lock onto was hiding out in Finn's bathroom. Was that why I was here? Had Finn lost it and attacked me?

Panic shot through my body and had me trying to sit up when I should have been content to lie there. Katrina appeared from behind the thin curtain, gripping my shoulders and pushing me against the bed. She was joined by Louis he gripped the other arm, each of them holding me, as I watched Sarah peek timidly the foot of the bed.

"Go get the doctor," Katrina instructed. "Then page Finn and tell him to get his ass down here as soon as he lands."

I let my body go instantly limp at her words. I tried to remember. I knew something was blocked or forgotten but what?

"Don't try to talk," Katrina encouraged in a soothing voice; her fingers lightly stroking my hair.

I focused on her face trying to convey my thoughts to her but as soon as I attempted to cast my voice into her head, pain erupted in my brain. Light, sound, touch; everything faded to black.

The second time around I woke to a different cast of characters, but everything else was the same, right down to the catheter and the tube down my throat. Finn loomed over me, rising from the bedside chair as my eyes opened. His face shaved but there was a weariness to his eyes. The whites were almost entirely red and the moment they landed on me welled with tears that spilled down his cheeks. He looked torn; his hands moved several times in an attempt to gather me up but stopped short as if he was afraid it would do more damage than good.

Kailani gripped my right hand; her upbeat smile looked none the worse for wear, and she seemed just as bubbly as her usual self. She squeezed my hand to get my attention on her the grin spreading.

"Don't try to talk," her words echoed those of Katrina earlier. "And don't try to cast either, not even to just project your thoughts, neither your body nor you mind can take it right now. You almost died... twice." She held up two fingers in the form of bunny ears for emphasis.

I nodded letting her know I understood. At least that explained why I felt like I was at death's door.

"Lucky I was coming to visit you yesterday or you might not be here now," she continued on. "And I'm so sorry about the basement," she leaned forward to whisper the word before settling back in the chair. "I held on too long. Fortunately I let go before it shattered your mind and body. I don't think any permanent damage was done," she winced, giving me large puppy eyes to signify how sorry she was.

I didn't understand much of what she was saying, hell I didn't understand any of it, but I couldn't convey that too her.

"It's not your fault, Kailani," Finn muttered though the words rang more hollow than sincere. "Would you tell the doctor she's awake again?"

Kailani nodded, smiled at me, pet my hand, and stood bouncing out of the door and presumable down the hall. I couldn't have been awake for longer than five minutes but I was already so tired.

"Try to stay awake," Finn whispered when I let my eyes drift close.

I opened them and looked to Finn again, wondering why he looked so pensive. Then I remembered that he or Simone probably mauled me, but why was Kailani here? And what did she mean she held on too long. It was frustrating as hell not to be able to talk mentally or physically.

"Miss Harlow," the doctor greeted entering the room and making his way to my bed. "Welcome back to the land of the living, I'm Dr. Walker."

He was good looking; at least Kailani seemed to think so as she stood behind him making little motions in his direction. I wanted to laugh, probably would have, had I not been positive it would have killed me.

"If you'll excuse me," he stated to Finn. "I just want to take her vitals."

Finn didn't speak nor did he move; he simple stared at the doctor with a look in his eyes that said he was welcome to try to move him out of the way. Dr. Walker chose to take his readings from the other side.

He did the standards first, taking my blood pressure, my pulse, listening to my heart beat, and my breathing. He took my hand and asked me to squeeze his fingers as hard as I could, which unfortunately wasn't very hard, then he moved to the foot of my bed and ran his thumb against the sole of my foot causing me to twitch lightly. All in all he looked please as he covered the appendage back up.

Silence fell in the room as he wrote out on the chart at the foot of my bed and Kailani checked out the back view, still grinning.

"I want to give it a few hours before we remove the tube, just to make sure you're on the right path," the first half was spoken as he wrote.

Clicking the pen close he placed that back in the breast pocket of his white coat while replacing the chart to hang at the foot of the bed.

"You've been in a coma Miss Harlow, for the better part of two weeks. When you arrived here you were legally dead," I watched his eyes flicker to Finn for a moment, a silent accusation in them. "Everything appears normal. Your muscles are a bit weak but that's to be expected. Once we remove the tube the police are going to want to have a word with you… get your statement of what happened the night you were brought in here."

I nodded letting him know I understood.

"I'll be back to check on you, in the meantime if you need anything just push this button here," moving closer he held up the red button connected to the white string. "Try to get some rest."

He cut one finally look to Finn before leaving the room. Kailani watched him leave before moving back to her chair and taking a seat.

With a mischievous smile she leaned over speaking softly. "I don't think he likes you, Finn."

"He thinks I did this to her," Finn replied casually. I closed my eyes for a moment when he lowered his lips to my forehead for a soft kiss before finally reclaiming his seat. "You really scared the shit out of me, baby. I thought I was going to lose you."

"Technically you did lose her," Kailani pointed out, her attention shifting to me.

"I'd like to talk about that ... when you can talk of course. I've never experienced a near death occurrence. I'm curious to know what it was like."

"Kailani," Finn glared at her, but whatever he was going to say never only left his lips on a slow exhale of breath.

"What?" the sea dragon replied innocently. "I'm just curious what it felt like. So many say there is a white light, others say there is just darkness, and others still report of an out of body experience."

He watched her for a few moments before casting his eyes back to me, his fingers moving over my face before he touched his lips to my forehead again.

"I have to go to work baby, been working the three to eleven shift, but Katrina and Luke will be here as soon as they gets off of work, and Sebastian will probably pop by sometime after dusk, alright?"

I nodded.

He bent down to kiss me again; at least I thought he was going to. Instead he just let his cheek rest against my forehead. "I love you, so much, Dani."

I closed my eyes as he drew away, listening to the sound of his retreating footsteps as he walked away.

"He really does love you very much," Kailani began once we were alone. "He's been staying at the hospital you know." Standing she moved to the curtain and pushed it back to reveal a cot set up in the one bed room.

She took a seat in the chair he occupied, grinning happily as she watched me. It was frustrating, so many questions I wanted to ask her but couldn't speak vocally nor could I shoot the questions into her head, nor could I even do something just mundane as writing it down since my fingers didn't feel like they could support a pen.

"He was performing CPR when Sebastian whirled us here. He didn't want to let go, even though the doctors obviously were capable of handling it. I thought he was going to pass out… that or change. He's had someone from his pack watching over you when he can't be around, but only Luke, Katrina, and Marco… though sometimes Sebastian takes over."

She continued to prattle on for a while; actually it was rather comforting to hear her voice. I fell asleep to the sound of it only to wake up some time later to Luke watching the basketball game on the television. He smiled, and talked softly to me, telling me about his day until Dr. Walker returned and removed the tube. As with Finn, he eyed Luke, or moreover they eyed each other. When he asked him to leave so he could have the nurse remove the catheter I thought there would be a situation, but Luke relented, assured me he'd be right on the other side of the door then walked out.

Dr. Walker wanted to say something that much is obvious, but the words never made it past his lips. He watched me for several long seconds before he just gave a nod to the nurse and left the room, leaving her to remove the other uncomfortable tubing.

Someone had removed the two IVs and the oxygen while I'd been sleeping. No sooner than the offending rubber was out did I hop up to go to the bathroom. I almost fell back down; my leg muscles not ready to fully support my weight after the long two week rest. The change in altitude did a number on my head as well, sending the room to a slanted skew for a few moments.

Relying on the use of the walls and furniture I made my to the bathroom, letting my body relax as I did what I had to do before making the exit back to the room. My reflection caught my attention but I'd just as soon it hadn't. My face was covered in tiny cuts in various stages of healing. It looked like someone had peeled off my face, cut it into different sections then stuck it back on. Stitches were on the deepest, white stripes holding others closed at the center, and some had just been left to heal on their own.

I turned away from my reflection, tears welling in my eyes. I never really considered myself beautiful, but I used to be pretty, now I looked like some sort of monster. Nothing that happened in the bedroom explained the face staring back at me. Finn wouldn't have done that, and he wouldn't have stood around for Simone to do it either.

I stayed in the bathroom for a while, waiting until I heard the sounds on the other side of the door die down. Turning the lock I stepped out to the smell of food and roses. A tray of food still covered sat on the rolling table positioned near the bed so all I would have to do would be climb in and pull it close. Two dozen peach tipped roses sat in a vase on one of the tables next to the bed, and Sebastian stood at the window, his back to me as he gazed out over the city.

He turned as I entered, a soft smile spreading his lips.

"It's good to see you up and about," he stated softly only moving close once I was under the thin sheet and blanket.

"I wish I could say it felt good to be up and about."

"Your strength will return," the smile never left his face as he rolled the cart close to the bed and uncovered the tray of food.

Some sort of turkey or chicken slices was on the menu, covered in beige gravy. There was a small dish of broccoli that had been steamed well past an inch of its life and looked about as bland as the sole of a shoe, and of course the ever present hospital jell-o and punch sitting in cups off to the side rounded out the meal.

"Looks delicious," Sebastian stated as he began to cut up the meat.

"Then you eat it."

"I prefer my sustenance to be red, a little darker, a little thicker, and a lot less solid."

After everything was cut he handed me the fork, but I had no interest in eating. I couldn't get the image of my patchwork face out of my mind.

"Kailani told me she warned you against casting for a while?"

"Yeah, said it might kill me."

I took a bite of the tasteless meat, chewed it a few times then pushed the cart away, my eyes meeting Sebastian watching him watching me.

"Sebastian what happened to my face?"

The question brought a frown to his lips, his right hand rose to brush across his lips before he took a seat in the chair nearest to him. "What do you remember?"

"The last memory I have is of Finn fighting to control his beast in his bedroom and Simone scratching at the door. Then I wake up here with a face that looks like something out of a horror movie."

"There's nothing wrong with your face," he spoke softly.

"Don't patronize me, Sebastian. I saw what I look like."

"Cuts," he waved his hand towards my face and stood only to take a seat on my bed. "It's nothing that won't heal over time; some of them will fade completely." He raised a hand and slowly moved it towards me, giving me time to stop him if that was my desire. His thumb caught one large tear as it spilled from the corner of my eye. "You're still beautiful, Danika. The scars don't take away from that."

I wanted to believe him, but I knew the kind of world we lived in. Scars didn't make a person beautiful, flawless skin did. I'd never considered myself one to care what others thought of me, or to care what society as a whole claimed was the perfect woman, but then I'd never looked like a patient of a plastic surgery gone horribly wrong.

For the next hour or so Sebastian relayed what had happened to the best of his ability. As he talked some of the holes filled in, others remained gaping voids. I had snatches of memory of the cemetery with Alexander but couldn't recall what had happened or what was discussed. I didn't remember going to Finn's house, or even being at Juan's manor, I sure as hell didn't remember saying to Juan the things Sebastian repeated as my words. I remembered seeing Finn in that god-awful contraption, and I remember running from the necromancer, but I didn't remember anything after that.

"I wasn't in the room," Sebastian finished, "But Kailani said you were magnificent."

I shook my head adjusting my position on the bed a bit more. "I couldn't have been that magnificent or I wouldn't be here."

"You fought a duel with an elder necromancer and won, Dani. Kailani said the magic that radiated through you body was blinding. She also said it was glorious."

"Did we kill him?"

His pause was all the answer I needed. "It is very unlikely he would have survived something like that."

"But…"

"But there was no body found." He watched me, his pale blue eyes locking with mine as his finger continued to lightly stroke my jaw. "The police are here," he whispered before he leaned forward, his lips brushing against my cheek. His feet finding the floor and standing the same time the door was pushed open and two officers walked in. "Get some rest," he instructed.

With a nod to the officers my friend the vampire, left the room. Both of the uniformed men looked me over carefully before the older one flipped open his pad. I could see the thoughts in their eyes but neither of them gave voice to anything.

In updating me with what really happened, Sebastian had also informed me the story he and Finn had already given. Apparently Finn and I had been out for an after dinner stroll when an occult group jumped us. Torture was the appetizer to what probably would have been a ritual sacrifice had Sebastian not happened by the deserted park where it all took place.

Finn just so happened to break out of his bonds at the exact time. Even though it was a completely fictional story, it still annoyed me that I had been reduced to the roll of damsel in distress saved by the big strong men.

They asked me to tell them what happened in my own words, which didn't take long. Good thing because my throat was starting to burn. Satisfied that the stories matched they thanked me, assured me they were looking into the matter, and bid me a speedy recovery before leaving.

I dozed on and off then; waking as my aching body struggling to find a comfortable position, falling back asleep when my recovering mind became too exhausted to sustain consciousness. Twice I woke to find Luke and Katrina in my room, talking softly, watching TV. Their voices brought a warming comfort and security, and lulled me to sleep again.

The next time I woke up in a silent dark room. Curled on my side facing the window I watched the pattern the water made. The room was quiet but I knew I wasn't alone. I could smell him; each deep breath in brought pieces of his musky scent into my nose. My body relaxed in response to it, subconsciously sending the message to uncurl and face him as he took a seat on my bed.

His fingers touched my face where the skin wasn't covered in gauze and bandages, pushed back into my tangled hair, and combed down to my shoulders.

"I'm going to turn the lamp on, okay?"

I reached out, catching the wrist that headed for the nightstand lighting. It was stupid, he knew what I looked like, he'd seen the cuts.

"It's okay Dani," he whispered softly.

I felt the heat of his body as he lowered his mouth to mine. All it took were those soft lips to bring back memories. His lips moved slowly as if he were afraid he would bruise me if he applied too much pressure.

He moved his mouth slowly against mine; his tongue running across my lips and encouraging them to part. It was transcending, we were no longer in a hospital room but in his bed, the smells of pine coming in through the open patio door, our scents mixing together in the warm room. I didn't realize he had turned the lamp on until he pulled away.

He caught my chin tenderly between his fingers when I tried to turn away, angling my face back until our eyes met. There was a circular scar around his neck where the silver band had burned against his skin. The skin was puckered and melted together like it wasn't really skin at all, but wax molded into place. Likewise under his chin were three symmetrical scars from the fork. My guess was a matching set was on his chest.

Two weeks had passed which meant the scars were his to keep, a side effect all werewolves suffered from silver.

My eyes stung as tears began to formulate behind them again; the more I tried to keep my chin from trembling, the more it quivered against his fingers.

"It's okay," he whispered those words once, than again, and again, repeating them in a mantra as he carefully pulled me from the bed into his embrace.

His hands and arms around my back held me close as I cried silently against his shirt. I still had a hard time conceptualizing all that had happened, but our scars spoke volumes. We'd been through a war and we survived.

He rocked me slowly; his hands and voice comforting me until I settled down. Once I had he lowered me to the bed.

"Nancy's been stopping by every other day," he stated softly. "She gave me some powder to put in your tea and some ointment for your wounds."

"They won't heal completely you know, at least the deeper ones won't," I stated watching his eyes. "If it had been a contemporary duel it would have been stopped before it got to the permanent stage, but now..." I shook my head, twining my fingers with his. "Now my nickname can be Scar Face."

"I don't want to ever hear those words come out of your mouth again," he reprimanded. His tone was almost angry. "You almost died Dani. I owe you my life and that of Simone's, so does the pack."

"Is that why Luke and Katrina have been walking on eggshells around me?"

He shook his head. "When you introduced her to Kailani..." his breath caught for a moment as he stared at me, a strange mixture of awe and longing in his eyes. "You introduced Katrina as you second."

"You keep telling me that's what she is," I pointed out.

"And you keep denying that you're part of my pack. Until that moment you never admitted it to us or yourself, let alone an outsider."

"I'm not. Just because I'm your girlfriend—" I argued.

"—you're my mate."

"Finn—"

"—No," he countered forcefully. "You don't get it. The only thing standing in the way of you being a member of my pack is you. It's always been you, baby."

I sighed softly; I didn't feel like having this argument with him, not here, not now. We were both alive, that was all that mattered at that moment.

"I love you."

The sound of his voice so soft and sincere, more than the words curved the corner of my lips into the beginnings of a smile. I was tired, but I wasn't ready for him to move away yet. I missed the warmth and security of his body, craved it.

"Lie with me until I fall asleep?"

He flashed that smile, the schoolboy grin that made him look like he was planning nefarious deeds. I scooted over making room for him while he leaned over to turn the lamp off. The bed gave a slight groan of protest at the additional weight, but it didn't stop Finn from settling down. He moved an arm around my waist, pulling my body back against the spoon his created.

He exhaled a long slow breath against my neck before his nose nuzzled deeper into my hair. "It feels so good to have you in my arms again. Spooning an unconscious body just isn't the same."

I laughed abruptly, reaching back and slapping his thigh. "Finn, stop tripping you did not."

"How do you know what I did? You were unconscious remember?"

"Keep it up and you're going to find yourself back on that cot," I teased even as I snuggled deeper against him.

"Will you stay with me, when they release you?" his question was soft against my ear. "At least for a while. I can take care of you while you recover."

"I think there are worse places I could stay."

The tip of his nose traced my ear and nuzzled my neck before he finally settled down. I could feel the hard length of him through the blankets and thin gown but he seemed contented to just hold me.

"Finn?"

"Yeah baby?"

"I love you."

One arm squeezed my waist; the other slipped under my neck and wrapped around my shoulders to pull me close. We still had plenty to tackle when I was recovered but for now I just enjoyed the quiet.